# Blue Jay's Night Club

## A Romance of Prohibition New York

Celeste Plowden

Blue Jay's Night Club

Printed in the United States of America

First Printing: July 2023

Paperback ISBN 978-1-960995-14-8

Digital eBook ISBN 978-1-960995-15-5

Published by:  Long Story Short Publishing Company

Albany, New York

# DEDICATION

In loving memory of Chris and Rollo.

# 1

The telephone was ringing. A young man walked over to where it sat on a coffee table in front of a faded aqua sofa, picked it up by the candlestick handle, disengaged the receiver and held it to his ear. "Hello," he muttered.

"Hi Baby! How's tricks?" a giddy female voice said.

He slumped onto the sofa, grimaced, brushed his disheveled mop of brown hair out of his eyes and held the mouthpiece closer. "Oh, hey, Mary Lou, what happened, did you get bored of your new beau?" He glanced across the room at his radio and wondered if he should bother walking over and turning it down or continue distracting himself with the tunes of Fletcher Henderson through this phone call.

"It's *Lulu*, now, I keep tellin' ya," she corrected him.

"Look, what do you want?" he growled.

"Let's go out, Baby, I've got Pop's machine," she purred. "What about that club you took me to last month, Blue something?"

The last time they were there a hot jazz quartet was playing *I've Found a New Baby*, and it was their first dance of the evening. He re-called her long strand of pearls swaying over her black sequin dress as she giggled as some other man bumped into her and said, "I'm cutting in to cut in, Babe," and how easily she allowed him to take Vern's place, for dance after dance without so much as a glance at Vern. Her body bent into the intruding man's torso as he whirled her around the floor. The thought humiliated Vern all over again as if it had just happened. "You mean the joint I took you to the night you broke up with me *again?* Blue Jay's," he snapped.

"Yeah, Blue Jay's. Let's go there again and make up this time, Vern."

He could almost smell her jasmine perfume over the phone, re-membering the last time he kissed her on the neck just beneath her ear lobe, a jet bead earring dangling over and tickling his nose, and wisps

3

of her soft, auburn hair grazing his eyelids. He paused and looked out into the dusky evening from his third story window onto West 48th Street and saw Blue Jay's large neon sign a block over on Sixth Avenue, all lit up with its sleek, electric blue letters and apple green musical note above the name, boasting an evening's entertainment for jazz lovers.

Vern was silent, still thinking of how poorly she had treated him several weeks ago, openly flirting with the imposing stranger after she had guzzled the little silver flask she carried in her red beaded bag. She had nearly fallen over while dancing with the fellow, and Vern had then insisted they leave. Instead, the new, other man pushed him out of the way, and held tight to his female prize for the evening. Mary Lou had giggled loudly, "Bye, bye, Baby," turned her head and allowed the new dance partner to move her across the dance floor to the other side of the room. It was an embarrassing scene, and though the floor was crowded with dancing couples, and very few people even noticed, he was stung by the incident, and left the club without her, as she wished. She had broken up with him several times before, in the past year that he had known her, and she always came back, with sweet, pouty apologies and smiles, asking for his forgiveness. He imagined her red, Cupid's bow lips curling into a smirk over the phone.

Was he still in love with her? No, she had killed that, he thought, shaking his head and rolling his eyes, remembering how he had felt about her in the beginning. How wonderful it had been holding her pretty fingers and yearning to kiss her, as they walked along the streets of New York on cool spring evenings, with the damp pavement glowing in the moonlight, after getting a bite to eat at one of the fancier clubs in the East Fifties. Though he had no real interest in her this time, he was itching to get out for the evening after a particularly grueling week at his office. He thought if he did not concede, she might very well show up on his doorstep or even at the club, unannounced, which could prove awkward and more irritating than agreeing to take her out for the evening. And she was pretty, and fun to be with, unless she decided to slight him, like last time.

"Ok. Come down and we'll walk over together, but get here by nine, or we won't find a seat, even at the bar."

"Gads, Vern, you're the sweetest! Can't wait to see yuz," she tit-

4

tered brightly. "I'm on the Parkway in 10 minutes, Baby."

"Your Pop's machine, huh? When's he gonna buy you a jalopy of your own now that you're outta Brooklyn, you rich Bronxville babe?" Vern answered, trying to buoy himself up into a jocular spirit before her arrival.

"Soon, Baby, but tonight I've got the red Chrysler. Bye!"

A few minutes before nine, the buzzer rang and he heard Lulu's quick footsteps creaking on the wooden staircase. He opened the door and was standing in the hallway in his grey flannel slacks, a pink shirt, and a gray and burgundy tie, as she walked towards him, cooing, "Oh, my favorite tie!"

She was all perfumed in her jasmine scent, and wearing a chartreuse dress covered in rows of silky black fringe, which draped just over her knees. Her bobbed, auburn hair bounced slightly as she walked, and around her forehead she wore a black velvet headband studded with rhinestones and accented with several pink plumes, which fluttered as she swayed down the hallway. She nervously fingered two long ropes of white pearls which showed under her open black taffeta coat as she approached. "Oh, I've missed you so much, Vern," she said as she reached up and kissed him quickly on the lips. "You're one in a million, Baby," she went on in a melodramatic tone as he opened the apartment door for her. "I parked just outside your building. Wanna walk, or drive over?" she asked, glancing around his living room. "Say, did you get a new sofa?"

"Not a chance. It's the same one I've had for three years," he answered, knowing she was just trying to fill up the air with her babble. He walked over to a small table near the door and turned off the radio. "Got a flask with you?"

"Sure thing, Vern, and it's full, too. I haven't touched a drop...just waiting for you," she simpered, and pulled it out of the red beaded bag she had carried it in the last time he had seen her. She took a quick sip and then offered some to Vern. Her wobbly posture belied her declaration as she stood and held out the silver container for his taking. "It's Pop's good whiskey," she whispered, drawing closer to Vern.

"Well, Lulu, it seems you may have been a little thirsty on the way here. It's only about half full," he chuckled, swirling the whiskey around in the half empty flask. "Let's walk over now. I'm sure Jay will have gotten in a supply for today. It's Saturday night." With that, he grabbed his suit jacket and hat from the hall closet and escorted her out the door. It was a warm September evening, with only a light breeze, and the sidewalks were becoming crowded with folks out walking to their favorite weekend haunts, enjoying the last of the warm nights. He glanced at the headlights of her parked car sitting in front of his building that caught a beam of light from a nearby streetlamp, and appeared like a pair of eyes watching them as they strolled towards the club.

The music had already started as the pair entered the club. It was a small space, and usually crowded when there was music. The lights were low, and the room was lit only by the small lamps with crystal beads dangling from the white shades, which sat on each of the tables. Jay, the proprietor, greeted Vern with a handshake and escorted them over to one of the little tables bordering the dance floor, where they would have a great view of the jazz trio playing their hot licks from a corner at the back end of the floor.

"What'll you have tonight, Vern?" Jay inquired as he pulled out a chair for Lulu, "I've got some of that rye you like." He held up two fingers and smiled at Vern.

"On the rocks," Vern answered. "Thanks, Jay."

Jay Jones had owned this place since before the blight of Prohibition tried to close him down, but this was New York. He was one of many club owners that fought to stay open, and still serve liquor to the pleasure-seeking clientele that came there to dance and drink and enjoy their evening. The regular agents were compensated in cash and drinks, and the new ones, or an occasional beat cop that did not know the drill, soon learned why it paid to be one of Jay's inside men.

Jay was in his forties, presumably, but he never told much about himself, except what he ate that day, or what band was hired to play, or that he would be glad to do a favor for some neighborhood widow, or that he gave the kids that lived on the block new gloves and hats when winter rolled around. He said his name was just Jay Jones, but no one really bought that story. He was a well-built man of medium height, had a full head of wavy, jet black hair, a large, aquiline nose, and piercing steel-gray eyes that honed in on the person he was talking to, appearing to size them up instantly. Though some people tried to listen to his accent when he spoke, to derive where he was from, no one could pin it down. "Hey. I'm a New Yorker," was his only answer if he were ever asked.

Jay Jones. Was it once Jacob, John, Jacques, or Giuseppe? Giuliani, Jacynski, Jameson, or Jaquette? Most everyone else told where they were from, or how their family came to New York, but not Jay Jones. He was just a New Yorker, "like everyone else," he would say before greeting an Italian couple in their native tongue, fluently and gracefully. Sometimes he served lox and pumpernickel bagels for a late night snack before the drinking into the wee hours caught up with his patrons, or handed out shots of Ouzo all around the bar and tables whenever the band played his favorite tune, *Everybody Loves My Baby*. Jay would clap his hands together in rhythm above his head and motion for a few men to dance the *Hasapiko* with him.

And he accepted everyone equally, whether in slick suits or shabby wool coats and dingy hats, Jay welcomed everyone like they were gentry. Broken English or acute Scarsdale accents received the same treatment from Jay. He was so glad to have them join him this evening. Ladies were all lovely to him, whether a factory girl in calico, or a Park Avenue princess in furs. And he always invited the musicians he hired, to join him on an evening when they were free, to come down from Harlem, or over from Brooklyn, and enjoy an evening with their wives and friends. Whatever their race or religion, they were welcomed not only by Jay, but the other patrons as well, who recognized them, and who frequently sent over drinks and smiles as they lifted their glasses to them from across the crowded room.

Jay was an example of what New York was, to all who came to this great city, whether to change their fortunes, or just to escape their humdrum lives and reinvent themselves and take charge of their future. Jay was truly a New Yorker, whether he had been born in one of the five boroughs, or in some distant land across the seas. No one ever found out where he was really from, or why he always dodged the question. One of his Prohibition Agent cronies was overheard as he sat at the bar and sipped his brandy, saying, "Irish, Italian, a Polish Jew, hell, it could be his name really is *Jones,* and he's just from some backwards Midwestern town that he doesn't want to admit to." The other guests at the bar chuckled at the comment, each nodding in understanding.

Vern and Lulu sipped their drinks and watched the trio in the corner set up. They were still in their shirt sleeves, but would no doubt begin their first set in their formal jackets, feeling free to toss them aside as the club heated up with more bodies and dancing. A very tall piano player donned his top hat and pulled out the piano bench, throwing his coat tails behind him as he sat down, while the bassist lifted his instrument from its side. When standing it upright, it was nearly a foot taller than he was. "I haven't heard this group before," Vern commented, smiling at Lulu, and beginning to feel relaxed in the atmosphere of the club. Lulu beamed back at him, apparently satisfied that he still enjoyed her company.

The band's drummer and singer introduced the group as the *West End Trio,* and opened with *Limehouse Blues,* as couples gathered on the dance floor. Lulu looked at Vern as if asking to dance, but he was not interested in revisiting her historic escapades on the dance floor, until he loosened up a bit more. He waved at Jay, who brought over two more drinks. Vern and Lulu exchanged a few words here and there, about the very lively crowd that evening, probably due to the frenetic energy of the band. One couple stole the show, with their mixture of Charleston steps and tap routines, as others moved off to the sides of the floor, in order to watch the act. "They've gotta be show people," chuckled Vern, who was content to simply enjoy the dancers, and listen to the music while they sipped their drinks. Lulu stayed seated at the table with him, but was swaying in her chair, awaiting the moment when he would decide to dance with her.

Vern's eyes were no longer on Lulu, as they once had been. He gazed freely at the jazz band and watched the dancers as they passed by their table, yet he was not indifferent to her, either. He knew she wanted to dance, but it was well into the band's first set, when they played *Charleston*, that he arose from his seat, smiled, and offered his hand to her. She laughed and threw her arms around him as they shuffled onto the dance floor together. "I thought you'd never ask!" she joked.

They danced several numbers in a row, and so far, Lulu was behaving herself and acting as though Vern were the only man in the room. He danced her into a corner at the outer edge of the floor, away from the band and the bar, where there was a bit more space. As he looked around the front area of the club, he noticed a striking young woman who was standing alone and staring at him. He believed he had seen her there before, but was not sure. She had a small frame, was wearing a sleeveless cocoa-brown satin dress and long, beige gloves, which contrasted well with her exquisite olive skin. Around her neck hung a very odd pendant of a pink scallop shell set in a gold rim, and three large pearls dangling from the bottom edge. Her amber eyes were luminous and direct like a cat's eyes, opened wide, from beneath a set of wispy bangs. Her wiry, black hair was worn long and loose, falling well over her shoulders, unlike any of the other chic ladies in the place, who wore chignons or the latest bob cuts. Her beauty captivated him, and Vern realized he was staring, and smiled at her as he passed by. He continued his dance with Lulu, who was showing no signs of fatigue, but was becoming a little unsure of her footing, as the whiskey began to catch up with her.

"Let's take a break, Lulu," Vern said, and danced them over to their table. The glow of amber eyes seemed to follow him as he moved back towards the center of the club. When he sat down, he could still see a glimpse of the woman between passing dancers. She was still staring at him, and he began to wonder who she was. Why had she fixed her gaze on him?

"Let's have another drink, Vern," Lulu hiccuped. "I think that's a good reason for a break."

"We'll have some cranberry juice this time, you've had enough booze," Vern announced, waving his hand at the passing waiter. "Two tall cranberry and ginger ales, please."

"I'll have a double whiskey in mine," Lulu retorted to the waiter, who stood there and awaited further instruction from Vern.

"Thanks, no whiskey this time." He smiled at the waiter, who started off towards the bar, but instead, Lulu grabbed the man's jacket sleeve.

"I want mine with whiskey," she insisted.

"Let go, Lulu," Vern snapped under his breath, but she refused, staring defiantly at the waiter, who carefully removed her clutched fingers from his jacket, and darted off without a word.

"I'm ready for more dancing," she barked, and clumsily shoved her chair back and tripped onto the dance floor, hailing the first man that looked at her, and slumped all over him as she tried to dance without falling. Vern got up as well, made his way through the crowd, and over to the bar, where he asked to settle up, glancing now and then at the drunken Lulu as he paid the tab.

Now he felt the amber eyes were closer to him. The unusual brunette was standing at the other end of the bar, pointedly looking at him, but he could only think of how to get Lulu out of the club before she caused a worse scene. He shoved his change into his coat pocket and looked at Lulu still dancing with the man, but barely able to stay on her feet. Vern shook his head and sighed quietly, wishing he had not agreed to take her to Blue Jay's this evening. He glanced back at the striking woman with the feline eyes, thinking that if he had come alone, he might have had a chance to meet her.

The petite onlooker, Carlotta, was also thinking about this young man with the wayward girlfriend. He seemed far too 'nice' in his efforts to put up with this drunken woman in public. She surmised it had not been the first time he had experienced his lady friend's sloppy conduct. He had a look of irritation but was nonplussed by her antics, as if he had expected the entire scene. Carlotta could put him to better use in her own scheme, and he would enjoy himself with her.

Her mind flashed through memories of her former lover, Geoffrey Northcott, a very wealthy Englishman who had shown her ecstasy through their passion and she craved to have him back in her life. But after three months of carnal pleasure together, he had told her he was finished with her. It was after a particularly long, delicious night of cocaine and brandy, spent in his hunter green bedroom on the heavily carved walnut poster bed in between its satin sheets. There was always a pungent smell of rose oil wax mixed with the musty smell of old wood whenever she had flopped over its mattress awaiting more of Geoffrey's kisses. The ceiling had swirled above her as she sat on top of him, swaying over his erection for an hour, and then again for nearly another hour, and even more, until the dawn began to spill into the room from behind the ivory velvet drapes. She sometimes kneeled at one of the posters, gripping it with both hands as Geoffrey guided her into rapture, the waxy odor lingering on her fingers through the next morning. She abhorred the smell, but enjoyed the memories it brought.

"Come on, Kitty, time for you to leave." His tone had been playful at first, but quickly wound into a bored speech of 'moving on to new things,' and she 'must understand that things had been interesting with her, but it was over.' He had picked up an Emory board from his nightstand and filed a pinky fingernail, then examined the rest of his nails for raspy edges before looking up at Carlotta. His eyes had blinked at her a few times but he gave no other explanation as if he were an employer giving her an expected task. She remembered his blonde hair, like a lion's mane falling over his shoulders as he sat up in the slippery bedsheets, feeling on his nightstand again for something, an elastic band, then catching his hair at the back of his neck and binding it into a haphazard tail as he all but ignored her. "Come now, be off. I must have some breakfast and attend to other things."

Geoffrey had waved her on with his fingers flicking towards the door, a slight smile on his lips. He reached into the crumpled sheets and handed her a diamond cuff that he had given a few her only a week after he had met her. "Oh, don't forget this momento, my dear." He had dangled the item above her head with a slight swinging motion like a master offering a treat to a dog. She intensely recalled the feeling of being kicked in the gut, and rushing out of his Sutton Place palace and standing bewildered as the red door closed behind her, looking through the remnants of the previous night's fog and her teary eyes for want of what to do.

That was six months ago and she was still stung by this treatment, but nevertheless obsessed with Geoffrey. The first time she saw him, he had picked her off stage one night at a downtown club after she played *Sweet Sue* on her violin in a duet with another woman on piano. She had been instantly attracted to him, and for three months she allowed him to introduce her to a world of decadence as his partner in a 'sex magick' faction that taught her to visualize her greatest

desires during orgasm, and how that energy would bring them to frui-
tion, namely that of becoming a famous violinist, much sought after in
the most dazzling of social circles. Then she would be in her glory, so
she had thought. But she was here now, in another club, eyeing a new
man through the throng of the club to fill her needs.  She pondered
his usefulness as she waited for a chance to introduce herself to him,
watching as Lulu's new man danced her back to her table and vigorously plopped her back down in her seat.

Lulu got up weaving, and tried to continue dancing while she
was holding onto her chair for balance. Vern stayed where he was
at the crowded bar, temporarily avoiding going back to the table to
collect her, since he feared more drunken melodrama if he were to
suggest they leave.

He looked again, over his shoulder to find the dark woman,
and this time she was standing right behind him. He had not felt her
squeeze in the tight space at the bar, but she met his eyes with her
lovely, round, orbs, and said, "You deserve better," in a low whisper.
He breathed in her enticing scent, which was a mixture of patchouli
and rose, and noticed the curve of her breasts as she spoke to him.

Vern paused and blinked several times, wanting to say something
interesting to her, but instead, he only sighed and shrugged his shoulders, declaring, "I usually come here alone." He detected a very slight
Eastern European accent beneath the more prominent Brooklyn pro-
nunciation.

"I've seen you before," she answered. "I'm Carlotta." She continued staring at Vern without showing any animation at all. She was
obviously waiting for him to introduce himself, but he did not know
what to make of this lone woman, who had so blatantly intruded in his
problem of the evening. "I come here sometimes to hear a little music,
but I never stay long," she continued.

"I'm Vern," he finally offered, "and yes, Carlotta, I think I have
seen you here before." He wanted to find a way of prolonging the conversation for just a few moments longer, before having to confront the
problem of getting Lulu out of the club.

"And you will see me here again," she stated. "I wish you luck with
the rest of your evening." With that, she clasped the gold encrusted

seashell around her neck, moving it distinctly three times, from side to side on its chain, and then with a sway of her hips, moved away from the bar and walked back to the corner where he had first noticed her. He thought her bold words and blatant stare were audacious, yet he was intrigued by her, and her serious, penetrating expression. There was an air of portent about her, which he felt even as he turned his back and walked towards the unpleasant obligation of getting Lulu out of the club.

# 2

**W**ith a few forced compliments about her lovely eyes needing to sleep and laying her gorgeous head on his pillow, he got the intoxicated Lulu to agree to let him escort her out of Blue Jay's without too much of a scene, although she turned her back on him when he first arrived again at their table, and began pointedly flirting with another drunken patron, who happened to be another one of Jay's regular Prohibition agents, who was looking for some fun between drinks. Though Vern supported her on his shoulder, the whole way out of the club, she managed to catch her toe on a bar chair leg, and almost toppled an elegant lady in a beaded dress of gray silk, who was sitting near the bar. Lulu crashed into her shrieking, "my foot, my foot, I broke my foot!"

Vern hailed a cab, and deposited the bombed flapper on the back seat, cursing his judgement in agreeing to take her out. He would simply drag her upstairs drop her on his sofa, let her sleep it off for the rest of the night, and send her home in the morning. He chalked the whole evening up to his bad decision, would offer her some breakfast when she awoke, and then be done with her for good. At the moment, all he wanted was a peaceful night's sleep, but before that could happen, he knew he had to call her parents' house and inform them that Lulu was safe, and would return home in the morning. He was not going to be accused of behaving irresponsibly towards her nor have her parents worry needlessly through the night.

When the cab stopped to let them out in front of the building next door, Vern told the driver, "Sorry, Pal, you'll need to drive right up in front of my doorstep. I need all the help I can get."

"Sure thing, Mister, I get it," answered the driver.

"Thanks," Vern said, handing the man a dollar bill. "Keep the change."

He opened his car door got out, and went over to open Lulu's door, on the curbside, trying as well as he could to keep from dragging her, but to no avail. "Wake up, Lulu," he said as he picked her limp body from the cab and carried her in his arms towards the front door. He fumbled in his pocket for his keys, but finding the building door already unlocked, he swung the door open with his foot, as he lugged her inside. "You've gotta stand up, Lulu," he said shaking his head, "I can't carry you up three flights."

She opened her eyes as he put her down and leaned her against the bannister. "Here, hold on to this," he instructed, placing her hand on the railing. "I'll be right behind you." From behind, Vern gripped her around her waist with one hand, and pushed with the other, forcing the sloshed party girl to maneuver herself up three staircases.

"I wanna lie down," she bleated, every few steps, until they arrived at his apartment door. Vern propped her up against its jamb, while fishing in his pocket for his key.

"Ok, here you go Lu," he panted, dragging her to his sofa and seating her there. She immediately slumped over in a heap. Vern took a pillow, tilted it against the arm of the couch, straightened her legs, and drew her arms down to her sides while her head fell into place on the pillow. "Thank God that's over," he muttered with disdain, grabbing a bucket from the kitchen and placing it next to the couch by Lulu's head in anticipation of her retching during the night. Then he picked up the phone to call her parents to let them know she was safe. He told Mr. Turner she had gotten sick on some bad seafood at dinner, and was too queasy to drive, but was he was pretty sure her father suspected it was drinking that had made his little girl sick. It was late, her father quickly accepted Vern's answer, and thanked him for calling. Vern then shuffled off to his bedroom and collapsed on the bed.

# 3

He awoke during the small hours, thirsty from the whiskey, threw off his covers and started to walk into the kitchen for some water. The bare floorboards creaked as he stumbled through the short hallway, and he glimpsed into the living room where Lulu had passed out on the sofa. It was dim with the curtains drawn, but by the light of the street lamps, he could make out her head resting on the pillow he had placed there earlier. He heard something rustle, like sheets being pulled back, but he saw nothing move over her body.

Still half asleep, he turned his head around and glanced back into his own room across the hall, and thought he saw something round sitting in the middle of his bed. He quickly reached out and pulled the cord to the hall light on the wall to his back but the bulb was out. The sheets rustled again and this time the object moved, as if it were a head nodding in agreement during a conversation. Two large black circles formed in the middle of the object, and stared back at him with emptiness, as a toothy grin emerged beneath.

Vern thought he was dreaming, shook his hair out of his eyes, and briefly glanced back at Lulu soundly asleep on the sofa, before re-visiting the sight of the round object atop his own bed. It was still there, looking like a ceramic replica of a human skull. "What the *Hell?* Where did that come from?" he gasped, shifting his weight a little, thinking it could be something that had fallen off the cluttered bookshelf by his bed. Sure, it was probably something ordinary he had forgotten about in the hodgepodge of his bedroom, which just gave off an eerie appearance in the dark room. The thing seemed inanimate and took on an alternately blue or gold cast from the street lights outside his window.

He took a deep breath and was about to start back towards the kitchen, his original purpose in getting up. He had probably bumped something on the bookshelf when he stumbled out of bed, like the snowdome he kept on the top shelf, or the stuffed Felix the Cat toy Lulu had bought him as a gag gift. The sheets rustled again, and this time the

16

object had changed its expression. It looked directly at him and moved its chin a little as if trying to get a better view of him. The corners of the mouth drew back and smiled at Vern, who was locked in fear and could not take his gaze from the grinning object.

"Lulu," he called out, still staring at the ceramic head. "Lulu," he said louder, but she did not answer or move.

The head opened its mouth even wider as if laughing at him, and the black holes of its eyes now glowed with a white light that seemed to dart from side to side as it mocked him.

"I'm dreaming," Vern told himself. "I drank too much, and I'll look away and it will disappear." The sheets hummed as the head moved forward over them. He watched it move closer to the foot of the bed. A twisted torso, no larger than a child's, began to grow out of the back of the head, and skeletal arms and legs, barely covered with flesh emerged from the deformed body. The creature now rested on all fours and crawled across the bed towards Vern.

"*Lulu, Lulu,*" he screamed with all of his might, "*I'm dreaming, help me,*" but barely a dull whisper passed through his lips, and the sleeping Lulu did not budge.

Vern ran to the door of his apartment, flung it open, hurled himself into the hallway, flew down the stairs, dashed through the main entrance, and spilled out into 48th Street. His heart was racing, his mouth, dry, as he glanced back to see what, if anything had followed him. All was silent. Not even the main door squeaked as it began to close of its own accord. The street, too, was empty and quiet at this hour just before dawn. Blue Jay's colorful neon sign had already gone dark, the windows on the entire block were pitch-black as well, and the street lights were the only thing that illuminated the midnight-blue haze of nightfall on this city block. Vern continued to look around from all sides, still fearful that the creature from his dreams would catch up with him. He saw Lulu's red Chrysler on the other side of the street, and he considered climbing in and passing the hour or so before dawn peeked out from behind the buildings, and melted away his nightmare.

He was just about to walk over and open the car door, when he thought saw something whisk out of a murky building entrance directly in front of the car, and move towards him. For a second, his heart caught in his throat as he gasped but when he saw it was a petite woman, he relaxed, assuming it was some night owl leaving her beau to return home.

"Vern," her voice echoed "Vern," she breathed again.

Before he could answer, the sexy brunette who had introduced herself at Blue Jay's that evening, was standing right in front of him. "What are you doing out standing in the street at this hour? Is your lady friend still drinking and sparring?" she asked while looking at him directly. She raised her hand to her throat and began to finger the shell pendant around her neck.

"No, she's passed out on my couch," Vern answered simply, pondering the same question about this woman being out on the street alone at such an hour.

Before he could toss the question back at her she continued, "Did you have a bad dream, or something?" Her wide, bright eyes stared at him like searchlights scouring his face for an answer, but a growing weight in his chest foretold an awareness that she already knew the answer, which shook him all the more. She continued to caress the pendant and each of the three dangling pearls as she spoke.

Tired and unnerved by having her show up in front of his building at the moment he was fleeing his apartment in fear, and his pulse now galloped, his throat was dry, and there was ringing in his ears, all increasing the eerie feeling he began to feel about her. Perhaps she had watched him leaving Blue Jay's at one time or another, and had followed him to see where he lived, but to what purpose? She was young, maybe a few years younger than himself, and lovely, even though strange, and he would have gladly spoken to her longer, bought her a drink, and danced with her, except for having to deal with Lulu's drunken antics that night at Jay's. And now here she was standing in front of his building in the middle of the night.

"Yes, I had a bad dream, and came out to get some fresh air," he answered, turning to cross the street and scoot back upstairs. Her face bore no trace of emotion. She blinked at him and nodded her head. "Look, I've got to get back to bed. Can I walk you somewhere?" he asked, "I'm just going to the other end of the block where my mother lives, but thank you." With that, she quietly fluttered past him, and continued down the block. Vern watched as she departed, but in seconds she had vanished behind the opaque curtain of the lingering night.

***

In the morning Vern walked into his living room to see Lulu sitting on the couch with her head in her hands. I feel really awful," she groaned.

"Sure. You had a lot to drink," he rejoined He took her hand and led her into his small, lemon-yellow kitchen and raised the shade over the single window above the sink. "I'll make eggs and toast."

He tossed some knives and forks on a seafoam-green table and quickly began cracking eggs into a bowl. Lulu sat in her chair with her head resting on her hands, and did not offer to help. She looked worse than he had ever seen her look after a night out, with her bloodshot eyes and puffed, ruddy cheeks. "This will help," he said as he placed a glass of orange juice in front of her.

"I feel worse than just hung over," she commented.

"Worse how?" Vern asked, his back to her as he cooked.

"I can't explain it, I just feel like nothing will ever be right again."

"You'll be fine, Miss Bronxville. You just need some food and rest," he exclaimed, attempting to sound cheerful. "I'm tired, too. Had an awful nightmare and ran outside for some fresh air. I even called out to you, but you were sound asleep through all the hubbub. Doors slamming, running down the stairs. You were out, even when I came back upstairs!"

Lulu drank the juice and picked at her eggs and toast, remaining fairly quiet and glum. "I'm sorry Vern," she expressed, however feebly.

"Ok, you'll be fine." He smiled, helping her to her feet, but ready to get her on her way. Are you ready to drive home?" he asked.

She nodded, and went to collect her bag and coat. He thought he had never seen her looking so awful, and it was not just her wasted appearance due to so much whiskey. It was something in her gait, her expression, a look of foreboding and melancholy. Vern held her arm and escorted her out, looking closely at her as they descended the stairs. She only watched her feet as she walked, saying nothing and barely glancing at him, as if in a stupor. "Are you sure you're ok to drive?" he asked.

With a weak smile, she looked at him and answered," Sure. I'll call you when I get home, Vern." She squeezed his hand and started the car.

An hour later, she called and said she had gotten home safely, and was going to lie down. Vern was relieved, and went about his Sunday as usual, getting his laundry ready to drop off on the way to work in the morning, relaxing on the couch with *Women in Love,* all while listening to a Tchaikovsky symphony on the radio. He didn't give much thought to the unpleasant events of the night before with Lulu, or agonize over the vivid nightmare. Bad night, bad dream, he mused, and went on with his day.

# 4

**M**onday came and went as usual, getting up, going to his office in Wall Street where he was a number cruncher at Morgan Bank. He liked his work well enough, enjoyed the pay, and looked forward to a long, prosperous career in that firm. He had been there three years, and had been promoted to accountant after only two years of working there. His thoughts were occupied by his work for the hours that he was there, going out for a quick lunch, with numbers still on his mind, and leaving at the day's end, usually stopping off at a neighborhood greasy spoon for a hot dinner and some coffee before going home for the evening.

The next couple of days followed in just the same way, and he was able to put any thoughts of the nightmare out of his thoughts. At eight a.m. he headed for the subway. He usually liked to walk along 7th Avenue to 42nd Street and take the train downtown from there. It invigorated him to have a brisk walk in the morning, seeing the hustle and bustle of folks hurrying to work, the sounds of car engines and the clatter of feet on the sidewalks. The air smelled of gasoline and coffee on a warm day and liquid concrete being poured somewhere, but today was an early October morning. Only the woody sweetness of damp, autumn leaves filled the air, as a cool fog rose from the sidewalk and enveloped the few city trees, as the foliage changed color and leaves dropped from their branches. He watched the office girls in their freshly ironed dresses, walking with each other and chattering brightly about their adventures over the weekend, and the men in suits with folded newspapers under their arms, hurrying to get a quick cup of coffee before going to their offices. He enjoyed listening to the echoes of the construction workers, soaring above on scaffolds as they climbed ever higher, to build yet another skyscraper in this great metropolis, while pounding away at the steel, as they drove each girder into its place in the sky.

But Wednesday evening came and brought bad news. The phone rang just before seven. It was Lulu's father, who informed Vern that

Lulu had been sick all week, and had to be taken to the hospital earlier that day. He wanted to know if anything out of the ordinary had happened to her on Saturday night when Vern had last seen her, besides the bad seafood, as she had come home the next morning, cheerless and exhausted, and had barely left her bed for three days.

"No, she just had too much to drink, as far as I know," he told the father. "I took her back to my place in a cab, and she slept on the sofa. In the morning I fed her some eggs and toast, and she seemed just very hung over." There was silence at the other end of the phone. "Why did she have to go to the hospital?" Vern asked after a moment.

"Because she wouldn't eat for those three days. All she would take was a little water, and she kept crying and saying she felt like she was going to die because her body ached so much. We asked her where it ached, but she said she felt it sometimes in her legs, sometimes in her head, her back, her stomach, but the worst thing was hearing this terrible screaming in her ears, calling her name and instructing her to 'give up.' So we called the doctor and he ordered us to get her to the hospital. It was like she was another person; she was so weak and cheerless. Her mother and I had never seen her that way." His voice wavered as he finished the last sentence. "We were hoping you could give us some clue as to what was wrong with her."

"She drank too much, Mr. Turner, but I've seen her that way before, I'm sorry to tell you." Vern gulped, uncomfortable telling the man his daughter was a habitual drunk. "Can I visit her? What hospital is she in?"

"She's right here at Lawrence Hospital," he answered. "Come after work tomorrow, if you like."

# 5

On Thursday Vern cleared his desk a little early to miss some of the rush hour traffic, and took the train to Bronxville, walking the few blocks to the hospital. When he arrived at her door, Lulu was asleep in her bed, an untouched tray of food on her nightstand, and a nurse just exiting the room. The nurse told Vern that the doctors did not know what was wrong with her. The blood tests revealed nothing out of the ordinary, but she was barely eating, and would have to stay there until she gained control of her faculties.

"Her *faculties?*" exclaimed Vern to the nurse. "What's wrong with her faculties?" he asked.

"She hardly speaks and when she does, she seems fearful of something, but doesn't say what. She just says she's afraid she'll die soon, but says she has no pain or discomfort anywhere anymore, but hears a voice calling her name and saying, 'give up.' She just looks frightened and says it over and over, 'I'm gonna die,' until she falls asleep. Her parents hope you can talk some sense into the poor young lady."

Vern walked closer to the bed and looked at Lulu. Her face was drawn, and the peachy tone of her lovely skin had vanished. It was dull and ashen. She lay flat on her back with her arms placed over the covers and straight down next to her sides, her trendy bob, now shapeless and drab. She looked as if someone had posed her the way morticians do before they put a body in a casket on view at a funereal. She was very still, her breath was shallow and her chest barely moving.

He took her hand and held it, but she did not wake up. He gently shook her arm, and said aloud, "Lulu, wake up. It's Vern." He called her name several more times before she slowly opened her eyes and looked at him. She smiled faintly and did not speak, but gave his hand a little squeeze. "What happened to you?" he asked "You were just hung over when you left my apartment on Sunday."

"I had a horrible dream about some monster chasing me, and I couldn't wake up," she confided in a low, but agitated tone. Lulu began to wake more fully, and her eyes grew wider recalling the fear she had felt. "It was a skull grinning at me, with arms and legs growing as it crawled towards me, and *I couldn't wake up*," she rasped. "It seemed so real, and I tried to scream, but I couldn't budge." Her whispered voice was growing shrill and Vern felt her arm shake as he held her hand. A flash of fear shot through him at this disclosure, but he did not want to tell her that he had the same dream. His rubbed his hands together attempting to wash away the sweat that began to heat his palms.

"Then I heard your footsteps walking into the living room, and the monster stood still, but kept staring at me, until I heard you call my name, and I woke up with a hangover, and you offered me some breakfast." She began to cry, and continued, "It was gonna kill me right then, Vern, but you walked into the room where I was and it stopped cold."

"Why didn't you tell me this on Sunday?" Vern asked, not really knowing how he would have reacted if she had told him then. He was unnerved by the coincidence of the two of them each having had a similar nightmare on the very same night. He rested one palm on a corner of her pillow, leaning over her, aware that his forehead was now heated, as well.

"I thought it was just the booze, and you were angry at me anyway," she answered, growing quieter, "but I couldn't forget about it, especially every night this week when I tried to sleep." She was silent for a few moments, only blinking at Vern when she finally spoke again. "I think something is going to kill me, a monster, or a car wreck, or food poisoning, I don't know." She wiped her teary eyes with her fingertips, and sighed with exasperation, still weeping all the while. "I don't know what to do," she moaned.

Vern sat down on her bed and leaned closer over her, hugging her to him. "No, Lulu, that's not going to happen. "You'll be ok if you just eat and forget about the silly dream." He was worried that if she continued to believe in this nightmare, that she could wither away and die, she was so shaken by it. "Hey, you have to get well, my princess, so we can go out to Coney Island next week, before it shuts down for the winter. Remember, you promised to drive us out."

He kissed her and stroked her cheek with his fingers, wondering how to breathe some life into her while recalling the day, just last year, when he first met her as Mary Lou Turner from Brooklyn. How pretty she had been that Sunday in Central Park when he had chanced to meet her chasing after a wide brimmed, pale pink hat that had blown off her head in the late summer breeze. He had retrieved it for her right before it flew into a large puddle in Sheep Meadow where they were walking, and where she and some other young women had been watching a group of people playing tennis beneath the late morning sun gloriously dripping its golden rays in joyous display over the park. She had blinked her blue eyes, those bright, cobalt blue eyes, and lavished her smile on Vern when he returned her hat. He was instantly enamored of this sweet, young beauty, stunning in her summer whites and lace gloves.

She was not a flapper then, and she wore her lustrous auburn hair smoothed into a low chignon. He remembered how he had waited several months before he would see her fine tresses undone, and run his fingers through the beguiling strands, which had draped over her creamy shoulders and ended on her naked breasts and pink nipples. He had loved her that first time, on his sofa, with the lights low and the shades drawn. She kissed him, sweetly at first, and then more passionately, slipping out of her garments as he caressed her thighs, feeling her garters and silk stockings on the way up and over her satin panties, until, at last, she drew them off, as well.

Whenever he looked back on the times of making love with her, savoring the feelings of affection and passion that rose in him, knowing that she returned them, this first time remained foremost in his mind. Her sparkling eyes had opened wide with excitement as he had first caressed her naked body, sitting there together, on his sofa. He kissed her, and his fingers slid upwards and touched her just between her breasts, gently pushing her to lie down, and placing her in a position for love. Each time he remembered that moment, his spine and fingertips tingled, for he was alive again, with that same feeling of excitement and craving as he had been that first time. Within that special memory he experienced yet again, her radiant smile and how it had captivated him on the sofa that day, carving out this moment in eternity for him.

No, he could not desert her during this illness, even though she had changed quite radically since her newly-rich father moved the family to Bronxville, just before her twenty-second birthday. It was not exactly a rags-to-riches story, but loads of stock market dividends and fancy new surroundings, had whisked Mary Lou out of her secretarial job at a downtown law firm, and into the life of flapper frenzy and Manhattan parties.

"Will you eat something now, if I stay here with you for a while, Lulu?" he coaxed.

She nodded in agreement, Vern summoned the nurse, and shortly a tray of roast chicken, mashed potatoes and some greens were placed in front of her. He helped her to sit up a little in her bed, and she ate nearly half of what had been brought, thanking him for staying with her and easing her fears. He stayed until visiting hours were nearly over, and Lulu had fallen asleep. "I'll be back tomorrow," he whispered, kissing her forehead.

The next evening proved a little easier, because she was awaiting Vern's visit. She ate again, while he was there, and began to look a little more alive. They made small talk for an hour or so, and then she closed her eyes in sleep. Mr. and Mrs. Turner thanked him profusely as he was leaving, and he assured them that he would be back the very next afternoon, as it was Saturday.

Lulu looked better still on Saturday, but still kept up the talk of her fear of dying. It was so unlike the reckless Lulu he had known over the past year with her increasingly devil-may-care attitude and her wild, irresponsible behavior, dancing indiscriminately with strange men while drinking heavily during the process, with no thought at all of his feelings, or even of her own safety. Vern left the hospital with the opinion that she was surely mending, and would be discharged in a day or two.

He would makes plans to take her to Coney Island as promised, but he doubted if he could reignite the feelings of passion he had once had for her, which made him quite sad. She had behaved so badly towards him, with her drinking and flirting, causing embarrassing scenes in public Vern was twenty-six, now, and had an excellent job with a bright future. He would have eventually wanted to settle down with Lulu and enjoy a comfortable married life with her, except that she had changed so drastically he could barely recognize in her, the young woman with the errant pink hat, who he had once fallen so madly in love with.

On the train home, Vern pondered the many times as he had dressed-up for her, with joyful anticipation of going out for an evening and sitting across a table from her looking into her pretty eyes. She had behaved charmingly in those early days of their relationship, with an affectionate way of placing her elbows on the table and resting her chin on her laced hands, blinking and turning the corners of her lips up, ever so slightly as she spoke to him about her day, and asking him about his. He thought she was loveable as well as beautiful, and he happily awaited the end of the evening, as well, when he could whisk her back to his apartment for a few kisses, and maybe more. Vern wished he could have those days of ardor back, the days before she had decided to reinvent herself as Lulu, the liberated flapper. Now, he only wanted to see her recover from this bout, and hoped she might mend her ways and stop the heavy drinking before it completely wrecked her mental and physical health.

But when he arrived at his block and headed towards his building, Vern's pace slackened. He turned around and glanced at Blue Jay's sign, almost swinging back to avoid being alone is his apartment. "What the hell," he muttered and continued his walk home. "It was just a silly dream." But his hand shook when he reached into his pocket for the keys, fumbling and dropping them on the top step where they landed with a sharp rattle. With a deep breath he unlocked the building door, rushed up the stairs where he dropped the keys again while attempting to open his apartment door.

Once inside he rushed to his ice box and sought out a cold bottle of beer. "Nerve-wracking evening," he mumbled to himself, and shook his head as if trying to jolt himself out of his fear of turning off the lights and lying down in his bed for the night. He picked up a magazine and flopped down on his couch, consumed his beer in several swallows and quickly got up to fetch another one. He ran his clammy palms over his shirt sleeves and flipped through the magazine, trying to sink into the comfort of the sofa cushions and relax before bed.

Finally, Vern walked into his bedroom, throwing his clothes haphazardly on a nearby chair. He sighed, brushed his fingers through his hair and took a moment to look out the window and onto the street where he had seen Carlotta that night after his nightmare. A streetlamp flickered just in front of the recessed doorway she had appeared in, and he thought he saw the shadow of a person there. A wave of nausea flew over him and he veered away from the window. The light stopped flickering and he looked again to see the area well-lit without a trace of anyone around. Rubbing his eyes, he pulled down the shade and jumped into bed with a loud groan, wondering at the meaning of Lulu seeing the identical phantom in her sleep on the same night. He closed his eyes in dread, hoping the beer would relax him enough to sleep through the night, feeling the fear of her imagined death from it all.

# 6

He passed the next workday with a growing dread of going home, recalling the distressing words Lulu spoke in the hospital the evening before. He slowly walked home from his subway stop as the skies were beginning to darken.

When nightfall came, the colorful neon signs of various eateries and clubs went on all over the neighborhood as usual. Vern looked out of his open living room window towards Blue Jay's and felt the cool breeze of early October on his face and hands. Sure, he would wind his week down at Jay's club, peacefully and unaccompanied by anyone else to look after or worry about. Some diversion from his worries over nightmares would be just the thing. He would have a couple of drinks at the bar, enjoy the band, and have a bit of chit chat with Jay or a few other regulars he knew by name, and after that he would easily sink into a sound slumber.

At 7:30 he strolled into the club with a newspaper under his arm, planted himself at the bar, and ordered a steak dinner and some whiskey. It was going to be a relaxing evening for a change, and he opened his paper to the last story he had been reading, about the prosperity on Wall Street and its never-ending bull run. The band usually did not start until at least nine, but he was in no hurry, and it was a quiet evening, with only a sprinkling of guests in the club, none of whom he knew. Vern ate his dinner, and sipped at his whiskey alone, staring idly behind the bar or glancing over at his paper.

A tall man with dark brown hair and large, brown eyes walked in and sat down next to Vern. "Hi, Vern, how's the steak tonight? I was thinking I might order one, too." Nick D'Angelini was a striking man, with lips that were full, and chiseled like a Roman statue. His prominent, aristocratic nose and high cheekbones were accentuated in the low light of the bar area, that seemed to dissipate in the otherwise darkened room. He was talkative, but soft spoken without the trace of any kind of accent, and his suit was of the best cut, showing off his trim figure.

"Hey, Nick," replied Vern, reaching his hand out for a quick shake. "The steak's great, and Jay's got some more of that rye, too." He held his glass up to the light and showed off its excellent color. "That's if Vinnie doesn't mind us having a few," said Vern, looking at a man two seats away and chuckling.

"Yep, great stuff, if I don't say so myself." Vinnie's jacket was off, his sleeves rolled up, and his hat was tipped back over the crown of his head. "Better save some for me, or I'll have to give Jay a summons for serving alcohol in this establishment." Vinnie reached into his jacket pocket as it hung on the back of the barstool, and pulled out his Federal badge in jest.

"We sure will, Vinnie, we don't want to see this dive closed down, do we?" said Nick, in his usual courteous manner, just as Jay was coming over to take his order. "Hi Jay, I'd like a steak dinner and a rye with just one ice cube. Thanks."

"I know how you like your drink, Nick," smiled Jay, as he poured out the favored bootleg rye over one ice cube. "I know how all my customers like their drinks, don't I?"

Nick pointed to the piano at the end of the bar and said, "Jay, may I?"

"Sure, man, it's all yours," he said to Nick. "We love your fancy fingers on those keys!"

"Thanks. Call me when supper's out," he answered and slipped out of his chair and over to the keyboard where he dashed out a spirited version of *I'm Just Wild About Harry*.

Jay ducked out of the bar area and stood near the barstools, just as Vern was finishing his last bite, so Vern turned his head to speak with him. Jay smiled affably at him and quietly inquired about his lady friend, Lulu. "No, she's taken ill, but she'll be alright in a day or so. I've had to visit her in the hospital the past few days, but they said she could go home tomorrow," he explained. "Just some bug she caught, nothing serious," he added.

Jay expressed his regret at her illness, and turned to go, but Vern still felt someone standing behind him. There was an aura of balmy patchouli floating around him, and he felt a strange warmth, as if candle flames were flickering very close to the back of his suit jacket, penetrating through to his skin. A finger tapped him lightly on one shoulder, and he turned to see two glowing spheres as bright and golden as a pair of harvest moons staring at him. "How is your lady friend?" the placid female voice inquired, her slight accent becoming more apparent as she formed with thickness, the words 'how' and 'lady.'

Vern paused and answered, "She's just fine." He looked at the woman and said, "Carlotta, isn't it? Um, how did you know she was sick? Did I tell you?" knowing that he had not seen her since Lulu's admission into the hospital.

"Carlotta, yes," was all she said, and looked openly into Vern's eyes, without any expression that he recognized as either congenial or malicious. She was wearing a taupe lace dress and a jeweled headband around her forehead, her hair falling loose and wiry, as he had seen it before. A pair of pearl earrings dangled beneath her tresses, and around her neck was the gold-rimmed, pink seashell he had watched her rubbing nervously, last week on the dark street.

It was Vern's turn to speak, or so it was implied. "May I buy you a drink?" he asked, not knowing what else to say, and caught off guard by her presence just while he was trying to escape any recollections of nightmares and Lulu's mental condition. Even through his uneasiness he could not help being curious about this strange, but attractive woman who had so completely invaded his space at Jay's. He offered Carlotta his seat, just as Jay whizzed by again, and wedged an extra, high-backed barstool next to Vern.

Jay stood behind the new bar guest as he helped her onto her seat. He leaned towards Vern and looked directly into Vern's eyes, gave a very slight shake of his head, then raised a finger towards Carlotta, disguising his negative gesture with a friendly, but telling voice. "I see you've met Cat."

"Sure, Carlotta, I met her here the other night," Vern answered still staring at Jay, a surge of queasiness jostling him while the back of his neck felt tight and heated.

"No, *Cat*," repeated Jay, swiveling Carlotta's chair around by its back, and grinning into her eyes. "Take a look at those golden cat eyes, my man!" He chuckled and added, "Watch out for those beautiful peepers! Ok, what can I get for you and the lovely lady tonight?"

Carlotta appeared nonplussed by Jay's comments, and only gave a brief smile, which Vern noted. He knew it was unlike Jay to make negative comments about any of the guests at Blue Jay's, unless he believed a very serious precaution was in order, regarding the well-being of another patron, and Vern had his own reasons for precaution where this woman was concerned. A fading bulb over the bar was flickering just above, blaring out harsh purple and green flashes over Carlotta's otherwise black hair, grimly reminding him of the skull creature in his dream as it grinned at him from the bed sheets. Vern took another sip of his drink and looked away.

"Excuse me," a barkeep said pointing to the dying bulb. "Lemme change it for yuz." Instantly, the new light shone a lovely glow of warm, white light over Carlotta, accentuating her flawless olive skin and enticing eyes. Vern's nausea began to calm and his limbs relaxed.

Although he took note of, Jay's cryptic warning, and still cautious of the eerie nightmare and her strange appearance on his street immediately afterward, Vern did not care to make any move to disengage himself from the dark lady Jay had referred to as "Cat." He was comfortable where he was, so he told himself, as he glanced over at her full, ruby lips and how they parted over her slight overbite. He wondered what it would be like to kiss that mouth, and touch the tip of his tongue to her front teeth. Would he tingle with excitement as he had with Lulu? He would have one drink with her, then excuse himself, and perhaps pick up a conversation with one or two of the other men seated there.

"Could we have a couple of Fallen Angels, please?" he requested, looking at his new companion for approval. She looked vacantly at each of the two men, nodded, and the tall gin and crème de menthe concoctions were soon served.

"Here's to a streak of good luck," she announced as she raised her glass to Vern, and took a sip of the green potion.

The band was just beginning their first tune of the evening. This quintet somehow managed to fit into the small corner space near their end of the bar. The drum kit was sparse, but with the pounding bass, and the resonance of the trumpet and soprano sax, and a burly male singer who was nearly standing on top of the piano player and belting out the lively tunes, it was almost impossible to have a conversation. Vern and Carlotta watched the combo and sipped their drinks, now and again turning to smile at one another. Vern watched the dance floor become more crowded as the band ratcheted up their lively set. The many beaded and sequined gowns of the ladies glistened magically, in frosty shades of yellow and violet, under the soft light of a tiered, milk glass chandelier with fluted brass fittings, that looked like a squat, upside down wedding cake with etched lotus flower designs on each of the three layers.

Vern finished his drink, and instead of thanking Carlotta for her company, and moving along as he had promised himself he would do, he found himself saying, "Would you like to dance?"

The band shifted from hot licks to a slower tune just as he made the invitation, and the singer was crooning out *Wild Women Don't Get the Blues*. Vern offered his hand and led her to the floor, where most couples had switched from Charleston to Fox Trot for this number. Vern felt a rush of heat in his chest as he took her hand in his, and with the other, embraced her back in proper Fox Trot position. He danced her around the floor several times, enjoying the smooth sway of her body close to his as they moved to the music. He glanced at her now and again, noticing the color of her eyes, growing brighter and more golden in the burnished glow of the chandelier, and he thought alternately of what she would feel like when her naked body was next to his, yet reflecting on Jay's telling introduction of "Cat," earlier at the bar.

After three slower tunes, the ensemble took a break. Placing his hand around Carlotta's shoulder, Vern led her back to their seats. "Thank you," he said, smiling, "I enjoyed that."

Carlotta peeked quickly, but deeply, into Vern's eyes and parted her lips in a brief smile, which showed her front teeth protruding over her full, lower lip, turning Vern's attention away from the warning Jay had hinted at.

"Would you like another drink?" he asked her, noting that she had not finished the first one.

"No, thank you, but I've enjoyed this evening with you, Vern, and was wondering if you would see me home to my mother's building." She blinked three times at him as she spoke, and touched his fingers lightly. "It's such a pleasant night for a walk, don't you think so?" Her general expression was bland, yet her luminous eyes were direct and boldly staring into his.

"Of course," Vern answered. "You're just down the block from my place, aren't you?" making sure to keep his tone casual as he fantasized more about kissing her full on the mouth and feeling her coarse black hair brush against his neck and bare chest.

"Yes, not far," she answered, keeping her spellbinding gaze on him as she spoke. He paid the tab, escorted her to the club entrance, where she retrieved her cinnamon red silk evening coat from the cloakroom, and out of the front door and into the dark night they went.

# 7

It was not quite eleven PM, still early for a weekend evening out, and Vern briefly wondered at Carlotta's motive in wanting to end their night now, or did she? The autumn air had kicked up a bit, and Carlotta drew her light wrap around herself and pulled a pair of black lace gloves from one of her pockets and quickly put them on as they walked down West 48th Street. Vern leaned into her slightly, offering his arm as they strolled. Catching a burst of her musky patchouli scent with a hint of rose, he fell into another fantasy about undressing her and running his fingers gently, all over her naked olive skin, and touching her upper thighs with the tip of his tongue.

They drifted along the quiet city blocks, passing Vern's building and continuing across Eighth Avenue and down another block, where Carlotta stopped in front of a red brick apartment building near 47th Street.

She quickly made her point. "I'd like for you to come in and have another drink with me before we end the evening," hoping she had found an unwitting conspirator in Vern tonight. If she could seduce him, and her mind found the sphere of trance during their sex act, then she would visualize her former lover, Geoffrey and his tawny mane of hair falling over her face as they used to kiss. In the vision his eyes would squint in pleasure, showing the mature lines of experience as she fondled him and offered herself to him. It would be Vern, but she would imagine Geoffrey and her intent would be set on him and their reunion.

She took his hand and laced her fingers with his focusing her widening eyes on his as if she meant to grip him in a trance, leaving him no doubt about joining her in her mother's apartment. Vern barely had a chance to nod his head in agreement as Carlotta led him through the entrance and up one flight of stairs, quickly unlocking the apartment door and bolting them inside.

The small, darkened living room was lit only by a few street lights from the window as the pair entered. Vern could barely make out its crowded appearance and nearly tripped over one of the overstuffed chairs and the large sofa which were all draped in heavy, red and gold fringed coverings. A couple of end tables were pinched in between the seats and the walls of the room. Tarnished, brass lamps that looked like elongated antique coffee pots, with large, bell-shaped shades of maroon silk, adorned with heavy fringe, rested awkwardly on the small tables. Several small red and blue oriental rugs were scattered over the worn, wooden floor, and behind the couch, the ample window ledge displaying a large, open bowl of dried rose petals. The place had a musty odor somewhat akin to the patchouli fragrance that Carlotta wore, as if the windows had not been opened in years.

Here and there were old photographs, mounted in blackened wood frames, excessively carved with scrolls and intertwining vines, with dingy glass, containing pictures of people in unusual costumes, standing with a horse, or in front of antique caravans, which caught Vern's interest. He leaned over to get a better look at the pictures, when he heard a quick rumbling over the floor, and saw a smoky puff of fur dart over the couch and tables, and lunge into his face. He heard a shriek, and then felt something soft and fuzzy rub over his fingers. Vern snapped his hand away.

"Boris, get down," commanded Carlotta to the intruder. A pair of eyes opened in Vern's direction, two large, yellow eyes, staring fixedly at him. He heard a soft, quavering breath as he looked at the creature in the dim light of the apartment, trying to make out what manner of beast had accosted him. The head thrust out and pushed into Vern's forearm. "Excuse my cat," she continued, beginning to chuckle. She reached under a lampshade and switched on the light.

In the new light of the lamp Vern beheld Carlotta next to the table, stroking the murky puff ball, who arched his back in pleasure, and turned his face towards his mistress' guest. Vern also reached out to pet the cat, paying close attention to the strange similarity of the cat's eyes and Carlotta's, as they stared at him in unblinking unison. Why had he agreed to come into Carlotta's apartment, instead of simply escorting her home? Before he had time to complete the thought, Carlotta bade him sit down while she walked a few steps away and poured some brandy from a glass decanter in a hutch on the other side of the room.

She handed a snifter to Vern, and toasted. "To Boris, my friend," she said twisting the creature's ears and rubbing his cool, leathery nose as he purred furiously.

"Won't we wake your mother?" Vern asked. "It's pretty late."

Carlotta shook her head and breathed in the vapors of her brandy. "No, she's back in Romania." She tapped on one of the photographs Vern had been trying to look at. "Her father, my grandfather, died, and my uncles have summoned her home to divide the property."

He scrutinized the picture of an old man standing with his hand on the back of a white draft horse hitched to a small, painted caravan. It did not appear to Vern that there could be much in the way of *property* to be derived from a person of such rustic means, but he nodded his head.

Carlotta continued an explanation of her grandfather and his worth as she drank her brandy. "He has several very old violins that are said to have cost quite a lot of money, and the family wishes to sell them, since no one else there plays. Only my grandfather played the violin, and had been given several of the instruments by a Polish princess that he knew. For many years he was a guest in her home, and entertained her daily with his talents."

"What happened to her?" Vern asked, still looking at the photographs.

"She died of consumption after having spent two decades with my grandfather. After that, he returned to his bohemian way of life in his caravan." Carlotta swallowed the last sip of her drink, and got up to pour out another one, continuing her tale as she reached for the decanter. "My mother, their only child, was just a girl when the princess died, and so my grandfather took her back to Romania and brought her up among the gypsies with her half-brothers."

"Will she come back here?"

"Yes, but not for some time, so I'll live here with Boris until she returns." Carlotta stroked the cat, who sat, sphinx-like, on the arm of her chair. She smiled languidly, her eyes half-closed, and sunk deeper into the overstuffed cushions pointedly shifting her hips and sighing deeply as she sat and told her tales of her gypsy family. All the while she and Boris the cat kept a close watch on their guest, their eyes staring in unison at him. He watched her lips as she spoke, wanting to touch them with his tongue and then feel them against his neck.

In order to divert his attention away from the growing feelings of lust he was having about her, he looked around the room. "What's that?" he asked, pointing to a small black violin case standing upright in a corner near the kitchen area.

"That's my violin," she answered. "My grandfather taught me how to play it during the years I spent as a child in Romania and France." Carlotta reached down into her purse which she had tossed down next to herself on the sofa when they first entered the apartment. She drew out a small black velvet bag with a pentagon embroidered on one side, and an eye on the other, causally holding it between her fingers and waited for Vern to speak again.

Still attempting to guide his thoughts away from the subtle, but voluptuous movements of her legs and hips as she sat in her chair, Vern said, "What kind of music do you play?"

"As a child I had a bit of classical instruction, but now I play the new jazz tunes." Her breasts shifted a little as she spoke, and Vern could not fight the wavering thrill that ran through his legs and arms.

"Maybe sometime I'll hear you play," he offered, trying to prolong the light conversation.

"No doubt you will, Vern," she cooed, smiling with her lips opened just enough to display her sensuous overbite to him again.

Still dangling the velvet bag, Carlotta sipped at her drink and touched her finger to her lower lip, brushing away a drop of brandy that lingered there. She then drew out a round, black mirror from the bag and checked her lipstick. Pausing a moment to look at Vern, she caressed her pink seashell, all the while peering into his eyes. He was silent as he gawked back at her, thinking of the evening he took Lulu on his couch and saw her pretty pink nipples and round, lovely breasts for the first time.

Carlotta again looked into the mirror as if inspecting her make-up, but this time she gazed a little longer into it before resuming her conversation with Vern, who had now fallen silent. She then held it up for him to see and said, "How do you like my little mirror?" Before he could answer she said, "Take a look and see how dark you look in its reflection." She smiled as if she were playing a curious game, looking into it herself again, then holding it up to Vern's face in some sort of ritual. "Go on, look," she coaxed with her hand out towards him.

He grabbed the mirror and briefly looked into it, sending it immediately back into her hand. "Yeah, it's dark," he said abruptly, brushing his hair off his forehead and grabbing his drink for another gulp. Vern looked away from her, but he felt her eyes on him, making him warm. He loosened his tie and unbuttoned his collar, wanting to leave her and her bizarre gestures, but something compelled him stay. Was it her seductive pose on the couch, her smiling red lips? Thoughts of desire overtook him, and he sat back again in the chair thinking of lustful acts, but not with Carlotta.

Here he sat now, in a strange woman's apartment, yet his mind was fixed in an hour from months ago with Lulu, that had crystalized into a haunting memory. He was torn between his carnal desire for this strange woman, and his past memories of someone who had been precious to him. He looked at Carlotta and knew he was only mesmerized by her, and her otherworldly, aureate eyes. He felt no love, no longing to know her; he only felt that he needed to get back the feeling of passion he had shared with his girl, and drown in the scent of Lulu's jasmine perfume, hear her short, breathy sighs as he kissed her and held her close, watch her smile in wonder as he undressed her and lay her down on his sofa, both of them tingling in the ecstasy of romantic love.

Suddenly Vern got up from his chair, and in two steps was standing over Carlotta, kissing her, pulling her to him and feeling the heat of her body as she stood and bent into him. She dropped her mirror on the couch, her hands now gripping his shoulders as she led him into her bedroom. With one hand Carlotta began to unbuckle his belt. Vern took over, removing his shirt, then his trousers, leaving them in a heap on the floor, while Carlotta wriggled out of her dress, tossing it on the pile. She pulled at Vern's hips they fell onto the bed together, winding their arms around each other, engulfed in each other's wet kisses. Vern pulled away just long enough to look at Carlotta's velvety olive skin, and saw a figure more curvaceous than he could have imagined under the straight, stylish dress she had worn to the club that night. She lay beneath him, her breasts separated, her brown nipples pointing upward, and her thighs slightly parted. Boldly, she leaned forward and began to kiss him all over, pausing briefly over his thighs and then continuing her lip's journey over his secret parts, then upward to his ribcage, dangling her tongue around his nipples and guiding his thighs with her hands, until he had penetrated her for a time. Then he abruptly withdrew and exploded over her throat and wild black hair in a frenzy of desire.

They fell asleep, and awoke several times during the short night, each time repeating the activities with more relish than the previous act. Vern quickly returned to sleep each time, giving into her hypnotic eyes and eager body. He finally awoke in the midst of heaving out a short scream and nearly fell out of bed onto the floor.

Carlotta sat up and pulled the bedcover around herself, as if in a sudden chill. "What happened?" she asked, "Are you alright, Vern?"

Vern rubbed his eyes and gasped. "I had a bad dream, that's all," remembering something about trying to open her bedroom window in the night and some very sharp little teeth piercing his fingers from under the sash as he lifted the pane open. There had been a scampering sound, too, somewhere on the floor. His eyes darted around the room as the morning sun tried to invade the closed window. "I need to be going," he stated, glancing at his fingertips, then reached for his clothes.

"Let me get you some coffee first," Carlotta offered.

"Ok, sure, thanks," he answered. He really wanted to leave and go home, and forget about why he had allowed himself to indulge himself with a woman he barely knew and had some apprehension of. He could blame her and her seductive ways, but he knew he had allowed her to make all of her rapacious advances, without resisting in any way.

Vern dressed. He was sitting on the edge of her bed as she brought him a cup of coffee. The two of them barely spoke, but Carlotta was preoccupied, holding her black mirror and looking into it from time to time, in between Vern's few words about getting to the office promptly. He noticed her toying with the object, but avoided additional conversation that might keep him from escaping her company. When he rose to leave, he took her hand and pressed her fingers to his lips, saying, "You're swell, Carlotta, but this can't happen again, ok?"

She looked up at him, with her usual bland expression, skirting the issue of the torrid acts that had occurred between them. "Sure, Vern, it was just one of those things, you know. And besides, you still have a girl, don't you?" Her fingers lightly caressed the mirror still in her hand.

Vern hesitated. "Yeah, I guess so," he mumbled, looking at the cat sitting upright on a little chest near the bed. Boris stared at him intently, and began to purr as Vern reached out to stroke his head. "Goodbye, Boris," he said, picking up his jacket. He opened the door, and moved his head away from Carlotta, avoiding any 'goodbye' kisses, but in a hasty movement she lifted the mirror to his face and said, "Remember me." He recoiled and darted down the stairs.

# 8

He had scarcely opened the front door of his own apartment and thrown his jacket on the sofa before hurriedly tearing off his pants and shirt on his way to the shower. He was disgusted for allowing himself to become so out of control last night with a woman he barely knew, and one he would no doubt, run into again at Blue Jay's, his favorite neighborhood haunt. He would have to find a way of handling this situation gracefully, but for now, all he wanted was to wash her scent off his body and out of his hair. The warm drizzle splashed on him like a pristine waterfall heated by the rays of the sun, cleansing and refreshing.

Vern stepped into his bathroom, and into another world of protective black and white tiles that covered the room from floor to ceiling, and dove into the cleansing water of his shower. This room had been his deciding factor in letting this apartment, especially because of the shower, which was as wide as a small tub. It had shiny new chrome and porcelain faucet handles, and a sizable sprinkler head, that, when turned on, spilled into the stall like gentle rainwater falling over a small pond, on a clear, spring afternoon.

He often remembered the day he let the apartment, after a long, hot train ride from his parents' house in Park Slope, and climbing up three flights of stairs on that humid, June afternoon. He had seen four other flats that day, and this was the last one on his list, and the one he had been the least interested in viewing, because of its location on the outskirts of Hell's Kitchen. The rest of the apartment was uninteresting, although the walls had a fresh coat of paint, and the wooden floors were newly varnished and clean. He was tired of looking, and thinking about how his life would be in any one of the places he had seen, and thought to simply thank the landlord for his time, and put the whole thing off for another week. But just before he uttered those words of *'no thanks, not this one,'* the landlord walked him into the bathroom.

The landlord had proudly announced, "I retiled this bathroom myself, only last month. I could have gotten a break on yellow tiles, but the missus insisted black and white was the way to go. And after she saw how it looked in this place, she wanted it done in our place down on the first floor."

Vern looked at the small, white hexagonal tiles that covered the floor, which were outlined in two rows of black tiles all around the edge of the floor. The walls were also tiled about halfway up, with larger, square ones in a checkerboard pattern. All of the facilities appeared to be new, as well, including a medicine cabinet with an etched mirror that hung above the sink and white torch lamps on either side. The room looked like a movie set to Vern, who imagined himself coming home from work and dashing into the shower, feeling the warm spray of soaking raindrops on his face and body, washing off the workday and beginning an evening of relaxation.

"I'll take it," said Vern. "I'm starting a new job, and I'd like to move in as soon as possible."

"Sure thing, young man," answered the landlord, counting the bills that Vern handed him. "You can start moving in next week, the last week of this month, and I won't even charge you for the extra week, how's that?" They smiled and shook on it, Vern delighted in his newly found home.

His mother had given him a set of slightly worn white towels and a shower curtain with a gray and white circle pattern. He could not wait to impress Lulu with his bathroom the first time she came to his apartment a few months after he had met her.

"Well, Vern Garvey, what a gorgeous bathroom! It looks like it belongs in a mansion, not a brownstone apartment." Lulu grinned and examined every corner of the room, touching the walls, opening the etched mirror to see the medicine chest, pulling the cords of the light fixtures and turning them off and on. Vern was glad that she was impressed, and had more than fleeting visions of what it would be like to have this lovely lady shower and dress in there, after having spent the night with him.

Soon afterward, Lulu and her mother took a train to Miami to visit her Aunt Alice, and when she came back two weeks later, she insisted upon meeting Vern at his apartment before they went out to dinner. "Ok, Mary Lou, but I'd be happy to meet you at the train station and we can take a cab to the restaurant."

She giggled and said, "No, I've got a souvenir from Florida for you, Vern. I'd like to bring it over first. Anyway, I can drive down in Pop's Chrysler and park on your street. See you later, Baby."

Vern had been so excited that she wanted to come to his digs again, that he spent that Sunday morning making sure everything was spotless — no old newspapers lying around, or coffee stains in the kitchen sink — but he took especial pride in cleaning his marvelous bathroom. He put out clean, white towels, folding them perfectly on the racks, sweeping the floor and getting the dust out of every corner, wiping down the mirror for finger prints, and gently tucking the shower curtain behind the lower edges of the shower stall.

At five o'clock, Mary Lou knocked on his apartment door just as Vern was dusting the window sill in the living room. He bolted to the door, running his fingers through his thick hair and giving a gentle tug to his tie, as a last effort in preening himself for his much awaited lady love. "Hey, Lu, it's great to see you, Honey," he exclaimed, hugging her, then pulling her inside and quickly closing the door.

She dropped some bags on the floor, wrapped her arms around him and kissed him, tittering "I missed you, Vern, it was such a long ride down and back, I thought we'd never get home." She looked around the living room and smiled. "Gee, it's great to be here." She kissed him again and again.

They walked to the couch, still enfolded in each other's arms, paying attention only to the other's eyes and lips. Vern's foot caught on one of her large shopping bags, dragging it a few inches before he really noticed it. "Say, what's in this big bag," he asked, "a new rug or something?"

"Yeah, something," she simpered then reached down into one of the bags and pulled out a large, folded plastic object, opened it up, and spread it out over the sofa. It was a shower curtain, with a lively design of several opera-red flamingos with black beaks and yellow eyes standing under a canopy of parrot-green palm trees, and had a row of chrome grommets at the top edge. Before Vern could comment, she pulled the other shopping bag open, and out came new towels in coordinating shades of green and pink, a round, black, looped rug and a white shaving mug with a green alligator for a handle. "Happy birthday, Vern," she laughed, her eyes shining brightly and her cheeks blushing. "I saw this, and I thought of your bathroom."

Vern was speechless, and hardly knew what to say besides, "You got all this stuff for *me*? I mean, I don't know what to say, Mary Lou, thanks so much." He leaned over and kissed her, but was having a little trouble visualizing his black and white bathroom becoming a nesting ground for plastic flamingos and zesty palm trees. "Oh, and it's not my birthday," he added.

"Happy birthday, *early,* then." She was still grinning, and taking Vern's hand, she led him towards the bathroom and teased, "You really don't know what to say? Say, 'Let's hurry up and get this new stuff into the powder room.'"

Vern grew to enjoy the bright, jungle colors of his newly decorated bathroom, and thought fondly of the day Lulu had surprised him with her packages of this colorful shower paraphernalia. He had enjoyed the fact that she wanted to add her feminine touch to his home. To him, it meant that she was not only comfortable there, but that she viewed him and his home as a long-term undertaking, a relationship where they could go out on the town as easily as stay in and read the paper and listen to the radio together on his couch. But today he planned to call on her at the hospital, and hope it would be the last time he would have to visit her there.

At nine a.m. the phone rang. It was Lulu telling him not to come that day, because she was being discharged. "That's g reat n ews," h e nearly shouted. "What time will you be home?"

"Not until later this afternoon. I'd love to have you visit me, but I might be awfully tired by then. What about tomorrow after work?"

"No, I have to stay late tomorrow evening for a dinner meeting, but I could see you Tuesday; how's that?" he offered.

"Sure Vern, Tuesday after work. Mother will give you some supper with me." She paused and said, "I'm feeling much better, just still a little weak. I miss you, Vern."

"I miss you too," he said. It was true, he did miss her, the way she used to be. Naturally, she had not had anything to drink during her hospital stay, and her manner reminded him of their first six months together, before she had gone to hell with her boozing and flirting.

Now he had to confront what he had done the night before, with Carlotta. He had thought he was finished with Lulu, but when he saw her so sick and weak in the hospital, his feelings began to change. Maybe there was no hope for them, but he still cared for her despite her being zozzled so often nowadays, and he would see her through this.

As far as Carlotta was concerned, she was unlikely to captivate his heart even though he found her physically very attractive and seductive. She was also sober and that was something, but she was quiet and emotionless, and it was disturbing the way she stared at him and massaged her shell pendant, or handled that black mirror she had shoved in his face as he was leaving her flat, as if she were casting a gypsy spell on him. He seriously wondered if she had been able to send telepathic thoughts that induced both himself and Lulu to have the menacing dreams about the crawling skull on the same night he had met her. And he had had an unsettling feeling when he had chanced to meet her standing across the street from his building, after his skull nightmare. He briefly looked at his fingertips again, wondering if rats really had been munching on his fingers during last night's sleep in Carlotta's bed.

Again he questioned why he had allowed himself to be seduced by her last night while sitting at the bar in Blue Jay's. He had never been like this with a woman before, a woman he was clearly not interested in getting to know any further, especially someone so close to his home and hangouts, who could make his world uncomfortable. *Yes, Why?*

Her quietude and deadpan expression made him feel detached from her, for she had no humor to share with him. There was no excitement in her conversation, only her body. He would have rather laughed over some ordinary phrase or incident with someone else, than become bewitched by her bold eyes, so full of mystery. Instead of reveling in the scent of her perfume all over his body and clothes, he had rushed home to wash himself of it and rid himself of the night of passion he had experienced with her.

46

Vern strolled out for a late Sunday breakfast at Mabey's, his favorite hash house just a few blocks down close to Times Square. He perused his paper and sipped a second cup of coffee, then spent the rest of his Sunday reading his book on his sofa, and going to bed early to prepare for the work week ahead, barely having another thought of Carlotta.

# 9

**M**onday at the office whizzed by, and he gave little thought to anything else but getting his week started, and preparing himself for the junior accountant dinner meeting at 5:00. He had worn his newest navy blue flannel suit, a white shirt, and a dark burgundy tie with a conservative diagonal gold stripe pattern, a veritable banking uniform for the other forty-odd young men in attendance, corporate and boring.

After the meeting, a few of the men decided to stop and have a drink rather than heading straight home for the night, but Vern was tired, and ready to go back to his apartment and read for a while before going to bed.

"Sure you won't change your mind, Vern, it's early yet," one of the other men asked. "C'mon," he smiled and motioned to Vern as he and the other three ducked into a dingy basement staircase and knocked on the gray iron door. The place hardly looked as if it housed a snazzy club inside, but that was often the way with gin joints popping up and closing down so fast no one could keep track of them. He hesitated, thinking it might be a good idea to have some diversion instead of rushing home to the prospects of more nightmares.

Vern smiled back, but did not enter. "Is this some new dive you guys just found? It looks like a warehouse storage room."

"Could be, but they've got pints, and that's all we need, right gentlemen?" he laughed, slapping a coworker's back as they filed down the stairs.

"Maybe next time," answered Vern, "I'm pretty tired." He continued walking towards the subway stop, hoping his fatigue would be enough to lull him into a sleep unbroken by dreams of grinning skulls.

When the train got to Times Square, he walked leisurely towards West 48th Street. The evening air was refreshing, and with the rush hour throng over, and the enchantment of a pink and yellow twilight settling in over the quieted streets, Vern began to feel more relaxed, allowing the familiar sights and sounds of the city to distract him. Muffled sounds of car horns sounded in the distance, and the neon signs were beginning to light up over the doors of fancy clubs and simple diners, alike. Echoes of laughter and cab wheels pulling up to a curb caught his attention, as several young women in fashionable cloche hats and sleek fall coats in black or gray got out and strolled down the street together, their red lips all moving at once, absorbed in animated conversation about their day of work in some department store where they were employed. Their high heels struck the sidewalk in a variety of clicks and clacks as they laughed and jested with one another about some incident concerning the glove counter one of them worked at. Vern took pleasure in scenes of this sort, of people enjoying their day to day lives in New York, because he too, had a sense of belonging to this world, this city he had embraced, from daybreak to sunset, every day of his life in Manhattan.

As he turned the corner onto his block and walked towards his building, he heard someone scampering away on the sidewalk ahead. He looked, but saw no one, and continued his relaxed pace. When he neared his building door, he heard a soft voice speak his name. "Vern," it whispered into the autumn breeze, and faded away. He turned around, and not seeing anyone, thought it must have been his imagination, so took out his key from his jacket pocket and was just about to pop it into the lock, when he heard the voice again. "Vern, wait." He heard the scuffling sound of feet again, looked around and saw a petite female figure running towards him.

"Carlotta?" His sense of ease and well-being slipped away like that of a carefree ice skater on a glimmering winter pond, suddenly losing one of the blades on his skates.

"Yes, it's me." She strode up to him and stopped a few crowded inches from him. He caught a whiff of her heavy, musky scent and noticed the blue sheen her dark hair had in the fading light. She was slightly out of breath from running, and her chest rose and fell under her light coat, as she spoke. "I thought that was you, Vern, I was just on my way home." She was quick in getting to her point. "Could you please walk me the rest of the way?"

Vern hesitated, his key sticking out straight in front of him, ready to plunge into his own front door and leave the city evening behind to enter the private world of his third story flat. "Sure, Carlotta," he answered not wanting to openly insult her. "Is there some sort of problem tonight?"

"Well, some ruffians were gathered just over there, and they all whistled, and a couple of them jumped out in front of me when I walked past." She pointed to the corner that Vern, himself, had just turned, where he had not noticed any such group as he passed.

He put the key back into his pocket and walked with her along 48th Street to her building on Eight Avenue. They said little on the short block over, and when they stopped in front of her door, Carlotta asked, "Would you mind escorting me upstairs? I've been a little uneasy here since my mother left."

Inwardly, Vern balked at her transparency. He knew for a fact that her mother had been gone for over two months, and Carlotta seemed to have little problem walking home from Blue Jay's at all hours on any given night. He said nothing, but smiled and nodded, holding the door open for her, walking behind her as she ascended the flight up to her flat.

Her heavy scent floated down on him as they climbed the few steps up to her door, and he began to remember the moment he had first seen her naked thighs. She unlocked the door with her key, and held it open for Vern. She peered into the dark apartment and then glanced back at Vern with a pained expression. "Would you mind having a look around before you go, Vern?" she asked.

He entered and waited for her to switch on a lamp, seeing only the bright yellow eyes of her cat from across the small, dimly lit room. The cat blinked at him, and pounced off the table on which he had been sitting, onto the floor with a heavy thud, and over to Vern, rubbing his whiskers against his pants and purring furiously. "Hello, Boris," he said, reaching down to pet the creature.

Before he could say anything else, Carlotta had whisked off her coat, displaying her bare arms, and lovely figure beneath a clingy, maroon chiffon dress. "Sit down, Vern, why don't you, for a few minutes?" she asked, smiling and opening her spooky eyes wider as she made her invitation.

Vern sat down on one of the draped chairs telling himself he would not stay long. She asked how his day was, walked into the kitchen and came out with a bottle of beer, which she handed to him.

"Thank you," he said. "Long dinner meeting tonight at work. "I'm pretty tired." But he took the beer and leaned back into the chair, the cat now sitting on the table next to him, staring into Vern's eyes with his wide, golden ones. Carlotta, too, stared at Vern, who pretended not to notice but slowly sunk into the memory of his pleasures with her just two nights before.

Things progressed quickly, with Carlotta sitting on the arm of his chair and placing her hand on his thigh. It was as if he had never left two days ago, with the thoughts of rushing home to wash off her scent, vowing never to repeat those unrestrained physical activities with her. This time, his thoughts did not even protest, but willingly surrendered, forgetting all intentions of maintaining only simple cordiality with her when he met her by chance at Blue Jay's or elsewhere. She hastily began pulling off her dress and slip and thrusting her naked breasts to his lips until he pushed her down into the cushions and repeated the actions of two nights earlier.

Afterwards, Vern fell asleep with Carlotta snugly beside him on her couch, waking only because the cat had decided to perch himself on the sofa arm, just above their heads, and rub his whiskers on Vern's forehead. Vern awoke with a gasp.

"You alright, Vern?" Carlotta asked. She laid aside the black mirror that was in her hand. I was watching you sleep for the past hour."

"Sure, I just had another bad dream." He sat up.

"What was it about?" Carlotta wanted to know. She again picked up her mirror and held it up to his face as she spoke which immediately made him suspicious of her motives and her unnatural powers. "Look," she said, "you're fine. Just a silly dream is all."

He shoved her hand and the mirror away from him. "It was nothing, really. Look, I have to go," he said, getting up and quickly throwing on his clothes and walking towards the door. "Goodnight, Carlotta." She positioned herself for a kiss but Vern stepped away and opened the door. "I have to get some sleep before I go to work in the morning."

"Stay here," she proposed, standing up and taking hold of his hand. She was still naked.

Vern grimaced, shook his head, and said, "I can't, and you know it. Goodnight now, Carlotta." Without giving her another word, he left.

Carlotta closed the door behind him and sat back down naked on the sofa, gazing into the black mirror for a time, thinking of her sexual prowess over Vern, Yes, she had made use of Vern's virility, and smirked while gazing into her mirror, noting the worn lipstick on her mouth while recalling the evening with Vern. She had imagined Geoffrey's face, focusing on the memory of his touch while Vern excited her into explosion, all the while imagining the sounds of herself as playing her exquisite violin. Carlotta the temptress would have audiences of the great stages of America and Europe roaring for more, and she would do it with Geoffrey sitting in a box seat smiling on and awaiting her kisses.

\*\*\*

On the short walk back to his flat, Vern recalled the eerie dream he had just had while sleeping next to her. He had been sitting in the passenger seat of Mr. Turner's maroon Chrysler, looking out of the driver's side window, and waiting for Lulu to climb in next to him, when he heard a heavy bang on the front windshield. It appeared to be an enormous black slug, or perhaps a giant cat, covering half of the glass. Then came another thud on the other side of the windshield, with one more slug covering the rest of the window. Both creatures flattened out like gigantic, slimy leeches, and he saw indistinct mouths with black lips sucking holes into the window, grinning wider and wider as they inhaled all of the air from the inside of the car threatening to suffocate Vern, who was gripped with fear and unable to exit the car, though he had repeatedly rattled the door handle which would not budge. At that moment, the cat's whiskers had brushed against his forehead, and jolted him awake.

When Vern reached his apartment, he tore off his clothes and rinsed off in his shower before flopping into bed, once again swearing never again to allow Carlotta to spellbind him. There in the dark of his room he tossed in his bed, unable to rest after his actions with Carlotta; actions which he could have resisted.

He was not a superstitious person, but he had a sense that there was something powerful about her knowledge of occult talismans and he could not dismiss the night terrors. Was she just testing her expertise on him? Surely, she had something to do with the evil dreams that had been planted in his head and in Lulu's, causing such fright in the poor girl that she believed she was dying. He jumped out of bed at every clang, murmur, thud, patter that sounded from the street below, carefully poising himself at the side of the window while lifting a corner of the shade and peering out to see only passersby, blowing leaves, or an empty box being tossed down the sidewalk by an occasional breeze.

After nearly an hour, he turned on the light and grabbed a magazine from his nightstand, flipping through the pages barely noticing any of its content before tossing it back on the table. He reached to turn out the light in case Carlotta ventured past to see that he was still awake in his bedroom. He then got up to wash the clamminess from his face and hands, and the faint smell of her musk that lingered behind his neck. Just before he entered the hallway, he rushed back and turned the light on again, remembering the night he had the dream about the skull as he looked back at his bed through the dark hallway. He shivered and walked briskly to the bathroom, careful to turn on the hall light, as well.

When he flopped back into his bed he did not even attempt to sleep, but repeatedly questioned his actions with Carlotta. At first, he had been captivated by her exotic looks and her attentions, and had easily succumbed due to his disenchantment with Lulu and her drunken conduct, so he told himself. Now Vern was actually repulsed by her and the potent allure she and her cat had over him with their matching feline eyes.

"Why did I go up there again?" Vern muttered, as he plumped up his pillow with a fist, crashing his down into it with a groan. He believed it had less to do with her seductive beauty than some preternatural trickery, for he had visions of making love to Lulu every time Carlotta made sexual advances towards him. While kissing Carlotta, he had again felt the irresistible attraction he had for Lulu in the very early days of their relationship. Like a drug, it overtook him and he caved in to Carlotta even though he had been wary of her since their very first meeting at Blue Jay's. He thought of his hands on her shoulders and breasts as he kissed her, and wiped his hands over his bedsheets with a scrubbing action. "Never again," he said aloud several times while staring at his dark ceiling. He eventually rolled over and fell asleep, waking to the sound of his alarm clock only a few hours later.

# 10

As his workday wore on Vern compelled himself to concentrate on the papers on his desk and look forward to the evening dinner he would have at Lulu's house, yet he could not shake the disturbing feeling he had about Carlotta and her forthright pursuit of his company. "Why didn't I say, '*no, I can't walk you home?*'" He fidgeted with his pencil, twirling it in his fingers, then rocking it on his desk like a rolling pin.

He sat absently and ruminated about it over and over again, and his feelings of being trapped and sickened by his own lack of will power. He could have said, 'no,' both times, but he responded to her lure with hardly a thought in his mind about the consequences. Vern picked up his pencil and forced himself to look down at his ledger, but he mulled over the bizarre way she seemed to relate to her cat, and how their eyes seemed to work in unison as they stared at him together. Again he dropped his pencil and stared out of his office window at the gray skyscrapers immediately in front of him and thought about the horrible dream while at her apartment the night before, of cat-slugs breaking through Lulu's Chrysler windshield. He shoved his chair back and left his office for a walk to the water cooler, hoping he would run into someone, anyone who would distract him from his thoughts.

At five o'clock, he took the subway to Grand Central, and immediately boarded the train for Bronxville and dinner with Lulu, finally able to leave some of the ominous thoughts about Carlotta behind. Besides, it was a fine, autumn evening for a walk, with a light breeze, which seemed to blow the waning sunlight in his direction, as he walked from the train station to the Turner's house just a few blocks away. He was anxious to see Lulu, and hoped that he would find her much recovered from her depression.

The Turner's house was not the largest one on their village street, but it may have been the most striking. It looked like a giant chocolate confection, delicious with its caramel-beige, wrap-around porch, and deep, cherry-red trim of swags and scrolls, which decorated the dark brown house and its several round turrets. A hedge of crimson barberry bushes lined the front of the house, ending with a rose bush at each side of the staircase leading to the porch and front door.

"Hi, Vern," called Lulu's voice from the open door, as she rushed down the steps to greet him with a smile and a kiss, nearly getting her skirt caught in the thorns of summer's leftover rose bush which hung slightly over the walkway. "How was your day?"

"Oh, just about like always, pretty good," he answered as they walked into the house. "Say, you look swell," he beamed.

She seemed to be more like herself again; her skin had that warm, peachy appearance, and her eyes were radiant. Only her bobbed hair looked a little out of shape, and her nails were not the polished red they were usually painted. She pulled at the chin-length ends of her hair and frowned slightly. "I need a trim, though," she said. She looked so lovely, in a simple blue twill skirt and white cotton blouse, with a pearl bar pin at the neckline.

"You'll get one this week," he answered, putting his arm around her, as they went to the living room to greet her parents.

The Turners put down their evening newspapers and smiled broadly at Vern. Mr. Turner got up and offered his hand. "Nice to see you again, Vern, thanks for coming out to visit Mary Lou," he said. He was a tall, well-built man with thinning blonde hair and a perfectly trimmed light brown, pencil mustache.

"Dinner's almost ready, Vern, can I get you a beer first?" Lulu's mother asked, clasping her fingers properly just below her waistline, and smiling. Mrs. Turner was an older version of her daughter, with sparkling, blue eyes, and auburn hair which was pinned back into a neat chignon at the nape of her neck. She was dressed in a buff lace blouse and an ankle-length camel skirt, and wore a light scent of rosewater.

"No, thanks, Mrs. Turner, I'll just have a glass of water when we sit down," he replied, not wanting to invite any hint of booze around Lulu, especially after her last bout of drinking.

"Well, you kids sit here for a bit. Pop and I will get the table set," she responded. "And Mary Lou needs only to relax and think about getting back to her life of leisure." A slight downturn of Lulu's mouth at this remark caught Vern's eye. Vern turned to Lulu when her parents had left the room, taking her hand and leading her to sit down with him, on one of the sumptuous fern green Louis XV style sofas that flanked the fireplace. "Is everything ok?" he asked. Despite the momentary frown, he was amazed to see her looking as she did months ago, before she had started drinking heavily. Her eyes darted over his face, her red, Cupid's bow lips curled again into a smile. They sat and held hands and gawked at one another as if they had only just met.

"Vern, I'm so happy to see you," she exclaimed.

"Me too," he chuckled. "It's so good to see you looking like yourself again." Vern moved closer to her and kissed her, moving back for a moment to behold her again, then repeating the kiss over and over. Sparks of excitement ricocheted over his heart, rousing him to believe that they could be as they used to be, but he cautioned himself to wait and see.

"Do you feel well enough to have dinner over the weekend?" he asked. "I'd love to take you to that Italian place on West 46th Street you liked."

"Oh, yeah, Fabrizio's, I loved that place," she sighed, smiling. "Sure, I'm ready, Sweetie."

"Ok, Saturday, then? We'll make it an early night, how's that?" he said, wanting to keep it short and avoid jazz clubs and drinking for the time being. "I'll make a reservation for 7:30, then?"

"Great, let's do it," she laughed, kissing him. "I can't wait!" Vern heard her giggle as he stepped off the porch and onto the front walkway. He looked back and saw her fading smile as she waved goodbye. "See you soon," she called out after him, still lingering as he turned the corner.

# 11

Vern started home in a cheerful mood, thinking of Lulu and her beauty, and how easy it had been to spend time with her that evening and new worries about Carlotta were momentary until he reached his subway stop at 42$^{nd}$ Street. He walked home in the dark autumn dusk taking in deep breaths of the cool air as he tried to keep his mood from turning anxious. As he turned the corner at 48$^{th}$ Street, he began looking about the buildings to see if Carlotta was waiting to pounce on him with some new excuse to walk her home, or worse yet, to entice her way up to his apartment. The streets were mostly empty and he heard only the sound of his own shoes pacing down the sidewalk and across the street.

Once inside, he made sure the living room curtains were drawn tightly together, but peaked out several times when he imagined a voice or scuffling footsteps on the sidewalk below, dreading to see Carlotta loitering outside, awaiting his appearance after an evening out. He went to bed relieved and fell asleep easily, but was awakened by what he thought was a crash in the street below.

Vern jumped up and carefully lifted the window shade, but saw nothing, only the dim light of a streetlight casting a blue haze over the doorway opposite his building. Still half asleep, he crawled back into bed and closed his eyes, allowing the sensation of drifting into slumber overtake him. Another crash. Again he opened his eyes, and attempted to get up and go to the window again, but his limbs were heavy with torpor. His lids closed again and disjointed thoughts of Lulu's lips and the faded roses at the Porter's front walk wavered and melted away until the crash came again and again. Vern did not open his eyes this time, but knew the sound was coming from his dreams, dreams of falling down an open manhole and screaming for help as water began to engulf his shoes, then his trousers. "Help is here," a female voice called. Then came the crash again of an iron lid being thrown over the open manhole and a burst of rusty odor as it fell, and he was now enveloped in the murky darkness of the damp pit, a gloom so black it felt like eternal obscurity. He did not awake until morning, remaining swallowed up the entire night in that Stygian despair.

Vern sat up in bed at the sound of his alarm clock, rescued by the rosy glimmer of morning's light peeking under his window shade. Still, he could not help taking a cautious look from beneath the shade to see if Carlotta was lurking outside, and might glare up at him with a chilling grin in acknowledgment of the nightmare she had caused him. But there was nothing there but his remorse at having engaged with her.

*** 

The next two days passed calmly, without any unsettling events due to Carlotta, although Vern continued to worry about the possibility of Carlotta following him again. He purposely stayed away from Blue Jay's for dread of running into her there. On his way home from work for those evenings, he would duck behind a parked car and scan the street for any trace of her before he bolted for his building.

On Friday afternoon storm clouds were muscled in by a high wind and blackened the heavens with heavy, steel-gray masses of smog covering the moaning sky, unleashing a dark, drenching rain over the city for hours. Vern trudged home, soaking wet as he went in and out of the subway stations, his umbrella, useless in the strong gusts of wind that pelted his back and hissed as he passed through it. Just before he got to his building, he heard a shriek, and saw a small object in his path that looked like a wet, crumpled up, black hat, or thick woolly scarf, flopping in the wind down the sidewalk. As he approached, he saw a head emerge, and a pair of eyes glaring at him. It opened its mouth full of teeth and shrieked again, looking directly at Vern, as if in warning. In the dim light and the sheets of rain that all but obliterated his view, he briefly wondered if this were one of the giant sewer rats he had heard tales of, but no one had ever seen. He looked down closer at the creature, and realized it was a wet cat; it was Boris.

"Boris, come here, little fella," he said, cautiously extending his hand toward the cat's nose. At first the shivering cat recoiled, but Vern continued talking to him, and very soon the animal bumped his head into Vern's fingers, in recognition. "How did you get out here?" he went on, trying to soothe Boris with his voice, but suspecting Carlotta of some twisted gimmick to get his attention. His heart quickened to think the chapter was not finished with her, but he picked up the cat and looked around. Seeing no one, except other soaked passersby returning from work, he walked with Boris in his arms to Carlotta's building.

Before he turned the corner, he heard a loud wailing and sobbing. It was a woman fluttering aimlessly about the sidewalk with her hands cupped around her mouth. She was yelling, "Boris," over and over between the sobs. Vern rushed up to her from behind grabbing her elbow and showing her the cat. She let out a startled screech and then more sobs.

"I've got him, Carlotta, he was lost on my block…. I found him on my way home from work."

The drenched woman took the animal in her arms and hugged him in the rain. "Boris, how long have you been out?" she cried, pet-ting his soaked fur. "I must have left a window open this morning, and when I got home, there was rain all over the floor and he was gone." She continued to sob. Vern took her arm and escorted her to her front door, and then upstairs to her apartment, uneasy about climbing that staircase once again, but determined to see that she was safe at home with her pet.

Carlotta, still crying and thanking Vern for Boris' rescue, retrieved a towel from the bathroom and began to dry off the purring creature. Vern stood and watched, waiting for her to calm down. Her eyes were dull and tinged with anxiety, unlike the brash, confident headlights that had mesmerized him with their brilliant power only a few days before. She brushed her sopped hair back with her hand, looking down at her pet, and whispering, "You're all I've got, Boris."

Vern glanced at the door and cleared his throat as if to indicate his departure. He looked at her still weeping, holding her pet, patting him dry, and kissing the top of his head as she did so. He had never imagined Carlotta as being anything other than a bewitching woman, and now, it began to occur to him how mistaken he might have been about her. Boris was just a cat, and Carlotta, maybe just an odd, lonely, young woman. Empathy for her swelled in his gut, his chest, and was spreading out over his arms, and into the hands that wanted to clutch her, despite his resolve not to.

One of her long, heavy earrings became loose as she was hugging Boris, and fell to the wooden floor with such an unexpected clang, it startled the growing sympathy out of Vern. He took off his hat, swept his hair off his forehead and replaced it as if attempting to take control of his thoughts again, deciding that perhaps her crying over her cat was simply another ploy to entice him to stay. Vern took a few decisive steps towards the door. The matching eyes of the two stared at him simultaneously as he waved 'goodbye,' and reached for the doorknob.

All of the sudden she stepped in front of him attempting to bar him from the opened the doorway, and said, "Can you stay with me for a little while, Vern? I'm so shaken up."

"No, I need to get home, it's been a long week, and I think you two are ok now," he said.

"Please, just for a little dinner with me," she implored him.

Vern sighed, still gripping the doorknob until his fingers turned red, the tension between his shoulder blades beginning to spread up the back of his neck and over his temples. He looked straight at her and asked, "Why *me*, Carlotta? You could have anyone." He hesitated and then said, "and I've got a girl."

"She's no good for you," she blurted out in a strained, high-pitched voice, "and you're nice, that's why. I saw how you treated her when she got plastered at Blue Jay's and embarrassed you." She paused, putting her hand to her forehead and rubbing it several times, struggling to find her words. "You're a gentleman, that's why I like you." She began to cry again.

Slowly Vern relaxed his hold on the knob and reached over to touch her cheek. "I'm sorry, Carlotta, I'm not the one," he said softly. He looked into her eyes and continued to reassure her. "You're ok, now, and you'll find your way. Goodnight," he said reaching again for the door, and opening it without another word before Carlotta could reach for one of her talismans and ply her spells on him.

## 12

Carlotta did think Vern was nice, but very inexperienced. She had been sure of gaining control over his sexual appetite and hoping to tear him away from the drunken flapper, who she was sorry to hear was recovering and out of the hospital. She badly needed more sexual activity with him in order to procure her dreams of Geoffrey, and she must find a way of weakening Vern again and draw him to her until her wish of having Geoffrey's attention again had become a certainty. She took the obsidian mirror out of its pouch and calmed herself by starring into it, all the while stroking Boris seated beside her. "Vern, Vern," she repeatedly chanted while looking into the mirror, "I see you here." Her voice trailed off and she closed her eyes from time to time, entranced by the mirror-gazing.

In a burst of energy as if something had just awakened her from her reverie on the couch, Carlotta got up and dove into a closet near the front door. While shoving coats and dresses aside she dug into one end of the closet and struggled with her hands and arms at something, tugging and using the weight of her body to wrench something out. It was a partition that had been made to look like the other plaster walls. With a heavy sigh she shoved into the closet again, and pulled out a tattered and scraped leather-covered violin case and opened it on the floor by the closet and carefully took it out of the black velvet lining of the case.

She took out an exquisite instrument of a deep red stain, and caressed its smooth curves, fingered the pegs and began tuning the strings, plucking each until the pitch was accurate. Getting up, Carlotta grabbed her bow case which was sitting near her other violin case that she kept in a corner of the living room. "Oh, my darling Boris," she said, "look what we have here--Grand Papa's finest violin, and it's ours now!" She winked at the cat who blinked back at her and turned his head from side to side as she began to play a florid baroque passage, one of Bach's partitas for solo violin. Carlotta closed her eyes tightly and took a deep breath as she started each phrase while the continuous drive of the rhythm propelled her into a musical rapture.

The tone had a richness incomparable to her other violin, a fine, modern instrument itself, but this one, this Gennaro Gagliano made in Naples in 1765, resounded with the velvety tones of a castrato singing Handel's arias in the Teatro San Carlo, near where the instrument was made. This violin had been shaped out of choice pine and maple, and it now bore the patina of antiquity in its aged, red varnish. Carlotta finished the piece and slowly opened her eyes, her face flushed and her lips parted in elation. "This will make me famous," she addressed the cat, "I will perform like no one else with this in my hands." Her shrill words erupted like tacks hitting metal, and the cat laid back his ears and gave a short hiss at her before turning his back on her and curling up on a corner of the sofa.

Carlotta gently placed the treasure back in its case on the floor and then went to her purse and retrieved the obsidian mirror. She knelt down and held the mirror over it over the instrument as if beaming a light on it and said, "Send this reflection with me everywhere I go." She got up and replaced the violin back in its hiding place in the closet. When she was finished she again held up the mirror rubbing the sides and back of it, all the while gazing into it and seeing her own reflection. Her forehead became relaxed and smooth, and her lips flexing into an open grin and a low rumble pushed up through her chest forming a distorted laugh as it exited her mouth.

Carlotta continued the mirror ritual thinking of the trip she had made to Romania with her mother upon her grandfather's passing some months ago. Her two uncles had squabbled over the violins and the few treasures that the Polish princess had bestowed upon their grandfather, the princess's lover of many years. A few jewels and the violins would bring good sums, but one of the uncles was reluctant to bring the pieces to an auction house. He insisted the 'Englishmen' would cheat them out of the true prices.

The strand of silver coins he wore around his neck jingled as he pounded his chest with one hand, exclaiming his word must be the only word in this matter since he was the oldest of the three siblings. He wanted the Gagliano for himself and his half-sister and other brother to take the rest to a dealer if they wished. But Carlotta's mother sneered at him and said he was just a stupid *zingaro* and had little idea of how business was done in the modern world. "Besides," she said, "my girl Carlotta needs a new violin to perform for the people of New York and she will have one of these as Papa wished." She cast a glaring smile at her daughter and said, "and she will make a lot of money for us, won't you my girl?"

Hearing this remark from her mother singed Carlotta as she recalled with resentment the many times her mother would dress her as a little gypsy nomad, in red and white costumes, heavily embroidered with colorful flowers and, strings of tiny silver bells around her ankles and wrists. "Dance for the people," she would hiss into the child's ear, picking her up and placing her on a yellow table cloth she had laid on the Brooklyn sidewalk along with a basket containing a few coins. "Dance for them, and they will throw money at you, my darling child. Let them hear the bells jingle---go now." And the mother would scowl at Carlotta and shake the girl's wrists until she danced.

As her mother and uncles drank and argued, Carlotta played each of the four violins giving them equal attention but never letting on as to which was the finest. Yet the bickering never stopped, so after quietly investigating the liquor bottles on one table she intervened with a calm suggestion. "Let's all go out by the fire and have a toast." She sent the three outside and carefully drew a small brown bottle from her travel bag, and poured a teaspoon into each of three glasses, and then a hefty amount of Drambouie into the mix of each. She nodded her head and smiled as she delivered the mixtures. "Here let's toast to..."

"Where's your glass my dear niece?" asked the younger uncle, kicking a log further into the fire pit with his worn brown boots.

"I'll just go and get it," she said. She poured out a shot of the Drambouie for herself and returned to the others. "Good stuff," she said holding up the brimming jigger. "To our family and our new fortune from Grand Papa," She clinked glasses with her mother and then the uncles, who all downed the shots and asked her for more.

"A little bitter," noted the older uncle, wiping his mouth on the cuff of his jacket and eyeing his empty glass, "but let's have another round."

After a night of drinking and squabbling outside their camp before the fire, and when she was sure they had all fallen asleep and slumped over in their chairs, Carlotta stole back into the caravan and grabbed the prized violin along with her carpet bag and coat. Off she went tearing down the little path that led to a village on the hill, following the few lights that were still on in some of the buildings. Once inside the village, she entered a church door, crossed herself, bowed to the alter, then quickly stepped into the side aisle and hid between two of the pews until the first light of daybreak broke the darkness. Before mid-morning she was boarding a train for Paris and then another to Le Havre for a ship bound to New York.

Once onboard the ship, she stopped to buy a snack in the breakfast room, but she dropped her change purse, spilling coins onto the floor. A young boy helped her gather them up. "Thank you," she said as she held the money in her open hand, "but I think there are a few pieces missing."

He was grinning as he held up his empty hands. He then closed them into a fist, opened them again showing her six or seven more coins. "Voila, Madame," he said, offering her the change. "Have you ever seen such a trick?"

"Yes, I have," answered Carlotta, handing him a coin, her lips contorting into a twisted smile. "For your trouble." She grimaced and walked up to the counter without another word, recalling the many times her mother had bade her play at such tricks for strangers and then stand and wait for a tip.

\*\*\*

Outside their caravan before the waning embers, the three sparring siblings awoke to find their young relative had flown, leaving them each with a vicious headache and one fewer violin.

"Curse that girl!" the eldest shouted when he entered the trailer and saw that his niece had vanished. "It figures you would have raised such an artful daughter to cheat us so." He raised his fist to the mother, but instead punched some skins of wine hanging on the back of the caravan door, dousing the floor with red liquid.

# 13

Saturday morning came and Vern headed down to Mabey's for an early breakfast of an omelet and coffee. He could smell the bacon and coffee nearly a block away, and was ravenous from the activity of the work week. It was seven a.m. and the diner was fairly quiet this early, but an hour later it would be jammed with local couples out for a leisurely breakfast, some with a child or two, and a few more solo men like himself, gathered at the counter with newspapers. He liked to sit at the counter and skim though his paper and catch up on the latest happenings around town while drinking several cups of coffee and savoring the cheesy omelet and steak fries he ordered every weekend. Mabey's was a small, but cheap and comfortable spot with chipped, black bentwood chairs, rickety, square white tabletops, and a worn canary-yellow linoleum floor.

"Say, Mac," yelled out one of the regulars to the hash cook behind the counter, "When ya gonna replace that beat-up yellow floor? Ya can't see the dribbled eggs on it to clean 'em up."

"Never, Ollie, *never,* "the cook retorted with a loud guffaw. "Why would I want my customers to see the mess?"

"That's why I like this dump," a woman in a moss-green trench coat and black silk scarf added in her eloquent Park Avenue accent. She looked at her husband and teenage son across the table from her and continued with a smile, "It reminds me of home," to which half the people in the place laughed.

Vern focused again on his breakfast and paper and was about to pop a bite of eggs in his mouth, when a loud bang on the plate glass front door startled him and everyone else in the diner. Looking up, he saw a large black mass spread across the door and it reminded him of the dream he had of the giant slugs sucking the air out through the windshield of the red Chrysler. He dropped his fork of eggs which went crashing onto his cup and splattering coffee over the counter top. The grill cook was too engrossed in the scene outside to notice and clean it up.

"Oh God, no!" Vern muttered, wiping the mess up with a few paper napkins as he looked outside the large windows, and saw a head of long wiry black hair over a dark coat. He heard screaming and saw the black hair convulsing and a man's face directly over it grimacing, as if shaking the owner of that mane by the throat or shoulders. Before anyone could in the diner dared to intervene, two other men walked up and crowded the screaming woman. With another loud thud the head of hair flew back into the plate glass window, and the first man forced his hand over the screaming mouth of the bearer of that hair. "Hand it over, Tootsie," he demanded.

A set of red manicured nails flew into the air above the wiry coif and a female voice growled, *"Here!"* She thrust a few small white packets at them, which they hurriedly picked up as they fell to the sidewalk. "But I'm *out* now, you got that?" she added.

"Hey! Where's the rest of it or where's the money?" yelled one of the men as he shoved the packets in the inside pocket of his jacket. "You'd better have it by tomorrow," he warned, glowering as he stepped closer to her, forcing her to again back up into the glass door.

"You'll get it," she shrieked, and they all hurried off without another word. No one in Mabey's, including Vern had budged to help the woman, but all had gawked silently as the rapid confrontation played out.

After that, the jolly morning scene in the diner shifted into one of anxious quietude. A few murmurs were heard here and there as patrons finished their meals and gathered their coats up, with one last sip off coffee as they stood and donned their hats, anxious to depart. But Vern was not in a hurry to leave, in case he might find Carlotta waiting for him in tears again near his building door.

He ordered another cup of coffee and pretended to read his paper for another thirty minutes or so, until a new crowd had shuffled in, unknowing of the jarring scene that had taken place earlier. But instead of noticing anything in the newspaper, he was plagued with thoughts of what grief Carlotta might cause him now that he had the poor judgement to get mixed up with her. How was he going to explain any of this to Lulu if they ran into Carlotta at Blue Jay's? He would just avoid taking Lulu there for the time being. But what was stopping Carlotta from hanging around on his block, say one night when he and Lulu were walking home from some other restaurant?

He took out his handkerchief and dabbed at his brow. "A little steamy in here, man, isn't it?" said another man with a newspaper who had just walked in and sat down next to Vern at the counter.

"Sure thing," answered Vern, trying to smile. His hands were so clammy he almost dropped his coffee mug when he reached for it, so instead just replaced it on the counter. He wiped his hands on his napkin and pulled out his wallet, paid the check at his seat and walked out.

On the way back, Vern picked up his weekly bag of laundry, and two freshly dry-cleaned suits and dropped them off at home, before heading to an Italian deli for some cold cuts, cheese and bread, all the while trying to forget about seeing Carlotta and her scuffle with the three thugs. He jingled the change in his trouser pocket as he walked and tried to take some deep breaths. "It'll be ok," he told himself. Things would brighten as the day wore on and he busied himself in his apartment getting ready for Lulu's arrival that evening. Maybe reading a book when he got home would shift him into another world—someone else's world, and not one like he had experienced in his own life the past few days.

Vern alternated his thoughts between the disastrous relationship with Carlotta and his anticipation of seeing Lulu, wondering how that would shake out. He was really looking forward to seeing her, but did not want to get his hopes up regarding a restart of their relationship, yet he wanted to do everything he could to make the evening special for her.

It was still fairly early when Vern had finished his Saturday errands, which included buying a bouquet of carnations. The sun was casting a peaceful, muted light through a mostly overcast sky, the perfect light for Vern to read by on the sofa, which sat just a few feet away from the two front windows. He first went to the kitchen and brought out a simple, round glass vase, filled it with water, and as if holding a bundle of pencils, hurriedly crammed the fresh bunch of pink carnations down inside and allowed them to haphazardly arrange themselves. He wanted to add a nice touch to his scantily furnished living room, in anticipation of Lulu's arrival.

**68**

He was excited about seeing Lulu, but a little nervous how she would act about having drinks, or not, since he had not discussed it with her. Vern wanted it to be her idea, one way or another, and he hoped that she had spent time reflecting on her actions in recent months, and would change her behavior. He would not offer her a drink, unless the restaurant happened to have received some bottles of wine for the evening, from a local supplier, which often, they did not. One glass of wine with dinner would be all he would offer, and he would send her home right after they left the restaurant.

Vern spent a couple of hours perusing several books in his cache of novels to read, not quite honing in on one in particular to settle in with. The D.H. Lawrence novel he had just read was excellent, but maybe he was in more of a mood for Fitzgerald or Hemmingway right now. He got up from the couch and turned on the radio to his favorite jazz program, now playing some wild horns and clarinet tunes. He continued flipping through the few books, but was too distracted about his upcoming evening plans to concentrate on any one of them, and still unsettled about the scene with Carlotta outside the diner that morning.

Vern jumped up from the couch and went to the window and stood there absently looking out over the street with his hands in his pockets. Maybe he did not really feel like absorbing himself in a book today, but he forced himself to put any thoughts of Carlotta's devious ways out of his thoughts, permitting himself to feel excited about seeing a fresh, sweet Lulu, and spending a dinner time with her.

Would she be the thoughtful, amusing young lady she had been in the first months of their relationship, or had that part of her forever vanished to make way for the indiscrete and reckless party girl she had lately become? He would be pretty certain by the end of this night out with her. He sincerely wished for a happy outcome, although he wondered if Lulu was having anymore repercussions from the skull nightmare, and contemplated whether to approach the subject.

The radio punched out an especially lively rendition of *Big Butter and Egg Man,* and Vern turned up the volume as he headed back to his couch. His focus on reading novels became toast, as he tapped his hand on his thigh to the beat of the music. He put the books in a stack on the coffee table in front of him, and hopped up and ran down to the newsstand a couple of short blocks away. He bought the most recent copies of *Vanity Fair, The New Yorker* and *Time,* and spent the rest of the afternoon picking out the latest stories about life and fashion in New York, but he could not help looking around every time he heard light footsteps following behind him, dreading the reappearance of Carlotta.

Seven o'clock was approaching fast, and Vern was busy straightening his orange and blue tie of an abstract greyhound design and checking the fit of his newly cleaned navy blue flannel suit from a long mirror on the back of his bedroom door. He combed his hair again, and took out a clean handkerchief from a dresser drawer and tucked it in his pocket, for one never knew when a lady would require one.

# 14

ulu buzzed his building door promptly at seven and for a moment, Vern's heart raced, almost as if this were his first date with her. "Hey Lu, it's swell to see you looking so grand," he called out as she was finishing her climb on the staircase up to his flat.

She was wearing a bottle green cocoon jacket with an abundance of matching green fox trim around the neckline and down the front, curving all around the hemline. The jacket fell dramatically over her hips and thighs, and ended near the middle of her coordinating short, pencil skirt. Her black bicorn hat boasted a languid white feather that fell almost to her shoulder, punctuating her stylish flair for fashion. She pulled at the fingers of a maroon pair of leather gloves she was wearing, and tucked them into her pocket just as she came face to face with Vern, leaned into him with the verve of a green humming bird reaching for nectar from a flower, and kissed him. "I'm so happy to see you Vern," she said, looking into his eyes and smiling, as the front ends of her freshly trimmed hair fell in place to the sides of her chin.

"Come in and I'll get my coat," he said noticing the absence of alcohol from her breath. Her posture was tall and straight, and her eyes were alert and attentive. "It's a nice evening. Would you like to walk over a few blocks instead of having to park again?"

"Yeah, let's do that. This way I can hold your arm the whole way," she answered, smiling at him. "Say, you got pink carnations, my favorite," she went on, noticing the bouquet sitting on the coffee table.

"That's why I got them, to spruce this place up for my favorite lady," he whispered into her ear as he put on his coat and escorted her out the door.

Moonbeams poured out from the round pumpkin that brightened the faded indigo sky and lit their walk over to Sixth Avenue and 52nd Street, where a red brick building with a black door awaited them. Fabrizio's was an excellent Italian restaurant, small and neatly furnished with wide, black upholstered chairs and starched white tablecloths, bearing little glass lamps with pink bell shades on each of the tables. The Maitre D' seated the couple at a table where a shallow marble fountain decorated with several cherubs and birds hung about five feet up on the wall, quietly drizzling a thin spray of water into the reservoir from a pitcher held by one of the cherubs.

Lulu smiled broadly at Vern, who reached for her hand across the table. "I'm so glad you're well, again, Baby," he said. He hesitated, then said, "Shall we see if Fabrizio has any wine tonight?"

"I haven't had anything to drink since that night I stayed at your place, hungover," she imparted lightly. "I don't know that I'm ready to have anything after that last bout."

Vern felt a sense of comfort begin to envelope his body, and hoped that this would be a new start for their relationship, and Lulu's realization that her free-drinking behavior was nothing but a downward spiral whether Vern was in the picture or not. "Sure, let's have some club sodas with a lime, then," he said.

"Great, club soda, then," she agreed.

"Good evening," the waiter said, "we have a nice white dinner wine in tonight. Would you like some with your meal?"

"No, thanks, not tonight. We'll have a couple of club sodas with a lime," Vern returned.

Lulu began telling Vern what she had done with herself while recovering at home for the last week or so. "I was never so happy to be home," she said. "Mother and Pop were wonderful. I read magazines and started reading a novel, *This Side of Paradise*. Mother and I went shopping at Saks on Friday, and had lunch at the Palm Court. I got two new suits, and helped Mother choose three new evening gowns for some upcoming affairs in Bronxville they've been invited to. It was so much fun! I miss shopping in the City, even just window shopping."

Vern enjoyed her lively gushing about her day on Fifth Avenue, and simply let her go on until she ran out of things to say about it. "I heard the windows at Bonwit's are all the rage, but we didn't have enough time to get down there before our train left. Mother wanted to get home for dinner with Pop, but I could have stayed until every department store was closed!"

Lulu's expression was livelier than Vern had seen it in months. She had been either hungover or tipsy ever since she had quit her secretarial job this past February. He wondered if she had any plans for her future, or if she was going to continue along as an idle daughter of a rich financier, and spend her days just shopping or planning evening entertainments to get herself out of the house. He was not going to bring that up to her, either, at least, not at the moment.

"Sounds like fun, sweetie. Your fashion sense is artistic."

"I got this on Friday, just to wear for you, Vern," she beamed, caressing the fur trim of her jacket that hung on the back of her chair, as she spoke. "Do you like it?" she asked.

"I love everything you wear. You're a knockout, Lu, especially in that hat," he answered, reaching over and teasingly pulling the luscious feather that dangled from one corner of the brim.

"Oh, my hat!" she giggled, taking off the item and laying it on the chair next to her, but then her look grew a little more serious. "Well, I'm bored, Vern. Now that I'm feeling better, I want something more to do besides going on shopping sprees."

"Like what?" he asked, a little apprehensive that she was going to hint at the need for returning to her party life.

"I was thinking I'd like to go back to work."

"That's great, Lu, but I'd like to know how you're feeling and what exactly happened to land you in the hospital in the first place. A bad dream doesn't usually make someone that sick and you said you thought you were gonna die."

"Yeah," she said, "it was like a curse had been put on me." She looked down at the table and straightened the knife and fork in front of her. When she looked up her eyes wandered around the room towards the cherub fountain, and then looked directly at Vern. "I felt so weak, like I wanted to let go of life, I don't know, but it wasn't just the hangover, it was something else. Lulu looked back down at the table top again and fidgeted with her silverware and straightening it several times again, "I didn't have any control over my feelings for several days," she ended, her eyes again wandering around the room and fixed on the gurgling fountain and the plaster cherubs spilling water from their urns. Vern thumped his fingers on the table and sighed. *What happened to me, Vern?"* she asked, now leaning back into her chair and drawing her coat over her shoulders.

For a moment he was silent, thinking about Carlotta and the black mirror, and the way she had startled him by shoving in into his face one night as he was leaving her flat. "I don't know," he said quietly, touching his knife with his fingers, twirling it around over the tablecloth like a hand on a dial. Lulu reached out to take his fingers and squeezed them. "You'll be ok," he offered as he squeezed back and made an attempt to smile. Vern stood up and leaned over the table momentarily, kissing Lulu and brushing a strand of her hair off her cheek.

"So, tell me more, did you want to go back to work downtown at Carnavish Polk again?" he said as he sat back down.

"No, I don't want to work for a Wall Street law firm, or any law firm."

"I'm sure you could find a nice corporate office job somewhere in midtown, then, and you could enjoy some shopping on your lunch hour anytime you wanted."

Her expression grew more thoughtful, and she paused, and said, "No I don't want to be a secretary. Not a shop clerk, either."

"Oh, what did you have in mind, then?" Vern asked.

"Well, when I was in the hospital the nurse and nutritionist that took care of me were friends and I would hear them talking about their day to each other."

"Oh, so you think you'd like to work in a hospital, maybe go to nursing school?"

"No, not that either. It was just I realized how independent they were, even though they were both married. They had a purpose, a real purpose in their jobs. They weren't just shop clerks or typists waiting to settle down with a husband, they liked what they did, ya know what I mean, Vern?" She was leaning over a little in her seat, her fingers on the edge of the table, and her eyes narrowed a bit, blinking. "I want to do something I can look forward to each day, some way of using my talents."

Vern straightened up in his chair, never taking his eyes from her as she spoke, awaiting her next words. "Go on, Lulu, tell me what you'd like to do."

"I want to be a window dresser at one of the nice department stores," she answered." Her eyes widened at this announcement and her fingers let go the table, her hands sprang up, palms open, fingers splayed, and a spirited laugh shot from her lips as she continued. "You know how much I enjoy fashion, and putting outfits together. I keep up with Vogue and all of the latest styles and couturier news, wherever I can find it," she said. "I know I could be good at it," she ended, her hair bouncing as she clasped her hands and grinned. Vern beamed, impressed by her earnest attempt to change her life. She was motivated, that was clear, and had begun to think seriously about having a career that she believed she could excel in.

"Wow!" he chuckled, nodding his head and pursing his lips. "That's a great idea, Honey, but how are you going to get started with this career?"

"Well, I thought I would interview at some department stores, and tell them what I would like to do. My friend Sue works for Lord and Taylor as a buyer's assistant, and she gave me some ideas about who to call." Lulu continued in a serious, but cheerful tone, adding, "She started there as a clerk at one of the apparel departments, with the knowledge that if she did a good job at that, they would train her to be a buyer."

"So, you've got a person there to call for a possible interview?" Vern asked.

"Yeah, and I'm going to tell them why I want to work there and see if they'll offer me some training in window dressing if I work out in the accessories department.....that's who I'm supposed to call, a Mr. Dalton, the head of ladies' accessories and millenary." She paused for a minute to look at Vern and see his reaction. "That's what Sue said to do, anyway, so I'm going to call on Monday." She cleared her throat and took a sip of her drink, as she told Vern of her bold plans. "Most window dressers are men," she continued, "but not all."

Momentarily, he wondered if she would return to being Mary Lou the sweet young woman who was ready to do a good day's work, instead of Lulu the flapper, with the fashionably bobbed hair, but he quickly dismissed the thought. Of course not, she was too stylish for that, and much more resolute about being an independent, career minded woman, than he had ever imagined she would become.

"I'm so proud of you, Lu. You'll do alright," he smiled. "Let's have a kiss, and then take a look at that menu." Vern leaned across the table again and gave her an affectionate peck on her lovely rouged lips. "You are glowing, Baby!"

Vern ordered lasagna, and Lulu had the shrimp scampi. All through dinner they talked happily about current news they had read in the papers and magazines. Lulu caught him up on the latest in men's fashion, including the new width of the lapel, and the rage for more artful ties with bold colors, that had striking and modern, geometric designs, while Vern told her about some of the cutting-edge wedding cake style skyscrapers going up, and big corporations that would move to New York to have their headquarters in the heart of the greatest, fastest growing city in the world.

For dessert, they ate Fabrizio's famous spumoni, and laughed and held hands under the table, all the while mesmerized by each other's eyes. At nine-thirty, Vern asked for the check, and they donned their coats and walked out into the crisp world of autumn, Vern mentioning how the leaves had seemed to turn such spectacular shades of red and gold, overnight. The simple walk back to his block became an excursion into the bliss of vibrant fall colors wafting in the intermittent draft, and collecting at the feet of the couple, like confetti from heaven during their happy chit chat.

Lulu stopped at her car, the maroon Chrysler, and Vern took a quick look around the street for any traces of a lurking Carlotta. "Say Lu, aren't you going to come up for a little while? We can look at the moon from the front window," he said playfully, more at ease now that he knew they were alone in the street. Still, he was mindful of either getting her upstairs to his flat or off in her car before that fact changed.

Lulu moved closer to him and kissed him full on the lips, and then said, "How about next time, sweetie? I'm still a little weary from the hospital and all."

"Sure," he answered, kissing her again and again and opening her car door for her, "Next Saturday, then? We'll go to Twenty-One, if you like."

"Ok, it's a date," she whispered, drawing him into a close embrace, "and I can't wait."

"We'll talk on the phone way before that, though, I wanna know how you're doing, and if you get that guy at Lord and Taylor to interview you, ok?"

"Every day, Vern, we can talk every day, if you want to," she giggled, her blue eyes sparkling and hinting at desire,

"Miss you," he called out, blowing her a kiss as she drove off. He stood on the empty street, watching as she drove away, marveling at how extraordinarily grand their evening had turned out. Lulu seemed well on her way to changing her vacuous life into a thoughtful, enterprising one, and once again their romance seemed to be flourishing.

He allowed the light breeze to sweep over him for a few more moments as he reflected on their conversation, her kisses still resting on his lips. Smiling, Vern went into his building, bounding up the stairs and unlocking the door that led to his island of fantastical flamingos, and a puffy red comforter and pillows on his bed, anticipating a peaceful sleep of candy-colored dreams of Lulu.

# 15

On Sunday morning Carlotta got up before daybreak and walked across town just as the magenta light of dawn of was beginning to bleed through the autumn fog. She crossed into Sutton Place and stood before Geoffrey Northcott's white front door and stood still. She took a deep breath and raised her hand to the brass lion's head knocker, but then withdrew it, turning around and facing the street which was lit only by a couple of street lamps that shone iridescent flares on the damp pavement.

She sighed again and turned around, taking the knocker ring firmly in her hand and beating it against the door. No one came. Again she banged and waited. Nothing. This time she beat the brass against the door and did not stop until she saw a light go on in one of the windows. "Oh, my *God!*" A high-pitched voice with a British accent wailed. "*Who* is there?"

At last the door opened and a perturbed man rubbed his eyes and began to open his mouth in a furious yawn. "What the hell…." He yelled, but seeing it was Carlotta, he changed his tone of voice and gave it his most refined English accent. "Oh, my dear, what *are* you doing out at this hour? Is everything alright?" Yet he blocked the door with his body and did not invite her in.

"No, it's not alright. I'm in a lot of trouble." She was trembling and glanced inside as if to initiate an invitation.

"But it's so early, my dear! Why didn't you ring me up last night, or wait until I'd had my breakfast?" His mannered pitch did not match the scowl that was spreading on his brow.

"I rang you, but you never answered and your man said he would give you the message."

He drew his satin robe more tightly around his waist and retied the belt. "Oh, I must have been out. Now what is it?" He pushed the door slightly as if getting ready to close it.

"I need money, Geoffrey," Carlotta seethed. "I have to pay off that drug boss--the mess you got me into because you wanted easy coke."

"Oh, my dear, I was only setting you up in some sort of business so you would have an income," he said in a sing-song pitch and rolling his eyes. "It was all for you, and now you come here in the middle of the night and accuse *me*, begging for money?" He put his hand to his heart and turned his head with an audible sigh.

"Look, they almost beat me up yesterday morning in the street." She stepped close to him on the front step, wedging her face into the door opening and glaring up at him, her pupils growing small under the porch light.

"What about the magic spells I taught you in the meetings we went to?" he demanded.

She said nothing but continued to glare at him as if she had heard none of his comments. *"Herald of Illusion,* our delicious magic clan,*"* he said in a louder voice, bending into her face. "Remember those lust-drenched nights with the mirrors and coke, all the members of the club congratulating you on your sensuous willingness to learn the ways of *Sex Magick?*" He gasped out a laugh and opened the door a little more and leaned on the jamb. "Oh, my dear, you were the star of the show with your little black mirror and your very vocal incantations during our passionate *crisis.*" He reached out and with only the index finger he gave one short stroke to her cheek, like a leopard teasing its prey.

"I need money," she hissed into his face.

Geoffrey stood back, swept his blond mane off one shoulder and allowed her to enter. "There. Now you're in." With a sudden cloying tone he lightly touched her lips with his and said, "Are you sure that's all you want, my dear?" She did not answer but walked ahead of him towards his bedroom. "I thought as much," he laughed. "I hope you have your little mirror….."

Hours later a disheveled Carlotta walked through the entrance hall to the front door, Geoffrey behind her and still in his robe. He swept his hair into a ponytail as he followed her and whistled as he searched in his pocket for a band to tie it in place. "So nice to see you, my dear, and I hope your spells are working. After all you got money out of me, and that's a magic trick for sure."

She opened the front door herself and without prolonging the exit, she simply said, "Goodbye and thanks."

But before her foot could reach the doorstep, he barred her with his arm across the opening. "It really was nice to see you my dear." He lingered a moment, looking at her with his eyes flitting over hers. "Those cat eyes, Carlotta, you always get me with those eyes of yours." With one finger he tipped her chin up to his and kissed her gently, then opened the door and watched as she hurried down the street like a nocturnal creature escaping the daylight.

# 16

I t was a dreary, cold Friday night in late March. Heavy rains had dominated the day, deluging the buildings, flooding the streets and gutters with oceans of water. Afterward, gale winds controlled the evening atmosphere with gusts so strong it sent many commuters chasing after their hats, or holding on to nearby railings or lamp posts, as it whizzed over the city blocks. It wailed and whispered adagio cries of great loss to passersby, some of whom may have answered back, screaming into a sky that was crying convulsively about desires and dreams that had been unmet in their day to day routines. Muted car horns echoed in the distance, and the trembling vibration of wet tires turning a corner splashed gray rainwater onto the sidewalk in great surges, catching a hemline or coattail as the evening work crowd streamed home, and out of the drenched streets. The wet, city smells were confusing and varied, as one passed a restaurant, a corner flower shop, or a cab stand, with scents that were gathered and mingled by the wind; the aroma of coffee and grilled steak, the fragrance of roses, or the stench of wet rubber and gasoline washing over the sodden pavement, all stirred together with the rank odors of decayed rubbish that drifted up from the manhole covers, and poorly hinged cellar doors. Together in the dampness, it became an unidentifiable stink that belonged in a dark, hidden place, like a sewer or a morgue, and not in the open streets of the City of Dreams.

At eight o'clock, a tall man wearing a long, taupe trench coat, and holding his tweed cap in his hand hurried down Fifth Avenue, continuously brushing his thick, dark hair off his forehead, just as the wind heaped it forward, into his eyes, those soft, brown eyes, which held off a touch of enmity that shaped his black eyebrows. He was trim and spry, but a closer glance would reveal his age, despite his full head of hair and youthful stride down the avenue, of a mature man nearing age fifty. When he reached E. 48th Street, he turned and headed west towards Sixth Avenue and Blue Jay's.

"Thought I'd never make it through the wind," he exclaimed," shaking his head at the coat check girl.

"Good evening, Mr. D'Angelini, looks like you had a quick walk," she prattled, taking his damp coat and hat. "We've got an excellent band here tonight."

"That's why I come here," he smiled, handing the cold garments over to her. ,"Thank you." He straightened his suit jacket and tie as he walked into the club and found a seat at the bar.

Jay was behind the bar, and greeted him with a handshake. "Hello, Nick, how's the weather treating you tonight?" he said, handing him a menu.

"Well, it stopped raining, so I made it over for some music and dinner," Nick answered with a warm smile as he spoke. "What's the special tonight, Jay?"

"Stuffed chops, roast potatoes, and green beans."

"Great, I'll order that, and have you got some of that rye in?"

"Sure he does," said a well-built tipsy man with thick lips and a prize-fighter's nose a few chairs down. He raised his glass into the light and said, "Look at that color, man." He tilted his head back and took another swallow. "I know you always like to check out the color, don't cha, Nick?" he said with a friendly chuckle.

"Hey Vinnie, how's business?" Nick asked, not wanting to ruffle the feathers of the federal agent, but at the same time, careful to behave in a jocular manner to this regular customer.

"Oh, I haven't seen a *thing* at this place," the agent said putting his drink down and raising his hands in the air, palms out, proclaiming innocence. He nudged his empty glass towards Jay, and announced, "Ok, I'll have one more and then I've gotta go."

Jay smiled and added, "Always happy to see you enjoying yourself, Captain Dawes. Why don't you bring the missus in again sometime?"

"Sure, next time you get one of those hot Harlem bands down here, she'd love that."

Jay winked and replied, "I'll let you know, Vince."

Nick watched Jay take a fresh bottle down from one of the shelves and pour his drink into a glass containing one ice cube. He placed the glass in front of Nick and said, "Just the way you like it, Nick, now did you want the special?"

"Thanks, Jay," he said. Nick barely had a trace of any sort of New York accent, despite having grown up in Brooklyn, and attended Brooklyn College. He was a second generation Italian, and his parents, although they were fluent in English, spoke mostly Italian at home, so Nick had not been as exposed to the heavy lilt of native New York accents during his early childhood. He ate his dinner and sipped his whiskey, making but a little small talk with a few of the other patrons at the bar, glowering slightly at nothing in particular, except the blank space of air immediately in front of his eyes, sometimes rubbing the bare third finger of his left hand as if he were fidgeting with a ring.

"Hey, Nick," said Vern who had just walked in.

"Have a seat." Nick shook his hand and motioned to the empty seat next to him. "Are you having some dinner?"

"Yeah, sure. I just needed to get out of the apartment tonight. What's up with you? Are you staying for the band?"

"First set, anyway, but first, some dinner." Nick turned his menu over to Vern.

"Hello, Vern," said Jay. Some rye? Say, haven't seen much of you lately, where ya been?"

"Oh, tired, mostly. Lots of late nights at the office." Vern shrugged and added, "I'll take a beer and your special." He smiled and then took a look around the club for Carlotta. He had already done so when he entered, but even though a few months had passed since he had run into her he was always reluctant to enter Blue Jay's for fear of her pursuit of him again.

At nine o'clock, three slinky gentlemen in black evening attire, walked across the dance floor, and quickly set themselves up in the tight, corner platform with the piano. One man opened up the keyboard cover, another tuned his bass and adjusted his microphone stand, while the percussionist sat down behind the drum kit, adjusted his seat and tapped the bass drum pedal. "Let's go, boys!" he called to his band mates.

Jay turned on the spotlight, and off they went with *The Sheik of Araby*. Another slim man with a clarinet walked leisurely over the dance floor, playing his accompaniment as he sauntered up to the musicians and joined them off to one side of the bandstand. Dancing couples, ready for the weekend to begin, gathered on the floor and stepped to this moderate tune beneath the frosty light of the wedding cake chandelier, which spilled its sugary glaze over the party seekers.

Most of this crowd had stopped immediately after work, having a drink and a bite to eat before the music started. A few women were very stylishly dressed, but most in workday attire of simpler short skirts, V-neck blouses, long ropes of pearls, and T-strap pumps. Others were adorned in chic suits of light wool in plum or navy with the new, shorter Chanel jackets or longer, belted ones, their sparkly lapel pins blithely catching sparks of light, as they danced beneath the chandelier. Shop girls wore the latest in tailored, dropped waist dresses in an array of subdued colors such as warm apricot and cornflower blue, hoofing over the dance floor in chorus girl pumps. Men of course, wore flannel suits, in navy or charcoal greys, with the only dash of color being their ties, fraught with lively patterns in abstract floral or geometric designs, displaying unusual color combinations in grays and pinks, and hints of sage green, or burgundy.

The dancers let loose and shook off the work week in every move, pounding out the rhythm with their feet, kicking their toes out, hands waving upward and out, hips and shoulders shimmying, whether close to their partner or a few feet away. As the tunes became more energetic, the dance crowd began to thicken, the ladies' red lips agape in frenzied jubilation, their darkened eyelids opened wide; the men's eyes sizzled with mad freedom from the confines of desks and coffee breaks, ready to win hearts and enjoy the weekend.

A woman in a tailored gray coat and man's fedora sporting some turquoise feathers walked in carrying a black leather briefcase. Her loose brown curls swung just over her shoulders as she turned her head to the back of the bar, took a few steps and then turned around again as a man's voice called out to her, "Gisela, over here."

Nick watched her as she strode over to the man, someone that he had met briefly one night, Lester, seated at a table. When she approached the table Lester got up and pulled the chair out for her. "May I take your coat and hat?" Nick heard him ask. She shook her head and sat down in her outerwear. Nick noticed that she was not like many of the other young women, there, and not so young at that. This one seemed more confident in her posture, the way she sat comfortably back in her chair, yet looked straight at the man with only a slight smile and a quizzical look in her eyes, her hand extended slightly for a handshake after he spoke a few words to her.

"Agreed, and now I should be going," she said after their brief transaction.

"Won't you stay for a drink or dinner and tell me how you are, Gisela?"

She looked at him hesitantly, but pushed her chair back and said, "No, Lester, not tonight, but thanks."

Lester nodded and patted the tabletop several times. "Ok, well take care of yourself, then." He raised one hand as if to wave, but paused as she walked away, her black pumps clicking over the empty dance floor towards the front door.

She turned around unexpectedly and turned up the corners of her full, ruby lips just enough to give him a droopy smile. She called back, "You too, ok?"

Nick had never seen this woman there before and wondered what the hasty bargain between the two of them had been about. He thought that had he been in Lester's place he would not have allowed a striking looking woman like that to leave so quickly, but as it was not his business, he turned around and minded his drink again, pondering his plight and waving at Jay for another round.

# 17

Luck seemed to have ruled against him when it came to meeting a woman closer to his own age, and with a similar education. Nothing had worked out for Nick since his wife's disappearance over eight years ago at the end of the Great War.

Roberta, a nurse at a Manhattan doctor's office, insisted on going to France to search for her cousin, Clotilde, who had lived with Robbie and her parents for several years when Roberta was a young girl. She also gave the excuse that she wanted to help as a medic, to aid the wounded American soldiers going home from France. Nick had forbidden her to go, infuriated at the idea of her putting herself at such risk, to leave the marriage and the comforts of their life together. Surely, she had no intention of really going, he had thought. She was eleven years younger than Nick, twenty-eight, and Nick, thirty-nine, when she left him. She kept mentioning Clotilde, who had been working in Paris and was part of the French resistance. Roberta had heard from her only sporadically since the war had begun, and felt a responsibility to try to find her, now that it was over.

"In the midst of all of that devastation and carnage?" he had yelled at her. "Robbie, *how can you leave me?*" He remembered covering his face with his hands, too shocked to sob, believing that she no longer loved him, or surely, she would not risk her life for this dangerous, laborious journey.

"I'm sorry, Nick, I have to go, I have to find her and bring her back here!" Her usually sweet voice was hard and shrill, and she was on the verge of tears as she tried to explain the importance of why she needed to go. "Anyway, I'm a nurse, and I want to help our men recover and come home, too. Since my parents died in that boating accident last year, Clotilde is the only family I've got left," she insisted, but to Nick, it all sounded like a bland, empty excuse to leave their marriage.

"*No!*" he screamed, with a roar that began from deep in his belly, and resounded in a horrifying rancor. "What about *me?* I thought I was your family!" He continued to blast her reasons, concerned for her safety as well as the loss of her in his life. "What about our marriage commitment, our life together? And what about the Spanish flu, Robbie? That could be more dangerous than anything, right now! It's insanity for you to think you're going to do anything but get yourself killed, and I won't allow you to go." Furiously, he added, "I've never heard such a hare-brained idea!" and stormed out of their apartment.

For several months they argued, bringing their once happy and easy relationship to a breaking point. Eventually, Nick hardened in his opinion that she did not love him, or even that she hated him enough to risk her life in order to get away from him. He tried endlessly to talk her out of it but she persisted, headstrong as she was. He begged her to reconsider, to wait until the treaty was signed and the Germans were well aware of their fate, and could do no more damage. Then they would go together, after the deadly flu had died down, and find her cousin. He would have said or done anything to get her to forget this plan.

"It may be too late, anyway," she said drily, staring at him with a callousness in her eyes he had never seen before. "But I have to find out what happened to her. We have heard nothing from her in nearly a year, since she hinted that she was living next door to a German spy."

"All the more reason *not* to go! Let Clotilde risk her life as a spy, then." Nick yelled, *"It was her choice to be part of the Resistance! I don't care if she's your cousin,"* he protested, desperately banging his fist against the lid of his piano, and making the instrument buzz in fear.

On a cold day in late November she packed and joined a few other Americans bound for France, who were also looking for their loved ones. Nick did not even see her off at the harbor. At the door of their apartment, he pleaded with her one final time not to go. "Love you, Nick, I'll be back if you still want me," was all she said when she kissed him goodbye and walked out.

That was the end of Nick's life. Although he carried on with his classes, his reading, and even playing the piano, he was tortured every day by her actions, and fully believed she had stopped loving him or thinking their marriage was important.

He thought back to the first day they met, a few days before Roberta's twenty-first birthday, on a late April day well over a decade earlier. She was walking down Fifth Avenue towards 42$^{nd}$ Street, wearing a white twill duster over a pale blue skirt, and carrying an exquisite, white lace parasol above her ivory straw boater hat. A wide, baby blue ribbon was all that decorated the hat, the ends of which waved slightly in the faint breeze. She stood out from the crowd like a wispy, snowy egret in the midst of a throng of seagulls as she ambled down the avenue alone, looking about aimlessly as though she were unfamiliar with the sights and hustle of the city. She paused in the middle of the sidewalk and gawked at a store window now and again, unaware that someone behind her might have to stop abruptly to avoid crashing into her.

She happened to glance at Nick as he was standing at the corner of 48$^{th}$ and Fifth, just as he had come out of a greasy spoon a few doors up. The young lady smiled at him, and nearly tripped over a woman walking her little black dog and the long, red leash that attached them, as she looked too long at Nick. He rushed over, and helped her recover her balance as the pet owner escorted the intertwined dog around the sightseer, and escaped. "Hi," the disentangled damsel said brightly to Nick, her cheeks beginning to flush. "Thank you for rescuing me."

Nick could have simply said, "You're welcome," and gone on his way, but was struck by the beauty of the young, slender woman. "Are you lost, miss?" he asked.

"Oh, no," she laughed, "not really, I rarely get to the city, but I'm going to be looking for a job and a room here, very soon." Nick bathed in the infectious sparkle of her round, gray-blue eyes as she spoke. "Do I look that quaint?" she giggled.

"No, of course not," he answered simply, while fantasizing about reaching out to touch her delicate pink lips with his index finger, then winding his hands around the lengths of tawny blond hair that spilled out from beneath her hat.

At that moment, another woman in a wide and very stylish black chapeau, laden with a profuse bouquet of lavender flowers, paraded by with two large, flawlessly puffed, brown poodles. As they came walking towards the talking couple, the woman paid little attention to where her dogs' noses wandered, more interested in the shop windows along the way. In a flash, the poodles yanked their owner towards the skirt of the talkative young sightseer, and began nuzzling it from top to bottom, slobbering and wrinkling it in a matter of seconds.

"Oh, I'm so sorry miss," exclaimed the dog handler, ferociously attempting to jerk her poodles by their leashes, away from the pale blue garment. "Chanel! Coco!" she howled at her dogs, finally leading them off to the next corner.

This time, Nick had an opportunity to whisk the young lady away with an invitation. "I'm just going down a few steps, to my favorite bakery. Would you like to come with me and have a cup of coffee and leave this avenue to the shoppers and dogs?" he proposed, wanting an excuse to prolong the conversation. "I'm Nick, by the way," he continued in a soft-spoken friendly voice.

"Robbie," she answered, "how nice, thank you, Nick." He took her elbow and led her a few doors down the avenue to Café Bianco, a cozy bakery with cracked and dented plaster walls which had recently been covered over in a spotless coat of pearl-white paint. The aroma of steaming espresso, and fresh, sugary pastries pervaded the small room, and the display cases were decorated with an abundance of chocolate dipped cookies, Italian petit fours in red and green, and cannoli. Nick offered her a seat at one of the empty tables in the window area, where they ordered cappuccino and some chocolate and pistachio biscotti, and was about to begin a conversation but was halted by a song. From a radio behind the counter burst the sonorous voice of Caruso singing *La donna e mobile,* to which the baker joined in, raising his arms in abandon, and motioning to the male guests to sing along with him, making low-keyed conversation amongst the clientele, impossible for the time being. The pair had no choice but to sit and enjoy the thundering performance, resonating all the way out the shop door, and into the street.

"I'm Nick D'Angelini. I'm a history professor at New York University," he said after the applause and laughter had subsided. He blinked his fawn-brown eyes, and tilting his head to one side, he slid the plate of biscotti towards his lovely guest, and chuckled. "I wasn't expecting an operatic performance, but I liked it."

"Oh, so did I," she answered, and added, "Roberta Grey." She smiled brightly at Nick, and he wondered if his older looks were of any matter to the young woman. Roberta did not break her gaze at Nick and her smile lingered as if she were awaiting further conversation on the subject. He felt encouraged that he might ask to see her again, improper as it was, having met her so casually in the street.

"I live in White Plains with my parents, and finished my nursing studies just last fall."

"Oh, congratulations," he said, "are you working now?"

"Yes, at a doctor's office near where I live, but I'm going to move to the city and work in one of the large hospitals," she said eagerly. "My parents don't like that idea, but I love the city and all of the things to do." Her independence and her enthusiasm for city life was clear. Nick had lived in either Brooklyn or Manhattan all of his life, very used to the metropolis, and sometimes numb to its many attractions.

"And what is it that you especially like to do, Robbie?" he asked, his eyes beaming. She hesitated for a moment and said, "I like the museums. I'd like to be able to go often, especially to the Metropolitan, and if I lived here, I would go there every single week," she said, the opalescent skin of her cheeks illuminated by the morning light which shone from the window as she spoke. "I love to look at the paintings, and the medieval tapestries, and the costume department." Her eyes grew wider as she spoke of her interests, and she continued listing the other museums she would see, as well. "Oh, and I want to go back to the beautiful new Library," she went on, "I haven't been since it opened a couple of years ago."

"So, you like to read? Me too," he said, wondering if he had at last found an intellectual companion in this refreshing young woman. "In fact, I usually take a book with me everywhere I go."

Their connection was growing quickly, like wisteria vines forever reaching upward, twisting, branching off to the sides, and burgeoning with sensuous purple florets. She spoke of her love of nineteenth century novelists, of Balzac, and Thackeray, and the new American writer, Dreiser; and he, of his love of poetry, especially Hardy and Goethe. Nick asked her about her musical interests, finding out that she enjoyed Tchaikovsky and his ballets, and that she longed to go to the Metropolitan Opera. She wanted to see *The Barber of Seville,* because she loved the comedic nature of Rossini's music, but especially because she wanted to see the grand spectacle of the opera stage. Nick told her that he played piano, and while there was a bit of Chopin in his repertoire, he was mostly interested in the new jazz that was coming out in the theaters, and a few clubs that were sprouting up about town.

In a little over an hour they had become fascinated with each other, and while neither told the other, they consciously delayed the ending of the afternoon. After a while, there was a lull in their conversation, and they simply gazed at each other, from across the little table in the window. Roberta was the first to speak. "It was such a funny circumstance, our meeting today, Nick, and I'm glad, but I think I need to head to Grand Central and catch my train back home."

He detected a touch of wistfulness in her voice, in her suggestion of parting. "I'll walk you, then," he offered, pulling her chair out for her and starting to walk away. "Don't forget this," he said, pointing to her white parasol leaning against the window ledge.

"Oh, thank you," she said, looking up at Nick, not even glancing at the voguish accessory as she took it from him.

They walked along to the train station, chatting about his classes, and her job search. Nick felt the electricity of their attraction when his hip happened to graze hers while walking close together on the crowded streets. He asked when she thought she might be back in town, and said he would like to take her to the art museum and lunch or dinner.

Standing close, he could feel her ribs expand, her breath seized as he offered the invitation. She beamed, and answered, "I'm free either Saturday or Sunday, Professor!"

"Next Saturday, then?" he said, grinning. "I could drive down here and pick you up, if you let me know your train time." Nick took out a napkin from his pocket and scribbled his phone number. In turn, he asked for hers, which he also wrote down, and stuffed back into his pocket, as they walked towards the entrance of the beautiful new, Grand Central Station, fabulously wrought with its French empire designs. He noticed Roberta looking up with awe at the magnificent sculpture group on the façade, the nearly nude Mercury wearing his winged helmet, and standing in front of the giant eagle poised for flight, with Hercules and Minerva to his sides.

"I adore New York," she said with such unaffected elation, that his heart flew instantly towards hers. They hurried though the main hallway under the celestial ceiling, past the big clock, down the white marble staircase to the train bound for White Plains at 4:30. Nick took a quick glance up at the turquoise ceiling, and felt the glow of the hundreds of golden stars beaming down on him, in the various shapes of constellations, as if to say, "You have found your heaven!"

Just before she boarded the train Nick took her hand and pressed it to his lips. "Next week, then," he smiled. He walked slowly backwards while looking at her through the compartment window, understanding that he was already in love with her.

# 18

Saturday at the museum came with great anticipation, and their exploration of it together, exceeded the expectations of both the history professor and the young nurse. They walked blithely through miles of galleries, not noticing that after several hours, their feet ached while talking about the sublime landscapes of Friedrich, the elegant French ladies of Lebrun, and the astounding seascapes of Turner. Nick sometimes guided Robbie by the hand, enjoying the gentle movement of her fingers intertwined in his as they wandered the shadowy Egyptian gallery together, then the foreboding medieval weapons hall, and into the opulent French and German porcelain rooms. In the presence of the exquisite curios, they fell into fascination with their own conversation and laughter, sealing off the rest of the universe, and living only with each other and the magnificent art objects in each of the galleries they entered.

Dinner was had at a nearby seafood restaurant, where they dined on tuna steaks and steamed clams, and a bottle of rose. Too soon, the day ended, with Nick driving her back to the train station, just as the full moon began to float above a swath of amethyst ribbon that divided the earth from the indigo heavens. Robbie's thigh pressed close to his while driving through the city streets, and though he felt the mounting heat between them, he checked himself by making small talk about the assortment of passersby who were strolling off to the theater in their top hats or silken gowns, pointing out the especially fashionable couples. But that was only mild conversation, intended to hide the intensity of the real thoughts that were flying between them, of each kissing the other.

Nick parked his car near Grand Central, and instead of getting out and opening the passenger door for Robbie, he leaned closer, and searched her eyes for a cue, while gently touching his finger to her cheek, and awaited her reaction. She swallowed audibly, and opened her lips as if to speak, but said nothing, her eyes quickly darting over

Nick's face. Nick leaned closer to her lovely, pink lips, and slowly touched them with his until she pressed into him, kissing him fully on the mouth. They sat in his car and continued their expression for a quarter of an hour, embracing, looking at each other and speaking without words, of their intense connection to each other.

Finally, Robbie drew a deep breath, and gathering herself, said, "I'll miss the last train if we don't go now." She kept her arms firmly around him, brushing her lips lightly on his cheek, a slight anxiety in her tone.

"Ok," Nick said with a nod, pulling away from her, then automatically straightening his tie. But he hesitated, and beneath a wealth of platinum moonlight, beheld her fairy-like face, and added, "next Saturday, then?"

A glow settled on Robbie, and like the tender bloom of a pale pink orchid unfolding, she parted her lips in a smile, and answered "Ok. Same time, then?"

Nick responded with an unexpected shout of laughter, giving her a decisive kiss, bounding out of the driver's seat, and over to open her door for her. Down they went into the white marble halls of Grand Central to the track bound for White Plains. They parted reluctantly just as her train was boarding, exchanging kisses, replete with blissful laughter.

He walked out of the station and over to his car, and stood there briefly to enjoy the night air and muse over the kisses he and Robbie had just exchanged inside the vehicle. Through the glow of the street lamps, he looked up at the hush of crystalline stars above the hazy city light. He was aware of his fingers grasping the chrome door handle of his blue model T, as if to hang onto something familiar that would ground him, and keep him from soaring into the expanse of the wide, free heavens that had granted his wish of happiness.

The next Saturday surfaced too slowly for Nick, who had noted his mental calendar every day since he had seen Robbie off at the last train the week before. It finally buoyed up into his life like a playful dolphin, rising from the misty ocean waves, glimmering brightly in the sunlight, and finally breathing in a gasp of earth's sweet air. Nick showered and dressed, and hurried down to a local florist shop that he had phoned earlier in the week. "Have you got it?" he asked. The florist looked at him with a slight, confused smile.

"You're mighty excited about something, young man—or *someone*," he chuckled.

"Oh, sorry—I'm Nick—I ordered the silver rose."

"Yes sir, one silver rose in a vase, packed in an open box for stability in the back seat of your car, right?" The florist walked over to an ice box and took out a single white rose that shimmered with silvery powder and was packed just as Nick had asked. "How does that suit you?" the florist grinned.

Nick looked with awe and delight at the gracious frippery and melted into a fantasy of presenting her with this blossom when he saw her. "It's perfect!" he answered. He paid the man, and dashed back to his apartment with the boxed rose.

He had called Robbie that Monday to say he could get tickets to a matinee performance of *Der Rosenkavalier*, at the Metropolitan Opera, if she would like to go. On the other end of the phone he heard flute-note laughter, and "yes, I'd love to!"

\*\*\*

Robbie strode into the opera house on Nick's arm, looking like a young queen entering her ballroom. Beneath a long, black velvet cloak, she wore a slim cut dress of raspberry silk, in the latest fashion of French designer, Poiret, with an empire waistline and a low-cut neckline. An impressive Victorian cameo of Psyche on a simple black satin choker was her only piece of jewelry, except for a silver pin in the shape of a bow, which kept an erect white feather in place, at the very front of her turban-style hat. Her cheekbones were highlighted in a lighter shade of raspberry, a ravishing contrast to her fair skin.

Nick watched as her color grew brighter with excitement, as she walked next to him inside the opera house, taking in the elaborate plaster swags and flowers that hung from the lobby walls. He handed his tickets to an usher who showed them to their seats in a lower box, and he met the flash of Robbie's vivid smile as she sat down. She was bursting with elation as the lights went on above the orchestra when they began performing the waltz overture, so tender and whimsical, whirling Nick into its melodious dance of *amour*. Fraught with affection towards this young lady he had only know for a few weeks, he took Robbie's hand and pressed her dainty, white fingers to his lips as the curtains parted and the singers gathered on the stage, in fine, period costumes of powdered wigs and lustrous brocaded coats and dresses.

The three hours of the opera flew like thirty minutes to Nick, who held her hand throughout the performance, and she, sometimes leaning over to kiss Nick's cheek. He was swallowed up in the sentiment of the story, of the young knight offering a silver rose to his sweetheart as a gift of betrothal. The undulating cadence of the music was much in rhythm with the swell of his own heart. His eyes were focused on the stage, but his spirit awaited that moment when, after the show, he would present her with his own silver rose, and behold a languid paradise in her blue-gray eyes. That moment would wait until after dinner, as he had earlier planned.

"I thought you might like to have dinner at The Gingerman, it's a French Restaurant," he said as the house lights were turned on and they walked out of their box. She nodded her head before the words could emerge from her lips, but another unexpected surge of waltz music floated up from the orchestra pit, and caught them in the hallway. Nick drew a long breath, and took Robbie in a waltz embrace, dancing her towards the staircase, lifting her down the short flight of steps, into the golden expanse of the lobby, and out the door.

"I have something for you," he said and rushed her back to his car, two blocks away.

"What is it, Nick?" she asked breathlessly, as they hurried over the sidewalks, and away from the opera house.

He opened his car door, and drew out something from a box in the back seat. "Close your eyes," he requested admiring her porcelain skin as she stood there, awaiting his surprise.

Gently, he took her hand and was about to place the silver rose between her thumb and fingers. She quickened and smiled, opening her eyes to the gift he had brought her. "Oh, Nick how thoughtful," she cooed, her eyes beginning to well up at his romantic gesture.

"Robbie, will you marry me?" he blurted out, still fumbling with the stem. Shaken by the boldness of his own words, he lost control of the rose, which plummeted to the ground, losing one of the outer silver petals as it hit the sidewalk. Embarrassed, he bent over and retrieved it, no longer a perfect metallic bloom, as a white area was now exposed where the petal had broken off. Forlorn at the sight of the damaged gift, he said, "I'm sorry, I just couldn't wait to give it to you."

"Okay," she replied with a quiet smile.

"It's okay?" he asked, replacing the injured rose back in her hand and looking into her eyes.

"No, I mean *okay*."

Puzzled and still flustered by the accident, his eyes surveyed her face, searching for her meaning. "*Okay,* I'll marry you," she declared, in a clear, decisive voice.

With that, his anxiety turned to unexpected joy, and there on the busy street, he gathered her in his arms, lavishing her with a confetti of kisses for all to see.

Dinner plans were changed, since Robbie, in high spirits and no longer hungry enough for a full meal, mentioned that French food might be a little heavy for this evening. Nick agreed and offered to take her to a little Greek café near where he lived, where they could nibble on kabobs and spanakopita and talk about their future. Nick ordered a bottle of white dinner wine, and they sipped and picked at the meal, too moved by emotion to require much food. To the sounds of a sizzling grill, and festive mandolin music pumped out from a Victrola in a back room, they sat side by side at their table, and made plans for next Saturday's excursion, that of choosing an engagement ring for Robbie.

"Sure," she agreed, with a playful laugh, "but there's something I want to do tonight."

"What's that?"

"I'd like to see your apartment, if that's where we're going to live."

With great warmth in his smile, he answered, "let's go!"

Nick entwined his fingers in hers, and off they went, noting that their hands were growing clammy and longed to find out if her body was effused with the same excitement, knowing they would soon be alone. They turned the corner at Fifth Avenue and 60th Street, and he stopped just before entering his building, a large square of brown brick with a white granite entrance, and looked at her for a sign of approval. She smiled, and kissed him lightly before entering. He reached to kiss her again, but they were interrupted by a young man who was entering the lobby, and fully engrossed in the front cover of a magazine he was carrying, appearing not to notice the kissing couple. They composed themselves while sharing the elevator with him, and got off at the third floor, where Nick led her down the hall to a door near the front of the building.

Robbie's luminous smile glowed up at him as he opened his apartment door, and led her into his spacious living room. There was a large picture window overlooking Central Park, an elegant fireplace on the back wall, and a spinet in one corner of the room. A simple green couch and two end tables with spindly black lamps were the only pieces of furniture. He briefly showed her his small, but sleek, mint green kitchen, a well-lit bathroom tiled in apricot and black, and two ample rooms; one, a study, and the other, his bedroom. Expressing her elation with laughter and kisses at her new residence, she asked if he might like to buy a few new pieces of furniture, a coffee table perhaps, and some oriental carpets for the bare wood floors?

"You may redecorate it any way you like, as long as you'll live here with me *forever and ever,*" he said. With that, he escorted her back into the living room where they collapsed on the sofa, engrossed in kissing. Kisses and words which sparked a fit of passion. Nick feeling unable to control himself, pulled away from Robbie, suddenly getting up and passing his hand over his face and through his hair, inhaling the trace of her lemony, floral scent that now infused his fingers.

"Would you like something to drink?" he asked, in an overly enthusiastic tone.

Robbie looked up and simply said," What's wrong Nick, did you change your mind or something."

He hastily sat back down and hugged her close. "No, my love, I'm just getting worked up, wishing I could make love to you, that's all."

Robbie hesitated, looking into Nick's soft, brown eyes, with self-assurance. Her voice rose slightly, as she asked a dazzling, stupefying question. "Wouldn't that be *alright?* I love you, Nick, forever," despite having known him for such a short time.

Robbie's words fell over him in silvery tones of a language he had never before heard. He reached out and touched her face, as if to be sure she was real, and not some phantom of tenderness he had dreamed up. "Yes, it *will* be alright," he whispered, leaning into her. There in the purple light of night under the streetlamps that seeped into his front window, he kissed her neck, and with a faint motion of one hand he tipped her back onto the length of his sofa, her silken gown rustling like a contented bird settling into her nest. Robbie leaned up to run her tongue along his lips, her sighs becoming light and evanescent as a growing passion took hold of her, and she murmured words of love in a rapt, andante melody. Soon clothes peeled away as though nothing had been fastened, the layers falling away until all that was left was skin and breath and ardor.

There was joy in their passion, the moonlight falling softly over her slim figure, as he kissed her nipples and glided his mouth slowly down over her belly, and onto her gossamer thighs. He rose over her, and melded his body with hers, intoxicated with the touch of her hands on his bare chest and hips.

Afterwards, they fell into a brief sleep. Nick awoke to the playful touch of her opened hands on his back. He looked over his shoulder and smiled, touching her lightly with his fingertips. She twittered like a bird when he tickled the side of her hips and ribs. "I love you, Robbie," he said, kissing her again on her throat and neck, but I had better get you home."

A few months later, when the refreshing breezes of early autumn vanquished the sweltering heat of summer, they walked through the majestic Gothic tracery of Trinity Church on East 87th Street, and were married. He kept this picture of Robbie in his mind, repeatedly playing over that day in his thoughts. She had worn an ankle length cream dress of lace and light wool, and her favorite scent of bergamot and freesia. The fragrance had bloomed over her fair complexion, as she slipped the ring onto his finger, a single tear falling from her eye as she gazed at him.

Theirs was an attachment that grew and flourished for the years they were together, or so he had thought, until that horrible day in November, nearly a decade before, when she had walked out of their home, and left him. Even now, Nick often took his wedding ring out of Robbie's jewelry box where he kept it, and caressed the words she had ordered to be engraved on the inside, *forever and ever.*

# 19

Despite his memories of her, bitterness always mastered him, and he continued longing for her and their life together. He smiled and behaved pleasantly in public, but his eye remained fixed on his loss, and it guided him like the North Star over an ocean of vitriolic green waters, with no wind to push his sails towards a clear destination.

"Hey Jay," Nick said, getting his attention as Jay poured out two glasses of wine. "You only have gigs booked on the weekends, right?"

"Sure, did you wanna play solo for us one free night next week, Nick?" Jay offered. "Everyone loved you last time," he said.

"Great! What about next Wednesday about eight? I don't have classes the next morning, so I'll give you two sets, he said with enthusiasm."

"Dinner and drinks on the house, my man," Jay grinned, happy to have a free night of music for his patrons on a slow week night. "I'll put up a few signs so folks'll know to stop in."

Nick had played the piano a few times during band breaks on the weekends, and it kept the crowd drinking and dancing. He banged out the latest jazz tunes with brio, so engaged in his performance that the band asked him to stay a few minutes into their set. "Do you know *Blue Skies?*" the husky bass player had asked him. "Let's play it in A minor," he nodded to Nick, and then motioned to a portly lady at the bar, in a formal, black velvet dress and full-length satin gloves, to join them. "My friend Doris, the opera singer," he announced to the audience, gracefully taking her hand and leading her to the microphone.

The impromptu Doris, belted out the tune with a heavy, but perfectly pitched voice, tossing aside her classical training and bending her notes, dropping her 'g's,' swaying her hips, and thoroughly enjoying herself in the freedom of the moment.

"Ain't jazz great? I have never had a greater love!" she said into the microphone afterward, in a supple, upper crust English accent, to which everyone in the crowd applauded or yelled, "Bravo!"

Nick remembered that night, and how it had buoyed his spirit, joining in with the throng at Blue Jay's. There was a certain ease of performing similar to lecturing at the university, yet unrestrained; showing off his musical skills was a way of putting his bitterness on hold. All he had to do was play the piano and revel in the clientele's appreciation. It was a reprieve from the ongoing sadness, concerning the loss of his wife, which relentlessly sliced into his soundness of mind.

It had been years since he had heard from her. Roberta wrote to Nick consistently ever since her departure, but at the end of eight or nine months, she wrote to tell him that she had found her cousin, nearly destitute, still living in Paris, and she was hastily making plans to bring her back to New York. He asked Robbie in his letters to her whether the flu epidemic was worsening in Paris, but she did not respond to that, only saying that she was coming back, and that she missed him, and hoped he still loved her. He held himself back from plunging too deeply into her promise of return, but prayed daily, that it would be so.

He waited for another letter detailing the departure plans for New York, but after two weeks, heard nothing. He telegraphed her at her hotel, but receiving no answer, he immediately boarded a ship for France. He scoured the rubble of war-ravaged Paris for his wife, beginning at the address of the hotel she had written him from, then asking at the American embassy, and every door in that city that would open to him. No one had seen her since she had written that final letter to him. At the hotel they said simply that she had ordered another room for her cousin, stating that they would be leaving in a few days for America. She had paid the bill that morning, and headed out to collect Clothilde, but had never returned to the hotel nor anywhere else in the vicinity.

Nick searched the whole of Paris and beyond, including all ports of entry, hotels, and hospitals, his nostrils full of the stench of decay, his eyes red with the dust of crumbled buildings, and his ears droning with the monotonous cries of faraway pleas for help. The effects of war on Paris shook him. The ominous burden of shattered buildings was a vision of the destruction of his own life.

No one had remembered seeing her, as they had their own losses to contend with due to both the Great War, and the Spanish flu. After several months, he forced himself to halt his search and came back to

New York, not wanting to believe that it was a great possibility she had died, either of the flu, or from some desperate mishap concerning the starving and sick French citizens. His thoughts turned dark again then, believing that she had intentionally left their marriage, and perhaps, had found a new life somewhere he could never find her.

Despondent, Nick mustered his remaining sanity and resumed his teaching, reading, and living a forlorn life alone, a life with no peace or mental comfort. In his jagged fury over her leaving him, he wavered between hatred and self-pity. But Nick was sorry he had been so harsh with her, failing to even see her off when she boarded the ship for France that November day. Relentlessly, he scorned himself in harrowing constancy, in between gracious public words and smiles, for those actions.

Nick ached for her, the memories of the happier days of their marriage gathering around him in both solace and torment, never knowing which mood would conduct his day. He missed her and the things they used to do together and the silly giggle she had whenever she wanted to surprise him with something, a gift of a book, or tickets to the opera; the way she liked an extra blanket on the bed, not for the warmth, but for the heaviness, to imbed herself into the mattress, for a deep, dreamy sleep. Now his life was lived only from one day to the next, trying to keep some meaning through his work and his reading. He wrote poetry and played the piano and went to Blue Jay's once or twice a week, for a detour from his road of sorrow, and afterwards always ended up arriving back at the door of despair.

During these empty years, Nick awoke every dawn so disoriented, that when he opened his eyes to the morning light he scarcely knew that he was in his own bed, and in his home of over two decades. He was perpetually bewildered by those devastating events that took his wife away, and the miserable outcome that had twisted his once happy life into the shape of a gnarled thorn bush, still alive, but devoid of all leaves and flowers. It was an existence he could hardly endure.

Nick had remained in the same apartment he had lived in for most of his years in Manhattan, a spacious flat, with a small balcony, and a view of Central Park. At his request Robbie had elegantly furnished it. There were two matching Chippendale style sofas in gold velvet, cherry chests and tables, an elaborately carved Louis XV lady chair in fern green, and an enormous oriental style rug in rich jewel tones which covered most of the oak flooring. The fireplace was outlined with dark green marble, and topped with a fine cherry mantle. On each side of the hearth were tall brass, antique candle sticks that he and Robbie had spontaneously chosen together one winter's morning as a very necessary Christmas gift for their abode. In one corner of the room was a spinet, which was scattered on top with a few books and pieces of sheet music, and the walls were hung with several landscapes paintings of the Hudson River, floral still lifes, antique portraits of ladies and gentlemen from past centuries, and an elegant horse standing on a swollen lap of green grass, that the pair had collected at various estate sales during their years together.  Each day when he arrived home from his lectures, Nick surveyed every object in that room, and recalled with longing, the peaceful evenings that he and Robbie had spent there together. He blamed himself for not fighting harder to prevent her from going away.

"Hello Blackie," Nick said, bending down to pet the little foxy-faced dog, who greeted him at the apartment door. "Let's give you a last walk of the night, ok, boy?" The fluffy orange dog bounced with joy as Nick reached for the leash, and pranced out into the hallway with his master, and entered the elevator. A few quick steps around the corner would suffice as a dog walk at this time of night. Blackie did what was required, and gleefully started towards home. "Come on, little man," Nick said as he walked his little pet back into the building and into the elevator.

On his way home from work one drizzling, chilly night in early winter, Nick had found the tiny creature standing at a puddle on the sidewalk and drinking the rain water. The soaked dog was shaking with cold in the wet night and seemed lost. He was missing a collar and tags. Nick gently gathered him up, and popped into a few bars and delis in the area, asking if anyone knew who the owner was, but no one did. He had a quick thought of Robbie being left without help in a foreign country, and hoped that if she were still alive a kind stranger might have taken her in.

He left his number with a few of the shop owners, and carried the lost dog home in his arms, dried him off, and fed him some leftover roast beef from his icebox. No one ever called about the dog. Nick had not wanted a pet to take care of, but now he was glad to have him, and looked forward to his excited barks and furiously wagging tail, when he came home from work every day.

He placed the dog on a large, green pillow next to his nightstand. It was one that Robbie had bought him for propping himself up in bed while reading. Nick undressed and flopped onto the mattress, glad to be home even though it had not been a particularly late night out at Blue Jay's. In the morning, he would go out and do his usual errands, visit his local news stand, and pick up copies of the latest news magazines. Maybe he would stay in and read for the rest of the day or play the piano, have an early dinner out at a nearby joint, and then perhaps go back to Jay's for a cocktail or two. He would decide tomorrow, but for now he just wanted to sleep and have a glimpse of his lost Robbie if only in a dream.

# 20

**M**orning came in, spilling buckets of pink and yellow light like glass beads over the early spring tree tops. Nick awoke in a fuzz of confusion, as was usual for him, due to the nightmares which frequently plagued his sleep. He sighed, opened his eyes to the glimmering light of dawn, but its resplendent beauty escaped his notice. He simply reminded himself that the dreams were over, all of his dreams, and that focusing on the days' activities would see him through his loneliness. He passed the day alone except for Blackie, ever at his side.

Although he was looking forward to that performance it was hours away. He repeatedly looked at the clock sitting on the mantle piece. It ticked fiendishly, counting out all of the empty seconds in the cosmos. Certainly, performing at Blue Jay's would be a welcome diversion from his empty nights, and with that proposal in mind, he decided to go back to the club this evening, as well.

The evening yielded a soft, golden vanilla sky and a filmy sun that looked like peach punch spilling into the dusky heavens. The late March air was unusually mild, and the breeze brought the sweet fragrance of fresh, new leaves and plum blossoms. There were many people strolling aimlessly home from their workday, enjoying the pleasant surroundings of the city drifting into a calm night, and lulled by the advent of Spring's warmth. Most of the shops along the avenues were closed, but the neon signs above the restaurant doors were beginning to light up with inviting appeal, enticing customers in for a bite or a drink. The greasy spoons like Mabey's, were lit from within, with intensely bright ceiling lamps that saturated the eateries with an artificial blaze. It radiated through the large glass windows, out into the darkening evening sky, highlighting the buzzing dinner crowd in every detail, like an enclosed stage crowded with actors at a disorganized rehearsal.

Nick walked briskly down the streets, entered Blue Jay's just before seven, finding an empty seat at the bar, next to the stage. Before he sat down, he opened up a worn file folder he had brought, pulled out some charts of his jazz repertoire, and leaned them against the music rack on the piano. A bartender with shiny, slicked back hair, in a white shirt and black vest, held a menu up, and smiled at Nick. "We've got some great swordfish, tonight, Nick."

"Swordfish sounds good, Joe, and a beer, please."

"Ok, comin' up. You playin' tonight?" he asked Nick as he wiped down that area of the bar with a damp towel.

"Yeah, at eight." He answered, and watched his beer being drawn from the only tap at the bar.

Nick ate his dinner and chatted with the barkeep and another man a few seats down, intently awaiting the hour of his performance, and feeling more cheerful tonight than most nights. Music spoke to him. When he was playing, he felt it in his chest and arms, all the way down to his fingertips, when they flashed over the piano keys, and exploded into a flame of lively tunes, rarely playing the same licks twice, dazzling all with his variety and zeal. He would have fun tonight, and become energized by the glow of the audience, whether they were dancing, or just sitting at a table and watching him play.

As he was finishing his dinner, a woman pulled out the barstool next to him, took off her tailored, dark gray coat, and draped it on the back of her chair. She wore a man's black fedora hat, profusely adorned with short raspberry and turquoise feathers and ribbon, topping off her loose, dark, shoulder-length curls. She was wearing a slimming, midnight blue, dress, with a generous V-neckline, and a simple pearl necklace was her sole piece of jewelry.

She looked at Nick as she seated herself, and said, "I know there's no music tonight, but the weather was so nice, I wanted to go out for a bit. What about you?" She smiled and put one finger up to the bartender, who brought her a glass of white wine.

"I *am* the music tonight," he said, recognizing her as the woman who had a brief conversation on Friday evening with his acquaintance, Lester. "Just me and the keys," he said, pointing to the piano. He paused a moment, and offered his hand. "Nick D'Angelini."

The lady's wide smile showed a set of elongated, very white teeth, beautifully outlined with succulent, crimson lips. "Gisela Bialek," she answered, briefly taking his hand and continuing to smile. "What kind of jazz do you play?"

"Oh, just some of the standard dance tunes," he answered, wondering what she meant by 'what kind.' He had noticed her long, smooth fingers, and the not-so-long nails that were perfectly manicured and finished with mauve polish. It was apparent she knew something of music by her mention that there were 'types' of jazz. It would not be surprising if she played piano, too, with a pair of hands like that.

"I play clarinet, myself," she went on. "Lately I've been working on the new gypsy jazz style that's becoming so popular in France."

"I haven't heard much of that," he admitted. "Where did you learn the clarinet?"

"My parents gave music lessons when they came here from the old country. My mother played the piano, and my father, ....." she made a comical motion with her fingers in front of her, as though she were playing and invisible clarinet. "It was assumed that I would learn piano, but I was drawn to the Yiddish dance music I remember from my early childhood, *so wild!*" She grinned and shook her curls, exploding into a short burst of laughter, then, taking a sip of her wine, as if to calm herself. "I'm sorry, I do like to talk about music." Her dark, sepia eyes lit up with merriment as she glanced over at him.

Nick joined in her mild laughter, thinking how pretty she was, and not so very young. "I wish you had your clarinet with you," he said sincerely, "you could join in on a few tunes. I rarely get to play with anyone else, I'm so busy with work and my studies."

"What work do you do?" she asked.

"I'm a history professor at New York University. I teach nineteenth century European history, mostly English history," he explained in his soft, tenor voice.

His eyes remained focused on Gisela, noting how interesting and well-spoken she was.

"If you live in the area, maybe you'd like to join me with some other people I play with for fun, most Friday evenings," she said. "We usually go to a guy's apartment over on 65th, off Fifth Avenue. He's got a basement we can rattle around in, with a piano and drums, and his wife invites a few people in sometimes, for coffee, you know, so they can listen."

"Maybe sometime I will, if it's ok with your friends," Nick said. "And I do live near there," he added.

"Me too, and I manage the fragrance department at Bonwit Teller, so on most days, I walk over there to work. Just a few blocks," she added.

"The fragrance department, *really*?" Nick leaned over slightly and inhaled. "You aren't wearing any perfume," he said.

Gisela smiled, seeming to openly enjoy the fact that he noticed something personal about her. "Well, I get tired of perfume, sometimes," she answered, "but I like the job."

Nick chuckled, too, then looked at his watch and said, "Time for me to go on." He glanced at her mysterious men's, black hat, and her loose, brunette curls, falling softly and just brushing her well-shaped, squared shoulders. "Maybe you'll stay for a while?" he asked.

"I wouldn't miss it!"

The club was a little busier than usual for a weekday night, probably due to the glow of the early spring sky, and the temperate evening air. No one was expecting any music on a Wednesday, but when they saw Nick sit down at the piano, and open the keyboard cover, some customers headed straight for the dance floor.

He started with a slow tune, *Tin Roof Blues,* as a warm up, then stepped things up a little with *King Porter Stomp,* and finally hit the keys with a lively version of *Charleston.* By that time, almost everyone in the club was up and dancing like it was Saturday night. Jay looked on at the spirited crowd and grinned with satisfaction at Nick, who was enjoying himself, as well. At a few minutes before nine, Nick took a break and went back to the bar, which was now packed with patrons ordering drinks between sets.

"Wow, Nick, look what you've done to a weekday night!" said Jay, as he handed Nick another beer. "And another for the lady?" he asked seeing that Gisela had an empty glass.

"Sure, Jay," she answered affably, and nudged her glass towards the bottle of wine Jay had just pulled out to pour. Nick took his seat next to her again, and she beamed and said, "I loved your set, Nick! I should be going, but I don't want to."

"I'm glad you could stay, but it would have been fun if you'd brought your clarinet tonight." He turned his barstool around at an angle so he could look directly at her and entangle himself in her lovely looks.

"Why don't you come down and play with us this Friday? I'll give you the address, and tell the others you're coming. We don't have anyone on piano right now, so you'll be very welcome," Gisela proposed, giving him another brilliant smile. "We start at seven."

"Ok, for a little while," he answered, a little unsure of what Friday evening would bring, playing with a bunch that were used to each other, and didn't know him or his style.

"Great," she replied, toasting him with her drink. "You'll have fun, I'm sure," she said. "You've got a first-rate repertoire. I loved the way you did up *St. Louis Blues,* and *How Come You Do Me Like You Do.*"

"Thanks, the blues tunes are my favorite." By now, Nick's interest in her musical abilities was really piqued. She had clearly been absorbed in listening to him play, and she gave an air of certainty when rattling off the names of her favorite tunes in his set.

Gisela stayed until the end of his second set and waited for him to come back to his seat next to her. "I enjoyed your playing so much, Nick," she said, gathering her coat and beginning to get up. "I can't wait 'til Friday." She smiled at Nick, with her engaging, lustrous smile, and she handed him a slip of paper with her number and the address of the 'jazz jam.'

"I can't wait, either." Excitement rippled through his fingers as he helped her on with her coat, elated that he would have another evening of music to look forward to, and an interesting woman to talk to.

"Goodnight, then," she said, and walked towards the door, turning around once more and giving Nick a wave with her fingers. None of the other women he had attempted to know had worked out for him, for one reason or another, but mostly, he had not felt any genuine love for anyone but his lost wife. He had not found anyone with whom he had as many mutual interests, or that he could speak as easily with. Things had seemed too forced and awkward to maintain a lasting bond with any of the several women he had dated. And as far as meeting other musicians to play with, even on a limited basis, had not be fruitful. Maybe he had not tried hard enough in either case, but Nick was weary of the effort it took for either situation. It had added to his bitterness over his loss, and he had given up hope of ever overcoming this vast, impenetrable prison of nothingness, crumbling over him in an endless succession of something which felt like cold dust, that had come to be his life.

# 21

Once at home from work on Friday, Nick looked at the slip of paper Gisela had given him the night he met her. "7 p.m. 22 E. 65th St. 1st floor, Kaplan," it read. That was only a ten minute walk from his place. He would walk Blackie, and then come back and dress. He nibbled on a piece of cheese and a roll as he opened his closet and decided what to wear, wondering if he should stay in his navy flannel suit, or change into some khaki trousers and a light sweater. Concerned about making a relaxed impression on the other musicians, he decided to change into the more casual choice.

At precisely seven o'clock Nick was turning the corner onto E. 65th Street, and looking for number twenty-two, just off Fifth Avenue. He straightened his tie a little as he walked up to the brownstone door, and rang the buzzer. He took off his wool tweed, newsboy cap as soon as he heard someone walking towards the door. A dark haired woman in a gray skirt and white blouse answered and said, "Oh, you must be Gisela's new friend, the piano player, right?" introducing herself as 'Mara.'

She showed him into the hallway and took his coat. He glanced around, and almost tripped on an antique empire chair with worn, gold painted swan heads for arms that occupied much of the floor space of the foyer. He followed his hostess down a set of stairs into a basement area that was lit up with two torchiere floor lamps. Several mismatched and well-worn dining chairs were placed haphazardly around the room, with a few music stands. A dark oak upright piano stood against one wall, adorned with Victorian style carved roses and leaves on the music rack and down the front legs of the instrument, and there was a small, black, drum kit on the other side of the room.

A slim man with graying blond hair and round, wire rimmed glasses was standing in back of an upright bass, and tuning the keys as Nick entered. He leaned out from behind his instrument and extended his hand, "Hi, Nick, I'm Mike. Glad you could join us."

"Thanks for having me," Nick answered.

Just at that moment, the buzzer rang and several female voices could be heard upstairs, greeting each other gleefully, and laughing. A petite, dark woman with a violin case sauntered downstairs, went over and gave Mike a quick hug, followed by Gisela, who opened her arms and smiled at Nick. "Glad you're here, Nick!" she said, her dark eyes opened wide as she gave him a light embrace. She looked over at the other woman, who was just taking her violin out of its case, and said, "Oh, Carlotta, I'd like you to meet Nick."

"Hello, Nick," she said, in a low sensuous voice, "so nice to have a piano man." She gave a quick toss to her long, wiry black hair as she stole up closer to him, and he was hit with a blast of her heavy, patchouli fragrance. She stared so pointedly at Nick with her cat-like eyes while shaking his hand, that he turned his eyes downward. Her short, scarlet dress draped alluringly over her voluptuous figure. Black pumps adorned her dainty feet, and she wore a distinctive, pink sea-shell pendant, encased in gold, with three pearls dangling at the bottom edge, around her neck. "I think I've seen you before at Blue Jay's," she said "at the ivories for a tune or two?"

"Sure, that was probably me," he answered with a nod of his head and a quick smile, before he headed to the piano and opened up his folder of song charts.

Soon, a short, muscular man bounded downstairs and greeted everyone with a wave of his hand, "Hi, folks," he gasped. "Sorry I'm late." And with that, he went to the drum set and picked up his sticks.

Everyone tuned up and played a few licks, filling the room with dissonance and uneven rhythms, until Nick started playing *Ain't Misbehavin'* as a warm up piece. "Let's try it in C," he said, to which everyone nodded and prepared to play. Nick thought it was going well, the bass and drums were in sync, and the clarinet and violin were filling in spots here and there, until each one had a turn for their solo. Nick went first, with his splashy, forceful style, and then Mike on bass, who played solidly and upbeat, not going much out of his way to play any hot licks. The two women joined in next, signaling each other with their eyes, their notes jumping back and forth with a duet of sorts, very flighty and colorful, for a piece like the Fats Waller tune Nick had selected and he was elated with the flair and musicianship of both Gisela and Carlotta.

"Ok, now for some gypsy swing! You ready, Nick?" said Gisela, smiling radiantly. "*Limehouse Blues* in G."

Nick was familiar with the tune, but he decided to step back and just keep up with the chords and hear what the others were playing. Carlotta played the melody, and Mike pounded out the bass for a few lines, then Gisela stepped out and played a frantic solo on her clarinet, with trills and unusual harmonies that astounded Nick. On the next tune, *Dinah,* Carlotta broke out into exotic, melodic passages, falling back into the steady beat of a shuffle with great expertise. They played for two hours, Mara coming down in between, with wine or coffee and slices of pound cake for everyone.

It had been an uplifting experience for Nick, and he told the group so, animated in his expression and compliments. "Please come back and join us," said Mike, laying down his bass and heartily shaking Nick's hand.

Gisela walked out with Nick as they were all saying their 'good-night's,' and chuckling in jollity, looking forward to the next Friday in Mike's basement. "Gisela, where do you live? Can I walk you home?" he asked her as they left the house and walked into the dark street.

"Sure," she answered, "I'm on 60th near Third Avenue."

Nick offered her his arm and they strolled down the blocks. "Your skill on the clarinet is amazing," Nick told her. He looked up at the heavens and shook his head in astonishment. "I can't wait until next Friday to do this again."

Gisela smiled, also caught up in the exhilaration of the music and replied, "I'm really glad you came tonight, Nick. How did you like the gypsy swing tunes?"

"Oh, I loved them! I'm not quite so adept at them as the rest of you, but I'm dying to learn," he said eagerly.

She continued to hold Nick's arm until they reached her building. Gisela turned to him, and smiled, as she bade him goodnight and started into her door.

"Oh, Gisela," Nick began, "Will you be coming out to Jay's any evening during this week? If so, I'd like for you to join me there for an early drink and a bite to eat, if you'd like." His heart was pounding as he awaited her answer. It had not been since his wife had disappeared that he had felt this kind of rapport with anyone.

"Thanks, Nick, but I have late meetings several nights this week with the buyer for my department. I'm just the assistant, and perfume buying season is coming up soon, and I'll be going to Paris in a few weeks," she said, her words ending in a sigh, one corner of her lips turning downward. But she continued and said, "Can we do it maybe the following week?"

Nick agreed, kissed her quickly on her cheek, and said, "Friday, then," and started for home with remnants of the lively music they had played, cavorting in his head, and causing the scowl that usually resided over his eyes to vanish from his expression.

# 22

Over the weekend, he played his piano furiously, dashing off some of the songs he had performed with Gisela's Friday night crew, wanting to improve his swing skills before the next ensemble gathering. When the work week began, he felt renewed, and went to his classes with a more relaxed outlook, and even discovered that he was less envious of his colleagues and their family lives. He now had a chance of having a life again, as well, even if it were only an involvement in music, with no romance at all.

On Wednesday, he came home, had a quick bite to eat, and decided to head over to Jay's for an early drink, just to get out of his flat for a bit. When he arrived, the club was already filling up with people stopping by after work for a drink or dinner before going home. He took a usual seat at the bar and ordered a beer from Jay, who was tending to the drinks.

"Say, that was some performance last week, Professor," he said heartily.

"Thanks, Jay, my pleasure," Nick answered.

"You can have an encore anytime you want," Jay said, "The gang loved it!"

At that moment, Nick got a whiff of patchouli and turned to see Carlotta standing next to him.

"Hi, Carlotta," he said. "Fun night on Friday."

"Sure was," she said without smiling, "You're coming back this week, aren't you, Nick?" She took the seat next to him, smoothing her slim, steel gray skirt, with the palms of her hands, over her hips and thighs as she sat down. With her fingers she preened the bristly ends of her long, black hair which fell over an acid yellow blouse. The satin fabric enveloped her breasts every time she took a breath, or made the slightest movement with her hands. She briefly touched her shell pendant as she continued looking at Nick.

"Can I buy you a drink?" asked Nick in his soft voice.

He noticed Jay standing by awaiting the answer, looking at Carlotta with a familiar, expression, his chin drifting downard and his eyes narrowing. Jay smiled and spoke. "Hey Cat, I've got gin tonight, how about a Bee's Knees?" he suggested.

She nodded to Jay, and gave him a very slight chuckle, before turning her eyes back to Nick, "Thank you so much, Nick," she said. Nick wondered why Jay had called her 'Cat,' if that were a pet name of sorts, not clear about the intent, since he had pronounced the word distinctly through clenched teeth as he had smiled at her.

Jay handed her the drink and said, "Let me know how you like it, *Cat*," to which she simply nodded again, and turned her attention back to Nick. Jay had his eye on her as he worked his bar, glancing over now and again.

"You are some wild fiddler," Nick said, smiling broadly at the petite violinist. "Where did you learn to play like that?"

She looked at him, casting a deep can over his face, while gently fingering her seashell. "My grandfather played the violin very well. I learned from him when I was a little girl living in France," she answered in a low tone, then added, "He was a gypsy." In that last word, Nick noticed her very slight Eastern European accent. She blinked her eyes several times and continued to trifle with her pendant, then settled into a fathomless stare.

Nick was beginning to find talking to her a little disturbing, even though she was quite ravishing, with her mysterious, untamed looks and luxurious clothes. He did not want her to have any ideas about the two of them being anything other than musical acquaintances. He would make a few more moments of small talk with her about music, only to be polite, and then he would excuse himself and hasten home to his dog and his new book.

Taking another sip of his beer as he watched Jay pouring a set of three, snazzy, red cocktails in wide-mouthed champagne glasses, he said, "Say, Jay, what are those lovely drinks you're making?" Not that he really cared, but he was looking for a diversion from talking to Carlotta.

"This? It's a Mary Pickford. Rum, pineapple, grenadine.....You wanna try one?" he asked as he placed a garnish of three skewered maraschino cherries on the top of each glass.

"Not tonight, I've gotta be going soon," he replied, taking another swallow of his brew, "but it looks like a doozy." In those few seconds of trivial banter he was thinking about the book he was reading, concerning Prince Albert and the building of the Crystal Palace. He reckoned he could get through a few more chapters before turning in, with Blackie at his bedside.

"What about you, Cat, wanna try one? This is great rum we just got in," Jay said, still looking at his creations.

"No, thanks, I'm still working on this one," she answered "but they do look classy, don't you think so, Nick?" she turned her head slightly towards Nick, with her eyes almost closed. Her red lips parted and gave way to a chuckle that sounded more like a sigh. She opened her eyes wide, and stared at him. "Sure," said Nick, as he met her gaze and thought how luscious her full lips looked over a slight overbite, which he had not noticed before now. He finished the last of his beer and hesitated. Carlotta was smiling at him. The dark strands of her coarse hair seemed to have a blue cast to them under the bar lights, catching Nick off guard. Even though he wanted to leave, he felt himself compelled to remain seated next to this beguiling woman. He felt in his trouser pocket for something and took it out, keeping it hidden in his clutched hand resting on the bar. "Sure, it's a work of art," he remarked about Jay's brilliant elixirs, "but I'm having another beer." He gently pushed his glass over towards Jay, and settled a little deeper into his seat, gripping the item in his hand.

He began to feel strangely complaisant, a sensation of having been transported into a hypnotic state, as if he were hovering over his chair, rather than seated in it. Was it the beer on a fairly empty stomach or something else? A warmth swelled up in his chest and was gliding up over his neck to his ears and temples. Carlotta was sipping her cocktail, but her head was turned directly at him, and she was looking at his hand on the bar and then openly into his eyes, without blinking, like a cat preparing to leap at her prey.

"When did you meet Gisela?" she asked in a dull tone. "She said she'd heard you playing piano here one night."

"Last Wednesday," he said. "I was sitting at that end seat by the stage." He pointed to the meager bandstand area where the piano sat. He seemed to have lost his usual suave bearing, and instead had a dry mouth, and felt the urge to gulp. He disguised it by taking another swig of his beer, and smiled briefly at her, cocking his head to one side and blinking. He felt as if his head was somehow not quite in alignment with his neck and shoulders. Turning his fist upward, he opened his palm, momentarily displaying a small, gold object, then closing his fingers over it.

Carlotta said, "Oh," but glanced at his hand, waiting for him to open it again. "She's a marvelous musician. Comes from the same area of the world that my people do, where they often shared each other's passion for the crazy dance music you heard us play." Nick found himself grasping for things to say to her, and simply nodded in agreement.

She looked again at Nick's hand and said, "What's that you've got there?"

"Oh, it' something my wife gave to me years ago. I always carry it with me." He opened his hand briefly, then closed his fingers over the object.

"Yeah?" she said. "It looks like an ankh. "Where did she get it for you?"

He cleared his throat and drew his hand back towards his chest and gazed at it. "She got it at a deacquisition sale at the Metropolitan one year, as a remembrance of our first date there when we had wandered many of the galleries, including the Egyptian one."

"Oh, yeah? So you went to the Egyptian galleries?" Carlotta continued to blink and then looked away taking a sip of her drink. "Deacquisition, though? It looks like the real thing to me." She leaned in closer to Nick, who had opened his hand again. "Can I see it for a minute?"

Instantly Nick drew back, turning his shoulder slightly away from Carlotta, quickly closing his hand over the ankh. "Had it been genuine, they would have never sold it in a public sale."

"I'll buy it from you," she stated.

"No." he shook his head several times and started to replace the ankh in his pocket, but hesitated and continued to grip it in his fist on the bar top. He avoided looking at her, but she was still staring at his hand.

"I guess your wife wouldn't like that, would she?" continuing the conversation.

"My wife disappeared some years ago after the Great War." Nick cast his eyes down and again displayed the object.

"You have never heard from her?" Carlotta asked.

"No, she went to Paris right after the war to look for her cousin against my wishes. She wrote to me for several months and told me she was coming home, after she got her cousin to agree to come with her, but then I never heard from her again." He opened and closed his hand over the momento several times and swallowed some more of his beer. "I went there to search for her, but it was no use. I never did find her, nor learn what became of her."

Carlotta stared at Nick and then the golden object and said, "Oh I'm very sorry for you."

"Thank you," he answered looking into his beer as he took another swallow, his hand reaching into his pocket and depositing the ankh.

She pulled out a small black mirror from her purse and held it up to her face as if checking her make-up. "Maybe you'll change your mind." She smiled and held up the mirror to Nick's face, then put it back in her bag.

"Never," he said sharply turning away, his grimace apparent as he dodged her little mirror.

Carlotta smiled in spite of his irritation, and held the mirror up again to his face. "Look at yourself, Nick, I think you have something in your eye." He ignored her comment, but felt a strange vitality, a tingling warmth growing in his arms and chest and then more heat crawl up his back in continuous waves. He wanted to leave for the comforts of home, yet he was locked in his seat, now imagining what it might be like to kiss her fevered, moist lips, and touch her flushed throat and neck after she had performed a spirited solo on her violin.

They exchanged a few more words while Nick guzzled the rest of his beer, his instincts advising him to go home immediately. It would be easy to stay here and allow her to make a suggestion that he walk her home, or meet her tomorrow for another drink. He could sit and fantasize about kissing her, or the way the skin of her naked shoulders would feel under his hands, but he knew it would all be a mistake. He pressed the pocket where he had placed his ankh, and pushed his empty glass away.

"Nice to have run into you, Carlotta." Nick stood up to pay his tab and go. With an obligatory smile, he added, "See you on Friday, then." He waved at Jay, who walked over and took a bill from Nick's hand. "Thanks, man, see you soon!"

"Sure thing, Nick," he smiled, glancing out of the corner of his eye at Carlotta, who was turning around in her seat to get Nick's attention before he could escape.

"Nick, would you mind walking me home?" she asked, "I don't live far from here."

Before she could continue, Nick said, "Let me put you in a cab, will you? I've really got to be going." He looked down, avoiding Carlotta, as he buttoned his trench coat, "Shall we, then?" he offered his hand to her and began to turn towards the door. Carlotta was now out of her seat and ready to make her exit with him.

"Hey, Nick, I almost forgot something," Jay called from the other end of the bar. He threw his bar towel over his shoulder and walked towards Nick, "give me just minute?"

Carlotta hesitated, waiting for Nick to escort her out, as promised, but Jay took the opportunity to change her plan. "Sorry, my dear, we don't want to keep you," he said, handing her a dollar. "Please, take this for the cab fare." He smiled at her and immediately turned his attention to Nick, as a cue that it was a private conversation.

"Goodnight, then," Nick said, as Carlotta reluctantly folded her coat over her arm and slinked away, her eyes narrowing in vexation, and her lips bent into a scornful pout. He shuddered at the change in her demeanor, and was aghast that he had earlier imagined her lips luscious enough to kiss.

Jay waited until she was out the club door then said, "Look, I don't say she's a bad person, but she's trouble." He leaned over and took Carlotta's unfinished drink and slung the contents into the sink, while shaking his head. He began wiping down the area of the bar with his towel. "I've watched her time and time again, making her same ploy with other men that come here. I mind my own business, but I've seen her try to corner men before, and if they get mixed up with her.....well, there's a price to pay, I can tell you that!"

"What kind of price are you talking about?" Nick asked. Jay was silent for a moment while he poured out a few beers for a table full of regulars that had just walked in, and another one for Nick. "She's a *gypsy witch,* or something, man. She thinks she casts spells on men with her eyes and that charm around her neck. I thought she was just crazy, until I heard some of the men talking about strange things that happened to them if they, you know, got to know her a little better, if you get my meaning?"

"Oh, c'mon, Jay, she's probably just a little lonesome and wants a steady guy. She's a great musician."

"Yeah? So what! Some guys have had terrible nightmares, one man's regular girlfriend ended up in the hospital thinking she was gonna die from the very same nightmare that he had, and on the same night. Another fella says one weekend he was here with his two sisters, who didn't take to that gypsy vamp, and she knew it. One sister tripped a few blocks from here, on an iron cellar door that was sticking up, and twisted her ankle, while the other sister bumped into her and fell down the stairs and broke her leg. One guy never told me what happened. He just looked damned scared to be around her anymore. Gets up and leaves without finishing his drink if she even walks into this joint." He looked at Nick and shrugged. "I can only tell you what I see in those savage feline eyes of hers, and she's always up to something." Jay raised his index fingers to his own face, and pointed emphatically at his eyes. "I'm not saying I *know* she's really behind these things, *I don't know,* but I wouldn't monkey around."

Nick was silent. He had never heard him talk about any of his patrons that way, and Carlotta seemed to be something more than just a little flirtatious. Her manner had given him an unnerving, creepy feeling, and he was not really sure why. It was more than just the fact that he didn't have any interest in vamps, there was something boiling under her provocative behavior, something murky and sickening, like a centipede crawling out of a mud pit, slowly and deliberately, until it senses live prey nearby, and then with the aid of a hundred legs working in harmony, it glides onto the unsuspicious morsel and stuns it with its venomous bite.

He closed his eyes momentarily and allowed the beer to guide him into a state of relaxation, and let any thoughts of her drift into the cigarette smoke of the people next to him, wondering how he could avoid her now that he was playing with her at the Friday night jams with Gisela.

Jay persisted with his rant. "Sometimes she doesn't come in here for weeks, and then there she is again, looking for some man to vamp. *All over him*, ya know? Then she keeps showing up for a while." He spoke in a low voice, continuing to mind his bar, smiling at the guests and making their drinks as he talked to Nick. "How do you know her, anyway? From here?"

"No, I'd never seen her until the other night when I went to a jazz jam. She plays a hellava fiddle." Something occurred to Nick just then and he said, "You know, Gisela had mentioned to Carlotta that she came here last Wednesday and listened to my sets...."

"Ya see! She tracked you down!" Jay gave a loud hoot and banged his hand on the bar top. "I don't much care for her antics, but she's free to come in here, ya know. Just *watch out*, man."

On the walk home, Nick thought he heard tiny, scurrying little footsteps, behind him at times. He turned his head, but saw nothing other than a couple strolling home, chatting and laughing as they walked. Occasionally, he would pass a man walking a dog, or carrying a briefcase, but he continued to hear the staccato footsteps intermittently as he walked. Whenever he turned around to look, there was only silence. He told himself he must just have been a little spooked by Jay's warning of gypsy charms, and the golden cat eyes of Carlotta.

He went directly home and was greeted by Blackie, who wagged his tail furiously and stood on his hind legs, awaiting Nick to attach the leash to his collar for the final walk of the evening. "Let's go, little man." The two walked into the elevator, and out the front door of the building, crossing the street to the park side, where the dog could have a bit a grass to relieve himself.

The park was quiet at that hour on a week night, and dark other than the street lights along Fifth Avenue that lit some of the lower tree limbs hanging over the sidewalk. Only a smattering of people were walking their dogs, or hurrying home from a late night at the office. Nick attempted to walk his dog up a few blocks, but Blackie hesitated, pulling in the opposite direction. "What's the matter, fella?" he asked. The dog turned his head and snarled into the air. Again, Nick heard that same echo of footsteps on the pavement, but saw no one. Blackie looked around cautiously, lifted his leg and quickly completed his task, then bounded in front of Nick, leading him home as fast as he could.

# 23

Friday night came, and Nick was ready for the jam. He had practiced some of the new riffs he had learned from the others the week before, hoping to improve his playing enough to fit the wild jazz style of this group. Gisela and Carlotta were already there when he walked down the basement steps. "Hi, ladies," he said, greeting them with a smile. "How was your week?"

Gisela beamed and said, "Hello Nick!"

Carlotta was bending over and taking her bow from its case and said a quiet 'hello.' She stole a quick glance at Gisela and Nick as they stood together for a moment talking about what tune they would start off with,

"No, not that one, said Nick. "Let's start off with *Blue Skies.*" They laughed as they said the title in unison, and Nick briefly took hold of Gisela's arm. "I need a familiar piece to warm up with."

Carlotta, now seated and holding her violin, looked up and whined "Shhhhh----I'm trying to tune up here." She looked back at her tuning pegs without smiling.

Everyone else was still unpacking and tuning up, while Nick took his seat at the piano and set up some charts on the rack. Mike dashed downstairs and informed them that they would be without a drummer that night, picked up his bass and began thumping on the strings. Everyone was in cheerful spirits, but other than a few greetings, no one said much else, they just took cues from Mike and allowed themselves to absorb the music. At the end of nearly two hours, the crew let out a round of howling laughter and compliments for each other.

"What a great night!" Mike said, laying his bass on its side and walking over to Nick. "You're really picking this style up fast, Nick," he said, shaking his hand goodnight as Carlotta and Gisela put on their coats and gathered their instruments. "Next week?" Mike asked everyone.

"I'm in," Nick said.

"Girls?"

"Yeah, so are we," Gisela answered, nodding to Carlotta.

He walked behind the ladies up the stairs, and then headed to the door, holding it open for them both, but turned his body towards Gisela as Carlotta was exiting .As soon as they were all out on the sidewalk, Nick smiled at Gisela and offered his arm. "Goodnight Carlotta," said Gisela with a quick wave of her hand.

"Shall I walk you home again?" he asked, as Gisela took his arm. "See you next week," he said to Carlotta. "Sounded great tonight!" Without another look or word, Nick guided Gisela towards Third Avenue and away from the gypsy vamp, who was already stealing away with her posture bent forward and her shoes clattering down the block.

They walked at a slow pace, Nick pointing to the steamy windows of a coffee shop on a corner they were about to pass, and said, "Do you have time for a cup of coffee?" His eyes and soft, mellow voice were inviting. Before she could answer he was opening the hash house door for her, as the smells of grilled burgers and onions accosted them upon entering.

Gisela chuckled, and flashed him a smile, her sepia eyes radiant with interest, beneath the brim of her feathery fedora. "I'd love to!" she answered, already inside the door.

They seated themselves at the counter and Nick ordered some coffee and a plate of shortbread sticks for them to nibble on. "How was work this week?" he asked her, "Did you have to work long hours?"

"Did I ever!" she answered, rolling her eyes and laughing. "And more of the same this week, too, I'm afraid."

"I was hoping you could meet me after work one night this week for a bite to eat. "I'd love to take you to a great Italian place I know."

Gisela paused momentarily and straightened her lips. "Hmm," she said, "I could meet you right after work, but I'll be working until about seven-thirty this week, getting ready for the Paris buying trip."

"Great, then, meet me at eight on Wednesday, if that's good for you, and we'll have a nice dinner and make it an early evening, how's that?" Nick winked and raised his coffee cup to toast hers.

They spent an hour talking about growing up in Brooklyn, he, in Prospect Park Southwest, and she, in Brighton Beach where her parents had settled upon leaving Russia, when she was a little girl. She told him of her childhood memories of running along the waves of the beach, believing that if she ran far enough, the shoreline of Brighton Beach would meet the shoreline of the Black Sea, where her family had often traveled to on holiday. It had made her happy to think her parents would have to chase her and follow her there, back to their homeland. Her mother had seemed sad, at first to have come to America, but her father was overjoyed, and instilled that feeling in Gisela. He found other musicians on his street in Brooklyn with whom to play his clarinet, and join in with the emotional music of their part of the Ukraine, where his people had sometimes crossed paths with the gypsies of that area, and each taught the other their festive music.

"Since a musician was a male occupation, the father would teach the son," Gisela informed him. "But since I was an only child, Papa taught me, his little girl, how to play the clarinet." She spoke happily with Nick about her early life with her parents and their lives which centered around the music her father played, and the many weddings and bat mitzvahs he was hired to play for.

"How did you come to play the piano, Nick?" she asked. "Did your parents play, too?" Gisela's eyes beamed while sipping her coffee and picking at the shortbreads now and again.

"No, they weren't musical, except for dancing, but they wanted me to learn the piano, so I could play dance music at the family gatherings we frequently went to." He paused and added, "I'm really looking forward to our dinner this Wednesday, Gisela. You're so much fun to talk to." Spontaneously, he leaned over and kissed her cheek. He then told her how his parents had moved from Little Italy to a modest house in Prospect Park, a mostly Irish neighborhood only a block from the park. He sometimes played ball there with other boys on Saturdays, but on weekdays he did his homework and practiced the piano after school.

After an hour or so, he walked Gisela the rest of the way home, thanked her for another wonderful evening, and kissed her goodbye quickly and softly on her lips. Her eyes were radiant as she stepped up to her building entrance, and looked back, throwing him another kiss.

Nick breezed down the block with hope at his side, for his bleak life was changing from misery and longing, to one of active evenings filled with music and new friends, and perhaps even romance. He was so enmeshed in the music of that evening, and it continued to swirl around him, as he thought of Gisela's rapturous solos and their conversations. He stopped short at a corner when the light turned red, almost stepping off the curb as a car whizzed past, and brought him inconveniently back to the reality of walking home.

Nick paused at the next block and thought he heard the same scampering footsteps he had heard when returning from the club, after his talk with Jay about Carlotta. Again, he looked around, but saw nothing except a couple walking out of the eatery that he and Gisela had stopped at.

"Lousy pastrami sandwich tonight, honey, it was barely warm on the outside, and cold as the North Pole on the inside. I'da gotten better at the automat," a man announced to the front window of that establishment, his arms outspread in feigned incredulity.

"Why didn't you send it back like you always do?" the woman standing beside him asked with a chuckle.

"I dunno. I wanted to get home to my newspaper," he laughed, as they walked down the street holding hands.

Nick forgot about the strange sound of running footsteps, and went on walking down E. 60th Street until he had nearly reached his corner at Fifth Avenue, when he heard the sound again. This time the steps were quicker, but he saw no one either behind him or in his path as he continued his walk. In a few more strides, just before he reached the entrance to his building, he heard his name being called from behind.

"Nick, Nick! Is that you?" A female voice stole up and vibrated over his shoulder, rattling him. It was Carlotta with her violin case in her hand, breathlessly running towards him, the patter of her shiny black pumps rebounding with every step.

Nick looked at her and asked, "What are you doing here Carlotta? I thought you left Mike's over an hour ago."

"I forgot my bow," she replied, holding out a long, slim bow case for him to see. "And now I'm wide awake." She grinned openly showing her overbite and white teeth, and suggested, "Let's have a nightcap, shall we, since we didn't get a chance to finish our conversation at Jay's the other night?"

Just as he took a breath to form his words, she interjected with uncanny timing. "I was on my way home again, and there you were." she simpered, her eyes opened wide and continuing to make a show of her teeth which began to form another sentence to prevent him from talking. "I'd really like to see your ankh again, Nick." She stepped in front of him and faced him.

Nick's chest rose and he groaned audibly, trying to step to the side of Carlotta and continue his walk homeward. Again he opened his mouth to speak but she interrupted and this time her lips tightened, her eyes flashed into his. "Look, I can help you get your wife back if you just give me that ankh." She reached her hand up as if to stop him from moving away, but Nick kept walking, trying not to step on her toes.

"Oh? Do you know where she is then? Are you going to go there and drag her back, because that would be the only way," he said, his face growing red and his hands tightening into fists as he fidgeted with his fingertips.

"No, I can work a spell that will bring her back, and your cost is only to give me your little charm."

"*No!*" he roared, leaning down and looking straight into her face, then stepping to the side and continuing his walk.

"The price is the Egyptian piece, and I will return it if it doesn't work," she clamored," keeping pace with him.

Nick halted, his lips pulled back tight, teeth clenched and his eyes wide as he listened to her rant.

"I can do it, and it'll be soon if you let me have the ankh."

"No, I can't, Robbie gave it to me and it's special."

"Not as special as having her back, though, is it?" she said, her eyebrows sharply raised and her open lips forming a hard square around her teeth.

For a long moment they stood facing each other, Nick's stiff posture began to ease and his jaw relaxed. He could still hear Jay's words, 'a gypsy witch or something,' recalling the distress in Jay's expression as he spoke. She carefully pulled her mirror from her purse and simply held it, caressing it and waiting for Nick's response as he debated her offer.

"Carlotta, I'm really tired," he said, turning towards the building door and away from her lips, which were softening, appearing to part like two engorged leeches on her face. He was irritated because he had to give his dog a last walk, and concerned he might find her waiting outside for him yet again, and wanted only to whisk himself into his building without further conversation. With great promptitude, he raised his hand and stepped into the street, signaling a vacant checker cab. Like a bad actor playing the part of a hero aiding a princess, he said, "Allow me," and helped her into the yellow vehicle before she could protest. He banged the car door shut so swiftly that her white scarf and the hem of her cinnamon evening coat got caught, appearing like choked ruffles along the rocker panel. He felt her glaring at him from behind the window, and he made a point of not looking up. Nick's lips formed a cursory smile, as he opened the door momentarily so she could adjust her garments, quickly closing it again. He hopped out of the street and back to the curb, rubbing his brow and groaning with exasperation

***

Once at home, Carlotta removed her coat and hat, then her dress and sat down on the sofa next to Boris in her slip and panties. "Look," she said, stroking the cat's head and taking out her mirror. "I've got someone new in here." She tapped the mirror with a red fingernail and then gazed into it until she grew tired and her lids fell heavily over her eyes, now barely opened. She sank down into the sofa all the while holding the mirror up to her face and softly spoke the words, "I see Nick….Bring him to me……and grant me his ankh. I see Geoffrey returning to me….. Geoffrey my love." She opened her eyes wide and starred again into the dark reflector for some time, until she finally let it fall onto the cushion next to her, and words now gushing out through her red lips in a low tone of another language. Her body stiffened, her arms twisting around her waist as she continued her rant until a great heave bellowed out from her chest like a raven escaping a cage.

# 24

There were daffodils in various shades of yellow and gold
assembled at the foot of an azalea, abundant with scarlet blooms,
and a sprinkling of forget-me-nots in a neat patch of earth to one side
of the simple black door at *Fabrizio's Ristorante*. Nowhere in the city
could there have been a more perfect spot for dinner on a clement
spring evening. The faint perfume of the flowers whisked over Nick on
a playful breeze, as he stopped in front of the crowded garden, while
awaiting Gisela's arrival.

He looked randomly east, and then west, not knowing from
which direction she would appear, shading his eyes with his hand from
the distorting glare of the fading sun. Nick glanced at the black door
of the restaurant wondering if she had already arrived, and was perhaps waiting for him inside. Then he looked west again, the blaring sun
highlighting a flaming red object with a white strip of cloth thrashing
around it as it seemed to be blowing down the block towards him. It
came closer and he saw a head with dark hair protruding above the
object, and gasped, immediately recollecting Carlotta with her red coat
and white scarf as he packed her into the cab a few evenings before. He
turned his head away, about to dash into the restaurant, heat scaling up
his spine, and the usual scowl returning to his forehead.

"Hello, Nick," the lady called out in a bubbly shout, as she sauntered up behind him, in a voice that was much too animated for it to
belong to Carlotta. He turned around, relieved to see the radiant smile
of Gisela. She dazzled in the glow of a gilded sun just over her head,
a tenacious ornament over the horizon's low, silver frame of vaporous
clouds that swirled upward into a rosy heaven.

His expression relaxed, and he reached out to take her arm
and said, "Hi, Gisela," kissing her in greeting on one cheek. She was
wearing a red coat of light twill, black patent pumps, and a diaphanous white scarf that draped long, and narrow over one shoulder.
A mulberry velvet cavalier hat with a turned up front brim, daring

in its newness, and its trapezoidal rhinestone pin, set the tone for some modern adventure. "You look like a Vogue fashion plate!" he exclaimed.

"I'm a famished one, then," she answered, "and very happy to see you." Nick did not take his eyes from her as he escorted her into the restaurant. At last, maybe this could be the connection he was waiting for.

They talked about their workdays; he, his lectures at the university, and how much the students seemed to be interested in the subject of the Crimean War, and she, of her upcoming trip to Paris the following week, for a busy, French perfume buying expedition, but Nick was fixed on getting her alone again and he felt it in his finger as he poured out two glasses of wine, leaning over the table and feeling Gisela's breath on his cheek.

"And I noticed you're wearing perfume tonight....Chanel?" He inhaled the mixed scents of citrus and flowers, the woody undertones lingering luxuriously around his face.

"Number Five, the most popular scent we sell," she said. "Do you approve?" She laughed spontaneously and she rubbed her calf against his, her fingers splaying out over the table as she caught his gaze. He met her fingertips with his, grinned and said, "What next? Would you care for some dessert?"

"Nick, would you like to come up and have a nightcap?" Her eyes darted over his face, her full, rouged lips curled into a seductive smile.

Nick swallowed hard and answered, "Why, yes, of course!"

Momentarily the check was paid and Nick was helping her into a cab, where they exchanged few words but an abundance of kisses until they reached Gisela's apartment. When she unlocked the door, her abode was like a small set of au currant Manhattan architecture, with a sleek, waterfall credenza, a gray easy chair with circular arms, a long, straight-backed red leather couch, and an enormous abstract painting above the fireplace. "Wow," said Nick looking down at the geometric patterned black and white rug. "Stylish place!"

A couple of brandies were poured even as the two were still taking off their coats, exchanging tame kisses in between sips and tossing scarves and hats on a nearby chair. Gisela guided him to the sofa beneath a picture window with a large, tropical plant on the sill. Still

132

embracing, they awkwardly clutched their brandy snifters while trying to settle themselves there. Nick caught a branch of the plant in his hair, almost toppling the interfering object, and spilling the contents of dirt all over the sofa. During some laughter and balancing acts, the pair replaced the nuisance plant, shoving it far to the other side of the window sill, and resumed their kissing, which quickly became frenzied with passion.

Nick was hopeful but timid in his approach, not wanting to appear pushy in any way towards Gisela. They continued kissing, until she pulled back from him just enough to smile into his eyes. She bent her neck back and slid her head down and rested it on the arm of the couch, her breasts plunging into Nick's face as she did so. He quickly took the cue and pulled her blouse up over her bosom exposing her white lace brazier, which he repeatedly kissed as she reached around her back and unhooked the foundation attire, enabling him to see her full, round breasts and erect, tawny nipples. She led his hand over the side of her skirt, to her thighs, and whispered, "I'm so happy you're here with me," to which he replied by rising up and covering her face with joyful kisses.

Vague words and hazy sighs followed, and eventually Gisela spoke the word, "bedroom," leading Nick with her fingers, still intertwined in his, to that luscious space on her mahogany four poster bed. Hushed layers of clothing fell to the floor, and the ivory satin sheets rippled with excitement as Gisela glided over the bed, her delicious fragrance falling around Nick in subtle waves, as they continued their caresses and kisses.

"I wish you could stay with me," Gisela said after the lull of sleep had briefly overtaken them after their passion. Her hand moved away from his bare chest, as she prepared to get up from the bed. She reached towards the closet, and pulled out a light blue chenille robe as she spoke. "I have to go in early tomorrow and Friday—oh, you are coming to the jam on Friday, aren't you?" Gisela walked back to the bed as Nick was getting up and pulling up his trousers, kissed him again and again, and said, "Can we make a night of it on Friday, after the jam?" Her voice was soft and her dark eyes darted over his face, awaiting his answer.

Nick answered barely before she could finish her sentence, "Well-- yes, yes and *yes!*" was his reply. With that, he finished dressing and followed her into the living room to grab his coat and hat.

"I can't wait to see you again, Gisela, but I've got to tell you something."

She drew back ever so slightly from him, and searched his eyes, still smiling, yet hesitant. "What is it, Nick?"

"It's Carlotta," he said, his mouth distorting into frown as he rasped the woman's name.

"Carlotta? What has she been up to?" Gisela began to relax again, her curls swaying easily over her shoulders, as if she had some knowledge of the gypsy violinist, and Nick's disclosure would not be much of a surprise to her.

"Yeah, *Carlotta*. She's acted rather strange around me.....I think she followed me on my way home Friday night, for one thing, and she stopped me in the street and wanted to have a drink. I told her "no," and put her in a cab. A few days before, I ran into her at Blue Jay's. It was last Wednesday. She wanted me to walk her home, but luckily Jay said he was waiting to have a word with me, so gave her a buck for a cab and sent her off. She was kind of weird. How did she know where I lived, anyway?" He fussed with his tie and collar, deliberately leaving out the part about Carlotta demanding his Egyptian talisman and how she had insisted she could bring Robbie back to him with a spell from it.

"Oh, I *have* heard a few things like that about her, but I don't really know her that well, just from the Friday night jams." She squeezed Nick's hand and kissed his cheek, smiling. "I wouldn't worry about it.....oh, but she did ask me how I met you, and I told her you had played at the club on a Wednesday evening, so maybe she was tracking you down for herself." Gisela winced and shrugged her shoulders. "Forget about it, Nick, she'll probably leave you alone now that you've turned her down twice."

"Ok, I'll think no more about it," he replied, relieved that his new lady friend was not concerned about the episodes. Nick hugged her close to him, and sniffed the woody fragrance that still lingered in her hair, even after their heated love making. "Friday seems so far away," he chuckled, drawing back and surveying the beauty of her contented face.

He opened the door and turned to leave, but her sigh stopped him.

"It was a wonderful evening, Nick, *really* wonderful." her voice rang with mirth. Could he really be so lucky, to at last have found love again? He kissed his index finger, and touched it to her lips. "Until Friday," he said, smiling brightly.

# 25

At the Friday evening jam Carlotta was noticeably quiet, greeting everyone while her eyes were fixed on her violin with a simple, 'hello,' and no smile. Although she was dressed in a slinky red skirt and a crimson blouse that billowed as she walked, her musical expression that night was subdued, with only a few meandering solo passages played skillfully but without expression. The party had little in the way of conversation, but spent most of their time going over charts for new tunes, and having an occasional laugh. Even though they did not openly kiss or hold hands, it was clear that Gisela and Nick had formed a connection as the frequent gazes and smiles between them showed. Carlotta seemed to glower when at nine o'clock, the group began to pack up their instruments and music.

"Have a good night, you two," Mike said to Gisela and Nick as they headed up the stairs.

Carlotta held back for a moment, and allowed the pair to leave ahead of her, not so much as waving or calling a "goodbye," as she let the door slam behind her. Nick was aware of her disgust, but paid it little mind, He caught a surge of her musky scent as he whizzed down the steps of Mike's brownstone building, and onto the sidewalk.

He and Gisela walked side by side on the way back to her apartment, Nick's arm tightly clasping her around the waist as they walked, and Gisela clutching her clarinet case in one hand, and Nick's fingers, in the other. They exchanged a sprinkling of quick kisses on the way, and a few words which ended in quiet waves of laughter.

Once inside her apartment, Gisela poured out two snifters of brandy, before even taking their coats. She brushed beside Nick as she was exiting her narrow kitchen, and he playfully grabbed a lock of her dark, curly hair as she handed him his drink.

He raised his glass and said, "To your exciting journey to Paris!" He smiled and took a sip. "Don't forget—I'll be waiting for you."

"And I'll be back for *you*," she replied, clinking her glass with his.

They retreated to her sofa, and Gisela began to tell Nick about her buying trip to Paris. She would be gone nearly three weeks. It was a five-day excursion across the ocean, each way, and the buying trip would take a full week. Nick smiled and let her go on about the details, but all the while he was wondering if Carlotta had followed them and was waiting for him to exit the building, like the week before. Worse still, she might be outside planning some harmful spell on them. She had wanted his treasure, his ankh.

"Nick? Are you still here?" Gisela chuckled and waved her hand in front of Nick's face. "It seems you're the one who has taken a trip."

"Oh, sorry, I was just remembering walking down the streets of Paris and looking in the shop windows." He took her hand and kissed it. "Yes, you'll have a wonderful time."

Gisela's smile faded, but she squeezed his hand and said, "I don't really think you were there to explore the shops."

"No," he answered softly while simply looking down at his drink. "But you will and I'll miss seeing you for those few weeks." He lifted his eyes up to hers and attempted to smile with one side of his mouth twitching upward, then falling again.

"I need a drink of water." Gisela let go of his hand and got up and walked toward the kitchen. "Anyway, I can't wait to see all the fashion houses and sample the new fragrances." Her voice trailed away in a sigh. "Can I get you anything else, Nick?" she called from the kitchen.

Nick swirled his drink and shook his head. Several times his fingers curled into a fist and unwound again. "No, I'm fine, but I envy your ocean voyage," he called back in a stiff chuckle. He felt the ankh in his pocket and imagined what might happen if he gave the piece to Carlotta in exchange for Robbie's return.

Gisela emerged from the kitchen and Nick stood up as she entered the living room. He leaned over and kissed her neck.

. "You're not wearing Chanel tonight," he observed leaning closer and delicately touching the tip of his nose to her neck. "What is it?"

"Arpege. Do you like it?" She briefly glanced at Nick as she sat down again on the sofa.

"Yeah, now let's see," Nick replied sitting closer, attempting to enjoy the moment with Gisela, yet his mind wandering back to the picture of Carlotta having perhaps followed them, hiding at times behind the corner of a building as she remained out of their sight. His lips rested on the nape of her neck, and he kissed her, as he said, "rose….. lily of the valley…what else?" Robbie had worn a lily of the valley fragrance. What if she really could be returned to him? He turned around and looked out the window behind the sofa.

"What is it, Nick?" Gisela asked while running her hand over her neck where Nick had kissed it.

"I'm sorry. I'm a little distracted wondering if Carlotta had followed us."

"So, what if she did? She's not gonna wait outside for you all night, is she?" Gisela turned to Nick and started, but allowed him to take her hand.

"Probably not, but Jay seems to think she's got a cache of evil spells she's been working on some of the men she's met at his club…."

"I'm sure you won't be a casualty. She knows she'll have to answer to me." Her tone softened and she caressed his fingers with hers. "Forget about it, Nick, it's our last night together for awhile."

"Ok." He moved closer to her and touched her soft curls with his lips and nose. He tilted his head back and grinned, saying, "I really wish you weren't going, Gisela." He then wrapped both his arms around her and repeatedly kissed her fully on the mouth. Excited by his kisses, she leaned her head back, allowing him more freedom to occupy her neck with his touch. "Maybe a little sandalwood….jasmine…" she tittered, her voice trailed off and she turned her head and kissed him again on his lips. The kissing was still in progress when she took his hand, and led him to her bedroom.

Nick unwrapped her from her black blouse and skirt, unveiling her figure clad in white lace lingerie, in all of its voluptuousness. She unbuttoned his shirt and ran her fingertips slowly up and down in a gentle, brushing motion that caused his stomach muscles to visibly quiver. They fell onto her bed and Nick heard the hum of the ivory satin sheets, reminding him of the passion they had shared only two nights before. The memory rushed out over him, firing him with even more fervor and enchantment than he had anticipated. Her fragrance of blended flowers spilled all over the sheets and pillows as he fell into a bewildering dream, not of Gisela, but of Robbie. The perfume was different, but he focused on the rush of jasmine and lily of the valley. The woman was different, too, but he closed his eyes and he imagined Robbie.

Afterward, they dozed but a little, and Nick awoke, feeling wonderfully awake and fatigued. "I'll miss you when you're gone," he said, caressing her cheek with two fingers, and then kissing her closed eyelids.

She opened her eyes, a clear light emerging from beneath her lashes. "I've been looking forward to it, but now I don't really want to go."

Nick smiled. "I'll be right here waiting for you and thinking about you every day that you're gone."

"You should go to the Friday night jams while I'm away."

"I hadn't even thought of that," he pondered, his forehead wrinkling. "Do you think Carlotta will try to pull anything, knowing you're out of town for so long?"

"I'm sure you know how to handle yourself," Gisela said, nodding her head and raising one eyebrow.

"Sure I do, but I just don't want to be confronted with it again."

"Forget about it, Nick. She might pull something else even if I were in town. Just go, and maybe leave a little early before she has a chance to corner you on the sidewalk." Gisela smiled and reached for her robe which was draped on the back of the only chair in her small bedroom.

"You're right, of course," he answered, also getting up and reaching around the floor for his clothes, "but I'll miss you at the jams, too."

With that, she tossed her brazier and garter belt at his belly. "Enough talk, kiss me goodbye, my darling. I've gotta be outta here before six tomorrow morning." She laughed and walked towards him, her black hair glistening under shards of fading moonlight that scattered in the room through her window. Nick's eyes claimed a last, loving glimpse of Gisela in her small, safe space, and departed.

He listened to the click of his heels on the empty sidewalks as he walked home through the early morning haze. Rhapsodic flashes of lightening lit the sky that was beginning to yawn into daylight in shades of gray and purple, above the flat rooftops of the Upper East Side. A fine mist flew over him with the breeze, scented with early green leaves, fuchsia blossoms, and clean, wet concrete, the way a city should smell on a spring morning.

# 26

A shabby white door on W. 38<sup>th</sup> Street creaked open from the inside and a petite brunette stepped out onto the street and stopped. She tossed her long, wild mane to the east and to the west, and upon seeing a lanky young man walking towards her, she re-entered the establishment and held the door open with her foot. The man entered and followed her as she resumed her seat at the tiny bar with worn black paint. There were no other patrons there at that hour, but the dank room smelled of last night's cigarettes and beer.

"You said three o'clock. It's nearly four." She looked him up and down, squinted and tossed her wiry locks behind her shoulders, noting his slicked back ebony hair and a scraggly Vandyke which amounted to nothing more than a few bristles over his chin. He wore an expensive but gaudy ivory silk suit with a black shirt and magenta tie. His beige Homburg was tipped towards the back of his head, and with his uneven swarthy complexion and crooked brown lips he looked distinctly like a person of low birth who had made good in some dubious occupation. The sunken black eyes amidst the web of fine wrinkles made him look wasted and malnourished, and much older than he was.

The man smiled, displaying his rather large, yellowed teeth, took off his hat and bowed. "Very sorry, Miss Carlotta," he said. "Anton Lupei," he said offering his hand. "May I refresh your drink?" His Eastern European accent was heavy and distinct, and his large eyes were direct and inquiring.

"Yeah, sure." She gave him a loose hand-shake and then finished the last sip of her cocktail and held it up to the young man. "Cranberry with a lime, please."

Still standing, he turned to her and leaned his elbow on the edge of the bar, staring at her with his wide grin. "So happy to be of service to you, my dear. Please tell me the nature of your desire and I will be able to assist you." He held up two fingers to the barkeep and pointed to Carlotta's empty glass. "I do thank you, sir, but I would like mine with vodka," he said while the man began making the drinks. He handed the barkeep a twenty-dollar bill and sat down, still facing Carlotta.

"It is a pleasure to meet you," he stated and offered his hand to her. She took his fingers and gave them a quick shake. Out of the corner of her eye she noticed his well-fitted suit, his black, perfectly slick-backed hair and pronounced widow's peak, as he took his hat off. He smiled again and looked deeply at her, even though she had turned her face away from him and focused on a painting sitting on a shelf at the back of the bar.

"What's that supposed to be?" she asked the barkeep while stirring her drink. "Looks like a rabbit going into a hole."

"That's right, Miss," he said. "That's the name of this place, ya know."

"Oh, this dive has a name?" she answered as she lifted her glass to her lips and glanced around the red painted walls and three small, bare tables.

"Yeah, the Rabbit Hole."

"Oh, I was only given an address," she smirked. "It's such an out-of-the-way dive, too." Now she was looking at Anton. "I'll get right to the point. I asked someone I know downtown if they had anyone who could help me with a special spell."

"You have the right man, Miss Carlotta, what may I help you with?"

"There's a man I know, another musician. He has a special charm, and Egyptian ankh, which looks like the real thing, but he won't sell it to me. I offered to bring his missing wife back to him if he would let me have it. She swiveled in her chair, turning her hips toward Anton and dangling her feet as she spoke, causing the fabric of her dress to ripple over her thighs as she moved.

Anton glanced down at her figure and then back up to her eyes. He took a sip from his drink and put it down closer to Carlotta's hand as she replaced her glass upon the bar.

"Those are two big spells, dear lady, but I believe there is something else you desire."

Carlotta hesitated and flashed her eyes over his face, flaring her nostrils and then turning her head away said, "That is none of your concern."

Anton relaxed his grin and moved his face closer to her, whispering, "You must tell me." His lips nearly touched her cheek.

Carlotta started, turned her face back towards him and felt the rush of his intensity looming in front of her. "I want a certain man back in my life and I wish to become famous with my musical talents."

"What talents would those be, Miss Carlotta?" he said, his face still very close to hers. He began to smile again, staring deeply into her eyes all the while.

Carlotta squirmed in her seat again, but seemed unable to move her face out of the intimate grasp his gaze held her in. "I play the violin, and I have a very special one. I play jazz."

Anton drew back and said, "Oh, I appreciate that, as I, too, am a musician."

Carlotta picked up her drink, took a sip and looked across the bar at the 'Rabbit Hole' painting, "Oh," was all she said.

"First, I will want to see any other objects you may have that you can use for these spells," he said. Carlotta took out her black velvet pouch containing the obsidian mirror and then she fingered her shell pendant, all the while looking at Anton. He noted the shell, nodded his head and then put his hand out. Carlotta then took out the black mirror and handed it to him.

Anton pursed his lips as he fingered its edges, then held it up and caught his reflection under the dim bulb above the bar. "Very good, Miss Carlotta," he said as he smiled broadly, his long teeth glistening under the lamp light, and handed the mirror back to her.

He nodded his head once again, closed his eyes tightly and took a deep breath. After a moment he said, "Give me your hand and look deeply into my eyes." He took her fingers and pressed them to his chest, and held them there for a very long moment as he stared back at her, growing ever wider while he held her hand in place. Centuries of bewitchment poured out from his gaze, and she heard the strains of her native Romani music running through her head, growing louder with each beat of his heart under her hand. She felt an urge to kiss him, to have his body bending into hers, allowing him to graze her neck with his teeth. "Be steady, my lady, I am connecting with your desires." His eyes darted over her face. "Continue to look into my eyes," he said whenever she blinked.

Carlotta twisted on her barstool and then she relaxed into his gaze again. She noticed him glancing down at her hips as she adjusted her skirt with her other hand. The warm flush on her cheeks expanded downward over her throat. "Yes," she gulped, still caught in his intense stare.

Several minutes later he slowly released his grip on her hand and placed it in her lap. "Very well, my lady, now come very close to me while I whisper a few secrets, and when you have your treasure in a few days, you will know what to do with it." Anton took her hands and pulled her to him, whispered something in her ear and clutched at her fingers. He leaned back, let go of her hands and said, "Do you understand?"

Carlotta relaxed her hands in her lap, nodded and looked at his lips as he spoke the words, "Now is there anything else?"

She hesitated, opened her mouth, then sighed, saying nothing but casting her eyes toward the dive's namesake-painting. With one of his fingers on her chin he turned her face forward into his gaze again. "What?"

"I would like to keep my mother in Romania for a very long time…." Her words trailed off as she thought of her mother praising her when she was a child, for her musical skills. *You will be famous someday, my girl, and you will take good care of your Mama, just as I take care of you now.* She remembered the way her mother had drawn back her hard lips and shooting a belligerent grin at her, pulled at her daughter's wiry hair until the child yelped. "Stop crying and get back to your fiddling," she had told Carlotta, slapping her bare legs with the instrument's bow. "A lazy daughter is no good." She lit a cigarette and walked out of the room clapping her hands once in the child's face as she spoke. "Now, play!"

Anton swallowed his drink, picked up his hat and stood looking at Carlotta. "We will take care of that next time we meet. But now, we must toast." He pointed to some jiggers on the bar and said to the barkeep, "Vodka, if you please, sir." Anton and Carlotta raised their glasses, entwined their arms in a hook, said, "*Noroc,*" and swallowed their shots.

"What do I owe you in return?" she asked, lightly licking her lips as she awaited his answer.

Again he locked eyes with her, drew closer to her and touched his fingers to her cheek. "To meet me here for another toast after your success," he said, with one hand pressing her upper arm as he donned his hat. "Goodbye for now," he whispered into her ear and walked out.

Carlotta remained where she was and fixed a blank stare on the 'Rabbit Hole' signage. "Geoffrey…" she whispered, transfixed, "you will be mine again." She tried to focus on his blond hair falling over her face as she kissed him, but her thoughts kept returning to the feel of Anton's murky eyes perusing her body, his grin catching the warmth of her desire as he hovered near her.

# 27

Saturday flaunted a brilliant spring morning in Central Park under a cerulean sky and a sprightly breeze. A bounty of daffodils nodded in unison as Nick and Blackie passed by, and the tree-lined Mall boasted a netting of young, apple-green leaves, resplendent with chirping blackbirds and chickadees, yellow warblers and sleek crows. Diaphanous pink and white flowers of the various kinds of cherry trees gave an ethereal aspect to the city park, enclosing patches of the sky with an abundance of soft petals held together with a mesh of half-hidden, wiry branches, some of which bowed to the passersby, and others that waved towards heaven.

Though it was a cool morning there were a few people seated on the park benches, one in particular that caught Nick's eye. Carlotta was staring right down the path at him and he had no option but to approach her. She had the morning paper spread out over her lap and her legs were crossed. He slowed down just enough to acknowledge her. "Good morning, Carlotta," he said with a nod and continued walking.

"Hello, Nick," she answered and waved, allowing him to escape her without another word.

Only a few paces later, Blackie stopped short, growling and lifting his nose into the air.

"C'mon little fella," Nick said, but the dog sat dawn and refused to advance, staring into the thin air, growling and sniffing. Nick reached to pick him up, but Blackie squirmed away, his eyes fixed on something that seemed close by but was not visible.

"Let's talk, Nick, shall we?" Carlotta said. She reached out to pet the seated dog who ignored her and continued to stare into an empty space immediately in front of him.

Nick grimaced when he heard these words, wondering if Jay had been right about her 'spells,' one of which appeared to be an immobilized Blackie.

"Sure, Carlotta, I guess we have a few minutes." He turned towards her but did not sit down, one foot still pointed down the path which he had intended to walk.

"Nick, I've been thinking about your ankh…."

"No, Carlotta, I can't let you have it," he interrupted, his throat tightening as he spoke.

"I know you have been thinking of what I said about Robbie. Nick I can bring her back, and soon."

"How could you possibly know what I've been thinking?" His cheeks began to redden and his lips grew taut over his clenched teeth. "What's in it for you, just this exotic charm, Carlotta? Is that it?"

"Yes. I will earn the ankh from you."

Nick rolled his eyes and pushed his hair off his forehead with a dramatic sweep of his fingers. "I don't believe you." He stared at her for a moment and then said, "Why do you want it so much, Carlotta? What are you going to do with it? Sell it because you think it's the real deal?" He stiffened and his free hand closed tightly, then opened again while he rubbed his fingertips together.

"I will make good use of it for myself. That's all," she answered calmly. Her eyes were focused directly on his.

Nick stood silently but did not break her open gaze. The tension in his expression slowly eased and he pulled out the talisman. But his eyes narrowed as he held out the object towards her. "Ok, let's see what you can do with it." He squeezed it tightly in his hand, then raised it to his lips and kissed it before handing it over to Carlotta.

As he placed it in her open palm he said, "How long will it take."

She looked down at the treasure, now in her hand and ignoring his question said, "Do you have a picture of her."

Nick pulled out his wallet and at the same time she retrieved the black mirror from her purse. He took out a photograph of Robbie. "Just hold it up to the mirror," she instructed while raising the seeing-eye up to the picture. She held it there for an eternity of seconds, and then up to Nick's face. "Come closer."

Nick leaned into her mirror and briefly saw his reflection in the black glass, but as she moved it away from him he saw the image of Robbie from the photograph. He gasped and felt his knees begin to buckle. He steadied himself with one hand on the arm of the bench on which Carlotta was seated, and continued looking. The image was distinct and unwavering. Carlotta followed his expression with her eyes, withdrew the mirror from him and put it back into her purse.

She folded her newspaper and rose to go. "Have a good day, Nick," she said as she turned in the direction of 59th Street. "Soon you will have your wish," She held out the Egyptian charm to him before placing it into her purse and walking off.

A faint, sweet aroma of spring flowers whisked by on agile zephyrs playing with the petals and new greenery of the Park. Nick breathed in the passing draft and looked towards his building just a few blocks down. "Come home to me, Robbie," he whispered as he exhaled, the corners of his lips drawing slightly upward.

Blackie, who was still seated at the foot of the park bench, had stopped growling and sniffing the air in front of him and was now calm. Nick reached down and petted his tiny dog and said "Let's go home, now!" With that, the two ran towards the nearest path out of the park, back down Fifth Avenue, headed for home.

# 28

Instead of walking back to her apartment, Carlotta swayed down 6th Avenue, taking notice of every young man that passed by her. A few of them smiled and she smiled back, but kept walking, for her eye was out for Vern, lest he should be out on Saturday errands or a bite of breakfast. When she turned the corner and walked towards Mabey's, she saw him just as he was entering. She waited several minutes until she was sure he had seated himself and placed an order before going in.

The place was abuzz with customers and there was barely a free spot to sit down. Carlotta saw him sitting at the counter and walked up behind him. "Hello, Vern, mind if I sit down?" Before awaiting his answer she quickly took the seat next to him. "How are you?" she asked.

"Oh, pretty good." He took a gulp of coffee and stared directly in front of him, watching the cook throw a couple of eggs on the grill. She ordered coffee and eggs, then pivoted the counter chair around so that her body was facing Vern's profile, and leaned an elbow on the counter to hold her position in the swivel seat. He turned his head only enough to look out of the corner of his eye at her and said, "Last time I saw you here, some guys were slamming you into the plate glass window." He raised his coffee mug in the direction of the front window. "What was that all about?" he asked finally directing his eyes on her.

"Nevermind. It's done." She opened up her napkin with a shake of her hand and tossed it on her lap. "I told you once before that a few ruffians had been following me and….."

"You wanted me to escort you home." He finished her sentence, nodded his head and turned back towards his plate and lifted his fork. "Somehow I don't think those were the same ruffians," he said, screwing up his lips into a contorted smile.

"I was in trouble, yeah, but it's done and it's nothing I care to talk about," she snapped, remembering the unpleasant visit she made to one of those men with Geoffrey's money. "We're *all done*, now," she had said, slapping the wad of cash into the man's hand and watching as he counted it.

Her lips twitched at the memory and she looked away from Vern, but still holding her seat in place so that her body was facing him. She reached for her coffee mug and then abruptly opened her purse instead and felt around for the ankh. When her fingers found it, she simply grasped it for a few seconds, and allowed it to drop back into the bottom of the purse. With an audible sigh, she turned to Vern and stared. She did not let up until he met her gaze. She dabbed at one corner of her lips with her napkin, all the while her eyes fixed on him.

She noticed his eyes straying down over her neck and throat, so she bent slightly forward while her hands smoothed her skirt over her lap and hips several times. Vern's eyes widened and lowered down over her figure, his breathing beginning to be heavier. Without looking up he said in a quiet tone, "I think I should walk you home this morning in case those men are waiting outside for you again." When he at last looked up at her, his eyes were glazed, his voice hoarse and dry. "Check, please," he said to the cook, never taking his eyes from Carlotta, who was by now smiling at him.

"Thank you so much, Vern," she said picking up her coffee for a last sip. "Let's go now, then if you're ready. I'm not that hungry anyway." She slid off her barstool and walked ahead of him towards the door, swaying her hips and briefly fingering her shell pendant.

Once inside Carlotta's apartment, Vern banged the door closed, and with his thighs over hers, thrust her back onto it. His hands wandered under her skirt and his lips pressed against her cheek until she angled her head towards his lips and ravaged him with her kisses, biting his tongue and lips. She slipped away from his grasp and pulled him toward the couch, hurriedly unbuttoning her blouse and then tearing off her skirt. She heard his zipper sliding open and he stepped out of his pants and flung himself on the couch next to her, pulling her against him while she wriggled out of her underthings, leaving nothing on but her black garter belt and stockings.

While he was attempting to draw her on top of him she quickly seized her handbag on the floor next to her and fumbled for the ankh, which she held tightly in her fist during the entire act. She wailed

150

during her 'crisis,' clutching the ancient charm and focusing on Nick and his desire for Robbie's return, imagining the energy of their first meeting. Vern sat up and spewed volumes of glossy white on her chest and belly and then looking up at her said, "I really cracked your marbles that time."

She started at his crude attitude, which he had never before displayed to her, yet received it with a laugh while still squeezing the ankh. Her hair fell wildly over her shoulders as she sat up and wiped the love juice from her chest with Vern's handkerchief which had conveniently fallen out of his jacket near the floor next her. She grabbed his hand. "Come," she said, leading him towards her bedroom. "Lie down and rest."

"I should be going," he said while walking into the bedroom with Carlotta and flopping down on her bed. He grabbed an extra pillow that had fallen to the floor, and placed it under his head and shut his eyes.

An hour later Carlotta clothed in her crimson silk robe sat on the edge of her bed where Vern was still sleeping. She lightly ran her fingernails over his chest. He opened his eyes and leaned up on his elbow. "I've gotta go," he said and began to sit up.

With one finger she pushed him back onto the pillow and held up her little mirror to his face. "Tell me what you see," she said.

"I see my face, of course." He shoved the mirror to one side, but she persisted, this time holding it a bit farther away.

"Look again."

"I really need to get going." He propped up on his elbow again and slid his legs towards the edge of the bed.

"Look again," she repeated, moving the mirror closer to his face.

Vern smacked the bed with his other hand, and rolled his eyes. "Ok, then. I see my......*Oh my God!* There's a picture of a woman in there." He reached his hand up to grab the mirror, but she snatched it away.

"Thank you," was all she said, and placed the mirror back in its velvet bag. In one move Carlotta tore off her robe, threw it to the floor and straddled Vern's naked body. He closed his eyes and took ahold of her hips. She turned her head as she gave herself over to lust, and stared at a small picture of Geoffrey that was lying on her nightstand for the duration.

\*\*\*

Again he dozed and was awakened by Carlotta crawling on top of him once more and draping her body over him. Vern opened his eyes and said, "Hey what time is it?" The late afternoon sun was glaring through the bedroom window and cast a shadow of the nightstand and a violin case on the wooden floor. "I have to go."

But instead of sitting up, he remained where he was, making no attempt to move. He placed his hands on her buttocks and pulled her hips closer to him. This time Carlotta fastened her gaze on the tattered violin case that she had positioned next to her nightstand. "I will be famous with you," she whispered.

"*What?*" said Vern.

"It's not important," She rose up and with the aid of one hand speared herself on his erection. "I need you once more," she said. "That's all." She moved her face over his and bit his lip, her black waves falling over his neck and shoulders.

When the act was over Carlotta simply got up and flung on her robe. She bent over and opened up her violin case and moved it into the sunlight, its red color glowing in the vibrant light from the window. Reaching down she felt the smooth finish of the instrument beneath her fingers and then looked at Vern. "Don't you have to be going?" she said, looking back at the instrument.

"Yeah, I guess I do." He got up and walked into the living room to find his clothing. Carlotta heard fabric rustling and a zipper being drawn. She got up from her spot near the violin and walked in just as Vern had finished dressing, tossed her hair over her shoulders and extended her hand towards the doorknob.

"Great seeing you," she said, leaning her hip on the frame of the open door and blinking at him. "I'll see you around then, Vern." Her eyes wandered over to Boris sitting on the arm of the sofa. "Are you hungry, my boy?" she cooed to the cat, while opening the door wider so Vern could exit.

"Goodbye, Carlotta," he said, hesitating, his hand gripping the edge of the door as if to keep her from closing it. "Look, I'm meeting Lulu…."

Carlotta groaned and placed her hand on the door, waiting to close it. She looked at him briefly and then back at the cat. "Don't even worry about it, ok?" She smiled at the cat and then slowly closed the door as Vern slipped out.

She led Boris to his bowl and then allowed her robe drop to her feet, picked up her Gagliano and began to fiddle, heated and rampant in the blush of the fading sun that fell over her naked figure.

# 29

Vern walked at a quick pace towards his building, and giving a glance at his watch knowing he had but a few minutes to get ready for his date with Lulu, who would be arriving at his flat shortly. But he was wrong. He had apparently misread the time, and there stood Lulu out on the street leaning on the hood of her father's Chrysler with her arms crossed. She did not smile as he approached.

"Hi, Lu," he said. "You're early, aren't you, Babe?" he made an attempt to straighten his jacket and ran his fingers through his hair.

"No, you're late." Her throat tightened over her words. "I thought you said six o'clock?"

"Sure, sure I did." He looked at his watch again and saw it was six-thirty. He closed his eyes and sighed. He reached out for her hand. "I'm so sorry, Lu, I looked at the time wrong." He took her wrist and drew her clenched fist towards his lips and awkwardly tried to kiss her knuckles, but she wrenched away from his grasp. He gave her a half smile, with only one corner of his mouth turning up. "Forgive me, will ya?"

"You look a mess, Vern. What were you doing, anyway?" she moved her head back and looked him up and down. His pants were wrinkled and so was his shirt.

"I was out for a long walk. Went all the way up to W. 72$^{nd}$ Street looking around, then walked back on the park side." He gestured with his hand in the direction of the park, then rubbed the back of his neck.

"And you smell odd," she said taking the hand he had just had on his neck and sniffing it. "What is that musky odor from?" Her eyebrows were raised and her lips were hard and straight.

"Oh, I don't know, c'mon, Lu let's go upstairs so I can change. I'm really sorry, ok?"

"It smells like perfume." She turned her face toward Vern's shirt and sniffed the collar. "Do they have patchouli trees on that side of the park?" Her eyes narrowed and her cheeks reddened.

"Oh, hell Lulu, quit looking for a fight, and let's go upstairs." Vern took her hand again and stepped toward his building, but Lulu stayed put.

"No. Whatever you were doing you had completely forgotten about me, and you barely said you were sorry." Her sharp words fell like broken glass over Vern's ears.

"Yeah, I *did* say it and I *am*, now forget about it." He clenched his teeth and scratched his neck and face, suddenly noticing Carlotta's musky scent made more pungent by the sweat that was beginning to leak from his pores.

Lulu again wrestled her hand from his, gave him an unflinching scowl, turned on her heel and walked away.

"Lu," he called out. "Where are you going?" He watched as she pranced down the block, threw up his hands and walked into his building.

After a quick shower and putting on some clean clothes, he took a look outside his window to see Lulu's car still parked across the street. It was now nearly seven-thirty. He sat on the edge of his couch and propped his elbows on his knees, placing his face in his hands. "Oh, God, what was I doing?" he muttered over and over, alternating between standing up to look out of the window for Lulu's return, and sitting back down on the couch with his fists staring at his apartment door.

Vern called to mind the strange compulsion that had come over him when he saw Carlotta at the breakfast counter that morning. He hardly remembered walking over to her flat and tearing his clothes off, or any incidents about the sexual act he had partaken with her, not her kisses, her touch, her eyes full of desire. All that he remembered was that driving force of lust that seemed to have begun when she first sat down next to him in Mabey's. "Why?" he said aloud, banging his fist on the lamp table, recollecting the aversion she had awakened in him after their last entanglement weeks ago. When he had bumped into her at Blue Jay's after that, he had felt not only disinterested, but repulsed.

Vern got up to check for Lulu outside again, but before he got to the window his buzzer rang. He hurried downstairs to catch her in his arms and apologize again. He found her sitting on the stoop and leaning against the railing. A flash of heat flew over his face as she turned around, her eyes half closed and her lips agape in a distracted simper.

"I'm starving Vern, let's go eat," she said, slurring her 'S's.' She was holding onto the rail and trying to pull herself up into a standing position. "Whoops!" she giggled as she slid back down on the step.

"Come on, let's get upstairs, Lu."

\*\*\*

After nearly dragging her up the three flight of stairs to his apartment, he plunked her down on his bed, held her seated body against his shoulder and pulled off her dress, allowing her to flop on his pillows in her undergarments, where she stayed the entire night. Vern laid himself out on his sofa and tried to read under the small lamp on his nightstand.

His mind wandered back to Carlotta's apartment and his motive for agreeing to go there so readily and give into her seductive charms. *No,* her seductive *powers,* he corrected his thoughts, for she held no charm for him, only fear. Was he going to have another nightmare, or was Lulu? He jumped up and looked out the window to see if Carlotta was outside his building, about to conjure something else.

He picked up Lulu's purse that she had dropped on the floor upon entering, held it in his hands and rubbed the soft leather of the lemon-yellow fashion item. "Oh, Lu, you were doing so well, with the new job and all." He fell back against the couch and slumped with a heavy moan, rubbing his forehead with one hand. He thought of her pretty yellow pumps beating down the street this evening after their fight, the short skirt of her dove gray dress flitting over her thighs as she walked away from him.

He reminisced about the night he had taken her to Fabrizio's and she had declined a glass of wine and told him of her intention to become a window dresser. Her eyes were sparkling, the dark green fur of her collar had set off the glow of her cheeks as she spoke of her dreams. No more would she be the useless little girl of a rich father. "I want to have a real career," she had said. "I don't want to stay at home like my mother and wait for parties to be planned." He had kissed her perfect lips as they parted that evening, and then watched her drive down the street in the red Chrysler.

Life would be good again, and he believed it that night that they had broken free of Carlotta's nightmare spells. But today he had fallen back into a dark cavern, and allowed himself to be overcome by an overwhelming physical hunger. Vern sat for a long time under the light of his table lamp, his book opened on the same page as when he had picked it up. He returned to the window but saw nothing except his actions of the early evening, and recalled watching Lulu walk down the street towards somewhere to drink.

# 30

It was a week to the day since Nick had seen Carlotta in the park and turned over his ankh to her. Except for a few errands, he had stayed in his flat most of the day, but at seven o'clock he put on his coat and hat and walked over to Jay's for some dinner and music. He had not seen Carlotta since then, not having gone to the Friday night jam the night before, and had the feeling that she would not be bothering him any longer.

The streets were heavy with people out walking and talking, crowding the pavement, ambling leisurely out to dinner, or home from the day's outing, none seeming anxious to reach their destinations on such an exceptional spring eventide. A few wispy clouds remained in the darkening blue-violet sky, appearing like white smiles from above, as they observed the strolling masses, and heard their gleeful comments to one another rising upward over the city streets. Ladies dressed casually in light spring coats of puce or khaki twill scuffed along together in groups of three or four, swinging a purse or twirling their long strands of pearls as they walked, giggling together about some comical secret they shared. Couples dressed for dinner walked hand in hand and stopped to look at menus in some of the restaurant windows before going in, and young men paraded down the city blocks, talking jovially to each other, as they headed out for a few drinks at one of the local bars or greasy spoons together.

Once inside Blue Jay's, he easily found his cherished bar seat, very near the tiny stage area. "Hello, Jay," he said, as Jay turned around from the back of the bar and headed towards him.

"Good evening, Nick," beamed Jay, his brown eyes bright with jollity. "What can I get for you?"

"Let's try the Scotch for a change."

Jay turned around and poured a generous shot of whiskey into an old fashioned glass with one ice cube.

"You gonna pound the keys here again this week?" Jay asked.

Nick replied, "How about the week after?"

"Ok, great," Jay answered, reaching around to grab four highball glasses and some gin. "Got a new trio here tonight. All ladies, I'm told" He took out his shaker from under the bar, and nodded to a man at the other end of the bar. "Four tall Southside Fizzes comin' up." Then he grinned at the Federal agent, Captain Dawes, who was just walking up to the bar with his wife. "You don't mind, do you Vinnie?" he laughed as he shook his mixture, and poured out the drink order into the tall glasses.

"I don't think I heard you, Jay," he bellowed back. "Or saw anything, either. Me and the Missus'll have some of that famous rye, if you have it."

"I might," answered Jay, grinning as he quickly filled two glasses with ice and reached for his bottle of rye.

Captain Dawes pulled out a chair at the bar for his wife, a buxom brunette with a friendly, puckered smile and thin lips.

"Hey Vince," Nick said, leaning over to shake the captain's hand. "So this is Mrs. Dawes?"

"Yep. Say hello, Mabel."

A small, diamond brooch in the shape of a firefly sparkled from the neckline of her black dress, as she leaned over and shook Nick's hand. "Nice to meet you," she said.

"You too, Mrs. Dawes," said Nick.

"Great band here tonight," Jay said, taking Mrs. Dawes' fingers in a loose handshake. "Glad you could make it."

"Hello, everybody," said Vern, just walking in and pulling out a barstool next to Nick and ordered a rocks and rye.

Nick eyeballed Vern noting the way he tapped on the bar and slumped over in his seat. "Lulu coming?"

"No, not tonight," Vern said lifting his drink.

"Friday night?"

"Yeah, it's Friday night," Vern said as he glanced around the dance floor, then back down at his drink.

"Everything ok, man?"

"Sure, sure it is….I guess." Vern blinked and added, "She had to work late. We'll be out next week." Nick nodded and watched Vern shake the ice left in his glass. "Make it a double this time," he said to Jay who was pouring out a beer for another patron.

At eight-thirty, the lights dimmed over the tables and dance floor, and three women wearing men's black evening attire and hot pink bow ties, slinked quietly up to the little stage, their high heels provoking a slight sway of their hips as they stepped onto the platform. A tall, brown-skinned woman with an elegant Nefertiti profile and long neck stepped behind the drum set and took several sets of sticks out from a pouch, while a blonde with a wavy bob pulled out the piano bench and set her sheet music on the stand. The last to enter was a diminutive lady with slick, blue-black, hair, tied into a chignon at the nape, carrying a tattered violin case. Her bright pink lips parted in a smile as she took her place in front of the other two and took out her violin. Nick barely recognized her with her hair pulled back and wearing the men's evening attire. "Look, it's Cat!" said Jay glancing at Nick. She caught Nick's eye and he waved at her as she poised her bow over the violin strings.

The spotlights were turned on over the trio, and she said, "Good evening, everyone. We hope you enjoy…. **Hot Pink!** With a wave of her hand, the music started, kicking into a lively version of *Down Hearted Blues*. Couples shuffled onto the dance floor, under the soft light of the chandelier, the ladies' glistening beads and glossy red lips flickering in a starry cluster of sparks as they danced. Another tune, and then another, one more frenzied than the last, until after several such songs were played, a slow tune for a foxtrot prevailed, and set a different mood of relaxation and balmy, tropical nights with *Dardanella*.

There was something different about Carlotta's playing tonight. Although he had heard her play splendidly at the Friday night jams, her expression and tone this evening was far and above that of just an excellent jazz fiddler. The evocative tone of her slow melodies sang mornfully of lost love to the point of bereavement and the lively tunes told tales of wild nights and passionate abandonment in a lover's arms.

After another foxtrot, the band took a break, and the house lights were brightened just a bit. Knowing he could not altogether avoid Carlotta, he put on his jacket and strolled over towards her while she was talking to a young man, who seemed very interested in her vamping techniques. The heavy scent of patchouli and rose water seemed to beckon Nick. He walked up behind her as she shifted her hips sev-

160

eral times smoothed her hair noticing how the young man's gaze was locked on her. Nick smiled, and said, "Hi Carlotta."

"Oh, hello, Nick, going so soon?"

"After a few more tunes. Wow, you sound great. Is that a different violin?" he asked.

"Yes, it was my grandfather's." She had a different look about her, with composed posture and eyes that seemed to wander the room casually instead of fixing them on any certain man.

"Well, you sound wonderful. Sorry I missed the jam last night. Did you have it with you then? Great band, too."

She shook her head. "Oh, I'm just filling in tonight, but this is the first time I've played that fiddle outside of my apartment, but I'm glad you like it. Thank you, Nick." Her eyes had a clarity to them that he had never seen, instead of the dusky stare she usually imposed to dominate her victims.

Nick stepped back as if to return to his bar seat, but hesitated looking at her well-coiffed hair, her sleek men's suiting covering her entire figure all but the very top of her neck to her open-toed patent leather high heels. "I was wondering—"

"Everything will go according to plan," she interrupted. "Excuse me, I've got to get back." She pointed to the stage and stepped away, motioning with her hand "Come take a look at my fiddle."

He followed her and she took her instrument of its case and held it up for him to see. "It's a beauty, very special isn't it?"

"Italian 1765. A gift to my grandfather many years ago from a Polish Princess." She turned it around displaying the back, and ran her finger over the scroll of the headstock like a jeweler giving a last touch to his masterpiece.

"Astounding, Carlotta."

She smiled at the violin and glanced at Nick. "Glad you were here tonight."

Just as Nick turned to leave, a lanky young man in an exquisite black silk suit walked up to the end of the bar where Carlotta stood holding her instrument. He took off his hat, nodded to her and took a seat at the end of the bar. Other than the time it took to order a drink, his eyes seldom strayed from her.

When Nick returned to his seat, Vern turned to him and said. "It doesn't seem like she's bothering anyone tonight. She's barely looked at me, thank God."

"Yeah, she seems to be distracted by her new band and whoever that man is at the end of the bar." They both watched Carlotta perform another piece, sometimes glancing over at the tall spectator, her cheeks flushed. Nick caught a glimpse of Vern looking at her as she played.

"She seems like a different person, and yeah, I'm relieved she's not all over any of us," Vern said, still watching Carlotta out of the corner of one eye.

Nick chuckled and clinked glasses with Vern. "Stick close to your own girl, Vern," he said tapping his fingers on the bar to the beat of the music. "I think this one's found a new enterprise besides vamping and casting spells on us mortals."

# 31

It was just before midnight when Nick left Blue Jay's. Carlotta's performance on her antique violin had immobilized Nick in his seat for the duration of the band's sets. Vern and Lulu had left in the middle of the second set, but Nick had fallen deeper into a reverie with each tune. The sounds of her instrument felt buried in his heart, and with her bow poised and dancing over strings, it brought memories of Robbie, in full force with every detail in his mind. When he turned his head to break the spell, his eyes rested on some female patron, who transformed into a living replica of his missing wife as she danced or conversed with friends. Then his eyes would wander back to Carlotta and her show, drawing him in deeper into a world where Robbie was just out of reach. Again and again Nick would turn his head towards the crowd and Robbie would appear, as if walking toward him, or waving to him. Jay continued to refresh his drink, and Nick told himself it was only the booze that was haunting him and nothing to do with Carlotta and her mastery of her violin.

After the last set was over he decided to leave while the band was packing up, without saying 'goodnight' to anyone. The chill of loneliness passed over him when he caught sight of a woman in a white duster and boater hat standing in front of the clock room as he was heading towards the exit. A sudden spasm caught in his throat and he steadied himself with one hand on the wall and briefly coughed. Looking again towards the coat rack, all he saw was a brunette woman handing over a navy blue coat, who turned around and waved furiously at some people at a nearby table. "I finally got here," she called and scampered over to them.

"Did you have a coat or hat, sir?" the coat check girl asked Nick.

"No, miss, but was there a woman here in a white duster and straw hat just now?" The girl stared wide eyed at Nick and shook her head as he looked from side to side and then hurriedly swung open the entrance door with such force that it crashed against the stone wall of the building. He peered outside and said, "Did she just leave?"

"No one in a white coat was here, Sir." The streets were lively with people scurrying about, going from club to club, or going out to a restaurant for a late supper. The chat-ter and the night air seemed to wake Nick from his fantasies, and he walked leisurely towards his building, trying to fix his mind on some-thing real, such as Gisela and her homecoming. As he approached the fountain at the Plaza, a few young ladies in shimmering black bro-cade or gold silk hoofed past him and ran up to a pack of young men in freshly pressed suits, several of them holding corsages. The wom-en prattled and squealed as the men each grabbed their own girl, and planted kisses on their lips and cheeks in greeting. Nick watched them and forced himself to imagine what was to come with Gisela, when she returned home in another two weeks, but he could not even picture the two of them kissing or walking arm in arm as they had done only a week earlier.

Just as he passed the group and was about to cross Fifth Avenue and walk over to his building, he heard the familiar sound of scam-pering steps behind him. He grimaced, wondering if he should turn around, or simply ignore the sounds, and hurry forth into his apart-ment. He had to stop for traffic just when he was going to cross 59th Street, and heard the shuffling noise growing ever closer as he stood there on the corner. "Oh, God," he thought, "not again!" Nick paused but shook his head, deciding not to turn around. He pushed across the street when the light changed and the cars stopped, trying to listen for the footsteps without having to turn around and look, but the din of the car horns and slamming doors of a taxi made it impossible to hear. In a few more paces he would be home, and safe, without having to acknowledge this gypsy stalker.

But when the cab drove off he heard the rushing steps again, tap-ping over the pavement, right behind him. "Nick, wait," a thin, clear female voice called out. The pitch seemed to travel on the light for what to say "Nick, please stop! I've been waiting for you." The dogs kept up and trailed off, and he stared, hesitating, to allow himself frightened. The sounds tumbled into his memory. He slowly turned around to face his pursuer, and beheld a frail blonde woman with despair in her blue-gray eyes waiting for him to recognize her. Chills ran through Nick's limbs. A spasm stabbed at his heart. *"Robbie?"*

A slow mix of mist and drizzle weighed down the fog that had spread and enveloped the night air, turning the ends of the supple, green leaves of Central Park mostly earthward. The dampness permeated Nick's sensibilities with a confusing fragrance, of sliced watermelon and freshly cut grass, as he contemplated his destiny with his lost wife. The expanse of Fifth Avenue in the dank night glistened with watery tire tracks that appeared to lead to his abode, and the wet sidewalk under the moonlight, seemed a silver roll of carpet, meant to cushion their feet as he and Robbie followed its path home. He stood still for a moment, beholding his beloved only a few feet away, conjuring up the many dream-haunted nights of destitution he had spent after her departure to France so many years ago, nearly a decade. The magic of their words floated in front of him. *"Forever and ever?"* he had asked her just after the first time they made love. Those words had been their pledge, but when was 'forever?' Forever is now.

Nick rushed to her nearly crushing her in his embrace, a great sob growing in his chest, and flying far into the night sky. "Robbie, my love….how's it possible?…..where have you been?….I searched….oh my God, Robbie!"

She lifted her head and started to speak, but her breath only rasped like the grating vibrations of a phonograph record that had reached the end of its cycle, with no more song to be sung. A startled expression and fine lines around her eyes exposed her years of hardship and pain.

"I still love you, Robbie," he breathed, his words streaming out beneath the tears that ran over his nose and lips. Nick kissed her and led her by the hand over the silvery pavement to their home.

# 32

When the Great War was barely over Robbie had arrived at the Paris residence of her cousin, Clotilde, on the appointed afternoon, feeling tired and weak, thinking it was just anxiety over the trip, and lack of a proper meal. She was determined to get Clotilde and take her back to her own hotel near the Tuileries and make plans for returning to New York as soon as possible. A bomb had gone off in the building on a quiet street that wound uphill towards Montmartre where Clotilde and a German officer had been living, just as Robbie was about to enter the open front door.

Robbie had arrived there immediately before the homemade device had been set off, apparently by a young man in a dust-laden white shirt and stained gray slacks, who came running out of the building right before she entered. Robbie unfortunately had run in to search for her cousin, not knowing that a bomb would soon explode. In the back of the apartment, Clotilde and the German were found dead, his head nearly covered with a pile of green plaster that had once been a wall, her cousin's torso crushed by a large, charred beam. Robbie had been seriously injured by debris from the falling beam, which grazed her head and knocked her out, as well as breaking her ankle.

Several days later she awoke in a stark, white room containing many narrow beds with dull metal pipes for headboards, and was told she had suffered a serious concussion, as well as having a broken ankle and the Spanish flu. She was unable to remember her name or from where she had come, and her purse and identification had not been recovered from the fire and rubble.

An English army medic, a doctor, had been traveling the hallways of the institution looking for several wounded soldiers in his troop, and inadvertently walked through the ward that Robbie was in, even though it was an all-female ward. He heard the periodic bursts of her crying as it carried through the long room, and took pity on the young woman, and listened to her vague, almost incomprehensible story about being caught in the blasted building. She could not remember why she had been there. In a weakened state, she was told she would soon be discharged from the hospital, which was overcrowded with wounded French soldiers, whose anguished cries penetrated the walls of the female ward, disturbing their sleep with dreams of bayonets and putrid foxholes. The English doctor, a slight man with flimsy, dusty blonde hair and blurry gray eyes, offered to help her return home, wherever that was. He would steady her and that would help her to remember.

Later that week he whisked her out of the ward and into his temporary rooms at a hotel on the outskirts of the City of Lights, somewhere near Notre Dame Cathedral where the shadow of its highest spires reached out towards the window of the room into which he brought her. She was not able to remember the name of the lodging she had taken a room in upon her arrival in Paris, and even though the doctor scoured the hotels looking for her former lodging, no one was able to identify her by his description, or so he told her.

More weeks passed, and the medic, Dr. Charles Bardon, who had fallen in love with the distraught patient, insisted she go back to England with him. She was now recovered from the flu, and her ankle was well on the mend, even though she still had brain fog from the knock on the head, and the trauma due to the extent of her fever. Eventually she would remember her identity and they would surely get her back to America, he consoled her.

Having no other recourse, Robbie willingly went to London with him, and he took her into his home in Russell Square, where neat brick row houses lined the four sides of the exquisite park, with the now bare branches of late autumn dominating the lawn and awaiting winter's snowy skies. He treated her as one of his own family, declaring his love for her six months after he had met her, and at first, catering to her every comfort trying all he could to ease her mind into a steady recovery. But it was three years before Robbie fully regained her memory.

When she realized who she was and how much time had passed, she immediately informed the doctor, Charles, that she wanted to return to New York, or at least contact her legitimate husband to tell him what had become of her. Charles, unhappy at this plea, suggested she write to Nick and describe the turn of events that had led her to London. In fact, as his tone and impatient sighs indicated, he had not been at all concerned whether or not she regained her full memory, and was tired of hearing her talk about things as she began to remember them, about the brilliant Isle of Manhattan and her former husband, the history professor. He insinuated that her husband might not be interested in hearing from her after such a long absence, and that he probably had found another woman by now. That comment stung Robbie and jolted her into a deep silence for several days. Yet her memories of Nick's warm smiles as they left for work each morning and their life in their cozy apartment facing Fifth Avenue haunted her relentlessly.

Robbie, having become dependent on Charles, and trusting his professional opinions about her health, faltered over his remarks. Perhaps Nick would no longer want her, and she questioned whether she was even the same person since the bomb incident. She felt like a whisper of who she once was, and therefore, let the matter of contacting Nick drop, at least as far as the doctor was concerned.

Yet finally, her memory began to improve and as thoughts of Nick and their life together grew stronger, Robbie ached to find him again. Every few months she would reconsider, determined to muster the courage to go against Charles. Three years turned into four, five, *nine*. Yet she hesitated, afraid that if he were right about Nick no longer wanting her, she would be left alone in London with a resentful man who might possibly decide to stop helping her altogether. Her silence grew as did her distance from this man, whom she now regarded as a warden rather than a rescuer. Time passed, but she felt emotionally weakened by the years of amnesia, and the slow recovery from it. Charles became increasingly exacting and cool towards her when she occasionally brought the subject of her husband and home back in New York up for discussion, so at last she stopped talking about it to him altogether. But she found the fortitude to leave the doctor's home one day when he was working an extra-long shift at his hospital.

She had gone on some early errands that morning for a few groceries and to drop off some dry cleaning. She walked across the Square, down Montague Street, past the British Museum, turning the corner onto Great Russell Street. Robbie had frequented the galleries there many times since her residency in London. The Egyptian galleries reminded her of her first adventure with Nick, when he took her to the New York Metropolitan Museum for their first date. She would always go alone on an afternoon when Charles was working at his hospital and reminisce about the time she spent in the museum in New York with Nick.

Today she looked at the building façade as she walked, and saw a tall man standing to the side of one of the many Greek columns which lined the entrance. His stood on one leg and then the other, frequently examining the large doorway as if waiting for someone to come out and meet him. Robbie noticed him glancing around the street, looking at his watch and then back at the museum doors. While repositioning his hat he dropped something on the granite steps. It bounced down several stairs. The man rushed to pick it up, losing his hat in the process, which he left sitting on one step while retrieving the object, kissed it and grasped it tightly in his hand and holding it against his chest.

Intrigued by this lone man standing there before opening hours, Robbie walked toward the museum, intending to climb a few steps at the corner of the building and have a better look at the man, who looked more and more like Nick as she advanced. She did not take her eyes from him and she moved ahead, watching him open his fist now and then, beholding something in his hand which she could not see. Once more he kissed it, finally replacing it in his trouser pocket. Although she steadily approached, going much closer to him than she had intended on going, he did not seem to notice her. Now only a dozen feet away, her heart pounded and she felt a rush of joy dash through her heart as she called out, "Nick?"

But as soon as she spoke the words his image vanished as if he had never been there. She darted amongst the columns looking for him, her hands reaching out to steady herself on each pillar as she paced through the colonnade, but there was no one there. Nearly in tears and breathing spasmodically, she sank against one of the pillars and tried to steady herself. Someone called out to her, "Miss, are you alright? Are you lost?" A woman was speaking to her from down on the street. Robbie saw her lips move, but the sound was Nick's voice. Robbie put one hand over her face, turned to the column and began to cry, recalling the first words Nick had ever spoken to her on fifth Avenue when she got entangled in a dog's leash while looking at the shops, *'Miss are you lost?'*

She slumped to the foot of the columns and dried her tears with her fingers, staring down the colonnade and wondering at her illusion. Was her mind still not recovered from her injury so many years ago, or did it matter? The fact was that she would never cease missing her husband. A single crow alighted on a step nearby, turned toward her and squawked several times. He twisted his neck and focused on her face, then fluttered his wings and flew across the street, again stopping to look back at her briefly before flying away. Robbie took a deep breath and arose, retraced her steps down the streets and through the park back to the doctor's residence. The crow was now standing on a park bench with his eyes following her as she walked past. He did not move as she approached. "I'm going," she said aloud, crossed the street and turned the key in the latch.

Robbie then gathered some of her things and stuffed them into a suitcase, concealing it deep within her closet for the time being, and rushed to the nearest ticket office. She was able to obtain a reservation on a ship bound for New York the very next day, paying the fare with money she had saved and hidden from her weekly household budget allowance. That evening she ate a bite of dinner by herself in the kitchen, all the while looking about the stark white room, finally able to admit her feelings of enslavement while living there. The place had seemed an odd sanctuary to her at first, before she healed and her memory was restored, but she assumed the feelings of unfamiliarity for the room would subside in time.

Each morning of her life there she would walk into the kitchen at six a.m. and prepare breakfast for herself and Charles before he left for the hospital.

And every day she had the same, unsettled feeling, a shock of not seeing the cheerful yellow walls of her kitchen back in New York. A chill crawled up her spine when this man with the dull eyes and limp hair would quietly stand before the white enameled metal table in his white jacket, awaiting her to serve him and take her seat across from him. It was an image of a doctor standing at an operating table, anticipating a nurse to bring a patient, help them onto the operating table, and hand him a scalpel. "Good morning, Charles," Robbie would say and serve his plate, trying not to look at him. "Tomorrow will be the last morning," she now told herself as she stared blankly into the cold, bleak room.

Robbie made sure she was in her bed pretending to be asleep before Charles came home. She knew he would arrive just before ten p.m. She heard him come in and undress in the bathroom, so as not to awaken her. The faucet turned on and off twice as he washed his face and brushed his teeth for the night. "The last time for this ritual, as well," she thought and turned her head deeply into her pillow. She would be asleep, so he would not touch her tonight, or ever again. One more deep breath was all she took before he entered the bedroom. Now she could await slumber to overtake her in peace.

In the middle of the night a startling dream awoke her. She heard a gasp come from her lips, but covered her mouth, careful not to wake the doctor, should he rouse and remind her to take something to help her sleep, which he often insisted on whenever she had a restless night. She looked over to see her captor fully out with one arm dangling over the side of his bed and softly snoring. Robbie huddled deeply under her covers and recounted her dream.

While standing alone in the center of Russell Square Park at daybreak, she watched a very thin man wearing a white silk suit and scarlet tie drifting out of the sky and downward toward the grass. He was suspended on a heavy gold chain that seemed to have no end as he hovered in mid-air in front of her, his dark hair slicked back off his forehead displaying a prominent widow's peak, his large dark eyes piercing her with his gaze. He opened his mouth over a set of long, yellowed teeth, and his lips formed words, but no sound came forth. The man smiled, then formed more words and pointed to the door of her building on the Square. She read his lips which said, "You must leave." Something from above drew the chain upward, rattling in short, sharp bursts as it moved upward, pulling him into the clouds. She could still feel his eyes upon her as he dangled for another minute in the sky before vanishing completely. A page from a newspaper suddenly fluttered toward her feet and caught on her ankle. She picked it up and saw a photograph of an ankh and below it a large title which read,

*'Go now.'* Heat flashed over Robbie's throat and she awoke just as her mouth opened to scream.

The next morning she got up as usual and made the six o'clock breakfast. She watched Charles standing in front of the white kitchen table as she brought his plate. "Good morning, did you sleep well?" she asked.

"Yes, but I thought I heard you stirring or calling out," he said while unfolding his napkin and picking up his knife and fork.

"Why, I don't recall. Perhaps you were dreaming." She answered and looked down at her eggs and toast, then up at the clock on the wall above the stove. "Late hours again tonight?"

"Yes, I'm afraid so."

As soon as the doctor left for work, Robbie grabbed her suitcase, hailed a taxi, and was gone. She left a note on the white table which said, 'Going to New York. Goodbye, Robbie.'

\*\*\*

"I'm sorry, Nick," Robbie sobbed into his shoulder after recounting those events. "I'm so sorry I didn't listen to you about leaving —I hope you still love me."

A crescent moon peered in through the large front window, shedding a velvety, mellow light on Robbie's distressed face as she leaned up and searched Nick's eyes. He beheld her, tormented and weakened, her pale face now gaunt with years of anguish. Stroking her silky hair with his fingertips and smiling, he said gently, "I love you Robbie; you don't have to keep saying you're sorry. I have you back in our home now, and that's all that matters." A light tapping sound came from a few feet away rushing over the wooden floorboards, ending with a small set of furry paws stretching upward to Nick's knee. He reached down and lifted the little dog in his arms, and held him up for Robbie to meet. "He will love you, too," he said as she smiled and stroked the pet, allowing Blackie to lick her nose in greeting.

The moonlight dimmed as a cloud passed over and covered its view through the window, as if to signal contentment with Nick's soothing words, and that the watchful eye of Heaven's golden orb was no longer needed.

172

# 33

"Ok, I'll be back soon, Sweetie." Nick said, giving Robbie a quick kiss at their apartment door. "Did you say you wanted some asparagus with the swordfish tonight?"

"Yes, and some more cream for coffee." She smiled at her husband and touched his cheek as he opened the door.

"And we'll take Blackie out for a walk in the park when I get back, so be ready." "Sure I will!" she answered, and walked into the bathroom and turned on the shower.

It had been a week since Robbie had returned to New York and Nick, but due to feeling exhausted from the ordeal of escaping her many years in London and the ocean journey, she had barely left the apartment. On the days Nick had gone to lecture at the university she remained at home and passed the time reading and resting with Blackie at her feet. As today was Saturday and Nick was not working, he planned to do some errands with her, but upon seeing the fatigue in her eyes at breakfast, he suggested she stay at home while he picked up some groceries for the week.

After bathing and dressing she walked into the living room, picked up her novel and was just about to seat herself on the sofa when there was a knock on the door.

"Nick?" called a female voice. Wondering how this person had gotten in the building without ringing, Robbie went over to the door and looked through the peephole just as the woman knocked again. All she could see was a head of dark hair nearly covering the peephole. "Nick?"

Robbie heard some rustling as if the caller was searching for an object in a purse. Then something was shoved under the door. It was a business card. Instead of picking it up, Robbie simply opened the door to see a woman with curly black hair under a man's fedora turning to walk down the corridor. Her red coat accentuated the black silk stockings that clung to her shapely legs.

When the visitor heard the door creak open she turned back with a wide smile and said, "Oh, Nick, I'm so glad you're…." Her expression of happiness transformed into one of disappointment. "Oh, I thought Nick might be at home, are you his sister?" the woman said with another attempt at a smile.

"No, may I help you?" Robbie asked. "I'll tell him you came by." She picked up the card on the threshold and read, "Miss Bialek from Lord and Taylor?"

"Yes, that's me." Gisela said, standing straight and holding her purse handle with both hands in front of her body as she turned to speak.

Robbie looked at the caller and then again at the business card. "Is there anything I can do for you? I'm Nick's wife."

Gisela froze in place, her eyes wide and lips pulled back over her open mouth. "Nick's wife?" she repeated.

"Yes. May I tell him the nature of your visit?" Robbie began to lean farther out into the hallway, her eyes moving from the fedora down the length of the brightly colored coat, over the knees and all the way to the black leather pumps which pointed in her direction on the hallway floor.

"I'm a friend…..I thought I might catch him…I've been away…" she stammered. She blinked her eyes as if trying to see through a fog while staring at Robbie. A tear rolled down one cheek.

"Why are you crying?" asked Robbie. She looked again at the card and back at Gisela, who was turning to go, but could not take her eyes from Robbie.

"How…how did you get back to New York? Oh, my God, Nick said you had been missing for years…..I never thought you would….." she gasped.

"Never thought I would return?" Robbie completed the sentence for her with a sharpness in her voice. "You don't seem very happy for your *'friend' Nick*," she added, her face beginning to feel red with heat. She grasped the knob on the open door and twisted it, her shoulders rising and her chest pushed forward towards Gisela. Her eyes narrowed as she spoke "Who *are you,* Miss Bialek?"

Just then the elevator door opened down the hall and both women turned their heads to see who would enter the hallway. A couple stepped out and walked past the two women. "Good morning," said the man, tipping his hat. But neither of the two women answered. Gisela turned on her heel and flew down the corridor towards the staircase, opening the door with so much force that it slammed against the wall. Her feet pounding the concrete steps downward echoed for a few moments and then a sob wafted upward, choking the staircase shaft with a rumble of echoes as it ascended, leaving only a whiff of coriander and geranium in the hallway of Nick and Robbie's home.

Once she was outside she ran down the block with one hand over her face still crying and not looking where she was going. "Excuse me, Miss," said an elderly man with a cane who backed up to a stair railing as she whizzed by. She stopped abruptly, put her hands to her head and drooped over the railing as if to steady herself.

A familiar voice called out, "Gisela, wait." It was Nick coming up from behind her. She arched around to glance at him, but quickly turning away while attempting to cover her eyes, crying all the while. He strode up and took her elbow and turned her around to face him. Silent tears ran down Gisela's cheeks as she raised her face upward to meet Nick's eyes. He let go of her arm and stepped back.

"Why didn't you tell me? Did you know she was coming back?" With the back of her hand she wiped her cheeks.

"No. She got back last week, out of nowhere," Nick said, shaking his head and taking a deep breath of the spring air as it rustled the leaves of a nearby maple tree.

Her lips began to form a question but closed instead as she watched Nick's eyes veer away from her gaze, blinking. He was carrying a bag of groceries in one arm, and the other arm was straight at his side. "I was going to tell you as soon as I heard from you and knew you were home." He turned one foot away from her and looked in the direction of his building. "She's my wife, Gisela," he said reaching his hand out and giving her arm a quick grasp before he let go and turned his eyes toward the street.

"Do you still love her after all this time?" Gisela's question slipped out in a taut, quick sound. She took one step toward Nick, but stopped when she read his expression, his eyes blurred and distant, his lips drawing up into a slow, quiet smile.

"Yes, I do," he answered, looking plainly at her as he spoke. He stood for a long moment waiting for her to speak, but she only stared silently at him. Her rigid lips parted several times as if beginning to speak, but said nothing.

Finally, as if awakening from a dream, Gisela composed her posture, relaxed the tension in her lips, and wiped one last tear from her cheek as she blinked and turned her eyes away. "Goodbye, then Nick," she said, and turned to leave.

Nick paused then took another deep breath and said softly, as he watched her curls sway over the back of her coat as she walked away. "Goodbye Gisela." He then shifted the bag of groceries and moved towards his building, his head erect but his eyes looking down at his feet.

# 34

When Nick returned to their apartment, he noticed an odd fragrance just as he stepped into the hallway. He opened the door and saw Robbie sitting stiffly on the edge of the sofa, her head bent down and her hands clasped over her lap. Nick walked in and stood silently a few feet away from her, the bag of groceries still in one arm. "How long did it go on?" she said. Her tone was placid but her eyes were dull, and the fatigue that he had noticed in them earlier in the morning was now more pronounced.

"Not long. About a month or so." Nick remained standing in front of his wife awaiting more questions, but Robbie was silent. "I was going to tell you, Robbie, but not just yet until you'd had a chance to recover from your journey and begin to feel safe here again."

Her hands were now stretched out palms down on her lap, her eyes fixed on them. "She came to the door when you were out, but I guess you already know that."

"Yes. I ran into her on my way home. She had just returned from a three week trip to Paris. I really didn't expect to have her knocking at my door like that."

Robbie got up and started towards the kitchen. "Let's put the groceries away, then," she said, walking in front of Nick without so much as a glance at him. Her heels tapped lightly on the kitchen floor as she went in and opened the icebox door, mechanically moving a few items aside on the shelves.

Nick followed her in and dropped the bag on the kitchen table, and Robbie began the task of taking the items out and placing them inside the icebox without another word about the incident with Gisela, avoiding Nick's gaze. After a few moments he started towards her, reached for her arm to turn her towards him and said, "Look, Robbie, I was going to tell both of you in another day or two."

"Ok, Nick." Robbie still refused to meet his eyes, looking down at the floor. "Let me go, please," she said quietly and tried to move away, but he persisted.

"You were gone for a very long time," he said, his cheeks beginning to flush. He squeezed her arm and looked down into her eyes. "I love you, Robbie, but you left me years ago when I begged you not to." He drew his head back a little, slowly shook his head and added, "And you lived with another man for nearly a decade."

"I understand," was all she said, and looked back down at the floor.

"You *don't* understand. I suffered too…all these years thinking I would never see you again." His throat tightened over his words and his grip on her arm intensified. "Robbie…." But his voice was silenced by the cry that pushed up from his chest as his eyes welled with tears. He let go of her arm, turned away from her and bent over the table, pounding a fist on it as if commanding the tears to cease.

After another moment of silence, soft tones flowed from Robbie's lips and with one hand she caressed her husband's back. "I'm so sorry, Nick, I've regretted it every day all of these years." Now she reached her arms around and placed her hands over his chest, holding him next to her. "Please forgive me," she said, holding him tighter.

"I wanted you back so badly I let someone cast a spell with the ankh you gave me to bring you home. I didn't believe it would work, but I was desperate." Nick finally turned towards her, his eyes now red and strained from the tears.

Robbie burst into sobs. "Oh, Nick, I finally had the courage to leave because I saw someone who looked like you pacing in front of the museum near where I was living. He had something in his hand, which he dropped, and when I got closer the man simply vanished." She clung to Nick, her head buried in his shoulder as she recounted the day she made her plans to escape her captor. "And in a dream I saw a picture of the ankh I gave you and the words written beneath it, *'Go now.'*"

"Come," said Nick, taking her hand and leading her back to the couch.

"Please forgive me, Nick." Robbie continued to weep, his shirt now wet from the flood of tears that poured from her eyes. "Can we mend this, Nick?" She looked up at him, her voice convulsing as she spoke.

He kissed her eyes, her cheeks and pressed her head against his chest while stroking her hair. "I do and we can, Robbie."

Eventually she calmed herself and wiped her eyes with a handkerchief Nick had pulled out of his pocket. "I love you, Nick, and I missed you so." She reached up and kissed him on the lips.

"I know," he whispered kissing her again. "And now we'll have a new life together, and be glad. No more feeling sorry, ok?"

She smiled, looking deeply into his eyes. "You said the ankh I gave you was used to cast a spell?"

"So I am told."

"I'd like to see it once again, Nick," she said pulling a little away from his embrace.

But Nick shook his head and touched his finger to her lips. "No, I promised to give it up upon your return."

"You gave it away?"

"It brought you back to me, so it truly was a good luck charm you gave me all those years ago." He was smiling at her. "I'd rather have you in my arms than your gift in my pocket." He reached out to pet his dog who was now wagging his tail and pawing Nick's pant leg. "Anyway, was that ankh really from ancient Egypt?"

"Doubtful, but they said it might be when I asked at the de-acquisition sale. I just knew it was special, so I got it for you," she said as she gulped back a final sob. She reached over and petted Blackie for a moment, her fingers gently smoothing his head then reaching down into his thick, fur coat before playfully tugging at one of his ears.

"Let's go for that walk," Nick said, taking both her hands and drawing her up off the sofa.

She reached up and kissed him again and again. "Ok, we'll go in a little bit, but for now, don't let me go."

"*Forever and Ever,* then?" Nick said gently pulling her back down on the couch. "I'd like to show you how much I missed you, Robbie," His placed his hand on her cheek then allowed it to slip down her neck and over her breasts as he continued to kiss her.

She pulled slightly back and undid her blouse and brazier, removing them before helping Nick to do the same with his shirt. And with a sigh that came deep from within, she pressed herself against Nick's bare chest as if he were the lifeboat of her deliverance from years of thrashing about in the storm her life had become.

## 35

The late afternoon sun glared between a row of brownstones and cast a purple shadow on the sidewalk in front of the Rabbit Hole. Carlotta's hair took on an amethyst glow as she stood in front of the establishment catching a quick ray of sunlight before entering the dive. The smell of stale beer greeted her when she opened the door. Anton was sitting at the bar alone and stirring a frothy blue cocktail in a tall glass. "Hello, Anton," she said as she approached.

"Carlotta, my dear," he answered, reaching his hand towards her. "What news do you have for me today?" He took her arm and guided her close to his face, kissed her cheek and then pulled out a barstool for her. "How long has it been since our last meeting? Two weeks, three weeks?" He winked at her and gave a low chuckle, the deep lines around his eyes accentuated by the overhead glare of the barroom lamp.

"Not three weeks yet." She did not smile back but turned her head towards the barkeep. "Cranberry with a lime, thanks."

"Any success yet?" He beamed broadly at her but she continued to look at the bar tender pouring her drink.

"Yes. On two counts." She took one sip of her drink and then glanced over at Anton and reached into her purse. "I was given the ankh and cast the spell as you explained." She held the Egyptian treasure in the palm of her hand for him to see.

"Very special," he said taking the piece and holding it up to the light. "I am pleased with you, Carlotta." Her eyes wandered his face as he examined the object, and she felt a wave of pleasure shoot through her body when he touched her hand as he replaced it in her palm. He turned and looked directly at her, touching his fingers to her chin. "What else, my dear?" he murmured. "You look very beautiful today in that beige dress." She put the treasure back in her purse and lightly caressed her throat, which was beginning to feel warm with flush.

"Thank you," she said, drawing away from him and sipping her drink. "I brought the wife back to the man I got the ankh from. I happened to get a glimpse of them in the park on Saturday walking their dog. It was her." Again she gave a quick glance in Anton's direction, but then turned and stared at the Rabbit Hole sign on the shelf behind the bar.

"Well done!" Noticing she had finished her cranberry juice, he said, "Now we will have a toast. He held up a finger to the bartender. "Two shots of Vodka, please, sir." Again Anton smiled at Carlotta, his eyes sparkling like polished French jet, which together with the profound crow's feet, caught Carlotta off guard as they seemed to penetrate through her like the action of an ancient sorcerer. She only glanced at him from time to time, her fingers lightly around her drink which she repeatedly stroked up and down.

The shots were placed in front of the pair and Anton stood up and stole closer to Carlotta. "Your patchouli reminds me of our homeland." He raised his glass as she raised hers, they locked elbows and said, 'Noroc,' and swallowed the shots.

Anton remained standing close to her. "I enjoyed your fiddling at Blue Jay's that night I saw your band. You have quite a talent."

"Thank you, but I was just standing in. I'm not in a band right now."

"Perhaps you would like to play in my band, then. We play jazz, but Romanian style. Would you like to join us for rehearsal and decide, Carlotta?"

"Yeah, maybe," she said. "Do you get many gigs? That's what I need….lots of well-paying gigs." She picked up her consumed cocktail glass again, leaned her head back and tossed an ice cube into her mouth.

"Sure, sure and in nice clubs all over town. We played a club in Harlem just last week, full house. "A beautiful talent like you would bring people of all sorts." He waited for her to respond but she just looked at him, now fingering her shot glass. "Another round, please, sir," he said to the barkeep.

"Will you come to our rehearsal tomorrow evening in my cellar?" He reached into his jacket pocket handed her a card. "Six-thirty. We will have food and drink as well." His voice was gentle, but it seemed to ricochet over the barroom walls and end in a tingling sensation on Carlotta's throat and cheeks.

Carlotta nodded, now focused on his lips and the length of his teeth as he grinned at her. "Ok, I'll come," she said, putting the card into her purse without taking her eyes from Anton.

The shots were brought and they toasted again, this time Carlotta leaned in closer to Anton as they latched their arms together and drank.

"What about your other endeavors with the charm you now possess? Your fame as a violinist is already in motion," he said. "Wasn't there a question of some man you wanted back in your life?" Anton leaned his hip into the bar, his hand in his pants pocket, looking plainly at her.

"I don't know yet. I haven't worked much on it." She was now unable to take her eyes from Anton, her palms grew clammy and her voice was raspy. In turn, he stared at her, his eyes darting about her face, fixing on her lips as she at last lifted them into a slow smile.

"Well he would be a very lucky man to have you desire his company," he said running his finger down her bare arm. Carlotta quivered at his touch and spontaneously drew her face closer to his, her eyes wide and her breath growing audible. He took her hand and kissed it, continuing to stare hypnotically into her eyes. "You must be mindful of using the gift of magic only for good results, and never for revenge of any kind." He gripped her hand tighter, kissed it again and said, "Agreed?"

"Yes, but I should be going," she said, slowing withdrawing her hand and picking up her purse.

"See you tomorrow, then, at my house." He smiled and added, "Oh, and 'Mama' will stay in our homeland as you wish."

Carlotta flashed a grin at him and turned to go. "Thank you."

"No one will ill-use you again for your talents, my dear." His eyes constricted slightly and he shook his head. "*No one.* You will be a star in your own right. Now off you go."

A wave of heat ran down her back as he said this, knowing she had not spoken a word to him about her mother having exploited her as a child to make money by dancing and playing card tricks on the streets for anyone who passed by. She left feeling the penetration of his eyes on her hips and calves as she walked out into the fading sunlight.

# 36

At six-thirty the next evening Carlotta stood at the corner of First Avenue looking across St. Mark's Place. Several doors down, she found number eleven above a green door on an orange brick building. She reached up to grab the ring on an iron knocker in the shape of a crow's head, its inky black eyes staring into hers as she rapped once. The door scraped open and Anton appeared in white shirt sleeves atop some finely cut gray flannel trousers. "Good evening, my dear," he greeted her, placing his arm lightly around her waist and leading her through a dark, narrow hallway to a set of charcoal painted steps that creaked as they tread downward and entered a cellar of whitewashed stone walls where a bowl of lemon peels sat on a small table near the staircase. Carlotta breathed in their scent that warded off some of the musty air of the antique basement. Several music stands and a few chairs were scattered about, and a man seated at a small drum set smiled and said "Hello." Another man bounded down the stairs and took a seat at a scuffed piano.

"Meet Carlotta," Anton said, "Our new violinist." He pointed to each of the men and said, "Max....Howie." Picking up a rather worn, black guitar with the painting of a white hand holding a circled pentagram on the upper part of the body near the neck, Anton took a seat near the piano. He motioned for Carlotta to stand next to him with her violin. "Did you bring it?" he asked pointing to her violin.

"Yes, this is the one you saw me with last week at Jay's place." She put the case on a nearby table and opened it, taking out the dark red instrument and began tuning its strings. "What's the first piece?" she said to Anton, turning towards him and noting the dark hairs of his chest pushing out over the open neck of his shirt.

"We'll start with a jam in 'A.' Just follow me." He smiled at her and nodded to the keyboardist, who began to play an upbeat tune with a moderate tempo. The drummer kicked in, then Anton followed with a few chords strummed on his guitar, allowing the piano to take charge.

After a few more bars, he nodded to Carlotta, who now took the lead with a dash of high notes.

Anton motioned to her to move in closer to him, until she was standing only inches away, facing him as she played. He looked briefly at her, then cast his eyes over his guitar, sometimes closing them as he played. With a flurry of arpeggios, he changed the tempo and escalated the piece with a modal strain from his homeland, which Carlotta instantly recognized and accentuated with a staccato lick, intensifying as they played. The drummer laid back with scant beats on his snare, and the piano now took over playing the chords as Anton continued with the lead, his face flushing a little, his eyes tightly closed as the music shot out of his fingers and over the guitar strings.

Still facing Anton, Carlotta noticed a fine layer of perspiration on his exposed neck and throat, creating a pearly glow on his skin under the soft light of the room. She fantasized about licking the hollow part of his neck and tasting the few beads of sweat that had formed there, imagining them tasting sweet and having the consistency of honey. At that moment Anton's eyes opened abruptly and beamed into her face. He shot a quick grin at her, winked, and then resumed concentrating on his playing. Although Anton's fleeting expression startled Carlotta, she did not miss a beat of the heated melody she was playing. Her fingers were fraught with electricity spreading out over her arms and down her chest, ending at her nipples, which felt strangely sensitive, her silken undergarments shifting over them as her torso moved to the music.

When the rehearsal was over, Anton invited everyone upstairs for lasagna and wine. "How nice," said Carlotta as she tucked her violin into its case and followed everyone into the kitchen at the back of the first floor. Its uneven plaster walls were covered in wall paper with a stylized design of mauve vines and leaves, abundant with an array of crows perched over all. A small, white table stood in one corner and four mismatched oak chairs were placed in a row against the wall.

A surge of garlic and basil blasted the room as Anton removed a steaming dish from the oven and placed it with some plates and silverware on the table. He held out a bottle of wine and nodded to the drummer, who took a corkscrew from a drawer and began to open it.

"Cheers," said Anton as he poured out glasses of red wine and handed one to Carlotta, stepping very close to her, his eyes lingering on hers as she took the drink and raised it to her lips. "Shall we toast our new band member?" he asked raising his glass and smiling directly at the lovely violinist.

She held up her glass to meet his and said, "Yeah, I'm in."

Again she felt physical sensations of desire flow through her body. Her weight shifted from one foot and then the other, unable to find a position of comfort. She reached one hand to her throat, now flushed and sensitive to her touch, catching Anton staring at it. He then turned and cut the lasagna, steam and a few bubbles of tomato sauce escaping from the hot dish as he did so. When he handed her a plate of it, he said, "We are happy to have you join our group, Carlotta. Would you be ready for a gig next week at a mid-town club?"

"Yes, just give me your calendar and I'll be there." She looked at him while she spoke, but immediately cast her eyes down towards her lasagna. "Thank you," she said, and took a few bites before placing the dish on the kitchen counter and picking up her violin. "Excuse me, but I need to be going."

"Wait, Carlotta," said Anton and turned to write down the date and place for next week's performance. He folded it, handed it to her and escorted her to the front door. His hand grazed hers as he reached to open the door. She felt another surge of desire fly through her body. "Thank you, my dear, and good luck with your next venture."

Once outside, she opened the folded piece of paper and saw the scribbled name and date of their next gig, but also a pentagram at the bottom of the page with a heart drawn at the center. She raised one hand up and hailed a cab. "Sutton Place, please," she said to the driver.

# 37

I t was now nearly nine-thirty. She approached Geoffrey's house and hesitated about knocking at the door. Just as she lifted her hand, the door began to open. "Kitty Cat, my treasure, what an unexpected surprise," Geoffrey cooed as he leaned outside towards her. His eyes swept over her and lingered on her violin. "Have you come from a rehearsal, my darling?"

"Yes. A new band I've been invited to join." She surveyed him briefly, noting his smoothed back hair falling over a black dinner jacket and pleated shirt. His breath smelled of gin. "Are you on your way out?"

He cocked his head to the side and frowned, blinking at her. "No, just coming home. Such a boring event!" He paused momentarily looking her up and down. "But don't you look splendid, my little doll, please come in, won't you?" He smiled with his lips only, his eyes darting and squinting with questions. "What brings you here tonight, Kitty? You don't seem very glad to see me. I've been wondering why I haven't heard from you."

She evaded the comment and stepped through the doorway, wandering down the hallway to his living room. "How about a glass of wine?" she said, putting down her violin case and walking over to a large mirror above the fireplace to check her hair and lipstick.

"Shall we make it champagne?" he asked, following close behind her and touching her shoulders as she stood before the glass.

"Sure, champagne," she said, turning around and meeting his lips for a quick kiss, then pulling away. She had momentarily thought of stopping at one kiss, finishing her drink and leaving for home, but instead leaned back and looked at him, his eyes fully opened, his breathing quickening, and a flush beginning to grow over his cheeks. She allowed him to draw her in to another kiss, awaiting the floor to become unsteady and the ceiling to fly away as their passion mounted, but her place in the room was solid and ordinary, and all the old feelings of intoxication turning to faraway memories that she could scarcely recall.

Geoffrey's kisses deepened and his intent and urgency was made clear by the caresses he imposed upon her back, her buttocks, her thighs, as his hands wound downward over her body. "I've missed you so much, Kitty," he breathed into her ear before leaning a back a little. He beheld her and went on, "Oh, those luscious, magical lips…" His words vaporized into sighs, and she felt his clammy breath on her neck and cheek as he turned his head to whisper something else in her ear about the first night he took her to the sex magick cult and her willingness to join in. For a moment her body stiffened, her eyes still opened wide, fixed on a marble head of a Roman lady that sat on a pedestal a few feet away. She stared at the flat, blank eyes. Eyes devoid of irises or pupils, with no lines at the corners to hint at the feelings of this ancient beauty, forever caught in a moment of hard, stone insignificance within the walls of Geoffrey Northcott's dwelling. Carlotta allowed him to lead her into his bedroom, and for curiosity's sake, she slipped onto his satin sheets, questioning the feelings of desire she once had for this man and whether they would once again envelope her, as she allowed him to peel off her clothes.

She went through the motions glancing at the bedside clock now and again, deciding what she had already known to be true during the first kiss this evening. She had cast her spell over Geoffrey at last, a yearning which had once been her focus. Yet now she had become as the marble Roman lady, cool and disinterested, her eyes displaying a blank expression each time they fell upon him.

Before midnight she arose from his bed, then swayed down the hallway towards the front door. "Kitty Cat, where are you going? Do stay with me tonight," Geoffrey called, "*Kitty?*" The sounds of the door opening and then closing again answered his question and she imagined him listening to the nimble step of her heels clicking on the deserted sidewalk as she walked away from his house.

The warm night breeze brushed over her and she caught a whiff of Geoffrey's cologne from her billowing hair. She started and coughed, gathering the blowing locks in one hand and threw them back over her shoulder, tossing her head and sighing loudly. She recalled Anton's long fingers on her hand as he had opened his front door and had imagined how they would feel on the uppermost parts of her thighs.

# 38

"Lu? It's me. I thought you were meeting me at Jay's after work." Vern took the phone off the table and pulled the cord over to the couch, sitting down and looking at his watch. It was nearly nine p.m.

"Sorry, I had to work late, and you were already gone when I called," Lulu said.

"So? I was waiting for you, why didn't you show?"

There was a pause before she replied, "I guess I was just too tired, Vern."

"Oh?" Vern got up and paced a few steps in front of the sofa, then sat down again. "It's Friday night, Lu." He sighed and brushed his hair of his forehead.

"You know we haven't seen much of each other lately, what's up?" There was silence on the other end of the phone. "Well?" he said.

"Yeah *'what's up'* is you and that gypsy witch. I don't like what I heard through the grapevine about her meeting you in Mabey's a few weeks ago, you know that Saturday you forgot about our date and walked back all wrinkled and smelling of musk?"

"I told you there's nothing happening there." He slammed the phone base back down on the table.

"Look Vern, I'm busy at work dressing the store windows like I've been wanting to. I have the start of a good career now so I don't need a man who is going to run around, ok?" He held the receiver away from his ear as she delivered this message in one long, sharp breath.

*"Oh, really?* Well what makes you think you're so perfect, with all the drinking and flirting you did last year when we were out together? You acted like a tramp instead of my girlfriend."

"See you around, Vern," the explosion of words rushed over the phone just before an abrupt bang from the other end.

The next morning he caught an early train to Bronxville and knocked on the Palmer's door just before eight a.m. Mr. Palmer answered the door. "Why hello, Vern, what brings you out so early? Mary Lou didn't mention you were coming for breakfast....."

"No, Mr. Palmer, I wasn't invited for breakfast, but I've got to see her." said Vern taking another step forward towards the doorway.

"Sure, sure," Lulu's father said as he stood aside and allowed Vern to open the screen door and enter the hallway. "Mary Lou? Mary Lou? You have a visitor."

He cleared his throat and showed Vern into the parlor. "She'll be right with you, Vern." Mr. Palmer looked down the hallway then turned back toward Vern, smiled weakly and said, "Here she is," and turned to leave.

Lulu rushed into the room, brushing by her father without a word. "What is it, Vern? Why are you here?" Her voice was tight and her lips were hard and straight. She stood in the doorway and leaned against the jamb, her arms folded over her waist.

"We need to talk, Lu, right now." Vern took her hand and led her to the sofa.

He sat down and let go of her hand. "Ok," he said pausing while looking directly into her face without smiling. "We're going to settle this one way or another today." Lulu's eyes darted over his lips as he spoke, but she was silent. He laced his hands together and leaned forward, he elbows resting on his knees as he collected his thoughts. He nodded his head and said, "Yeah, I slept with her, ok? I wish I hadn't, and I don't really know why I did, because I don't like her much. I'm sorry I did it for my *own* reasons, and not just because I'm sorry I hurt you."

He sat up straight again and looked at Lulu's watery eyes, her lips quivering. "But you've got stuff to be sorry for, too, Lu. We can make this right if you want to, but if not, then I'm done." He took her hand and gathered her closer. "I love you, Lu, I really do and I'm proud of you for taking your life in your hands and jumping into a wonderful new career, and facing your drinking."

Lulu whimpered and said nothing. Vern gave her his handkerchief and she dabbed the corner of her eyes. "I don't know what to say," she murmured.

Vern shifted closer to her and squeezed her hand. "Tell me how you feel about me....about us. Do you want to fix this, or do you want it to be over, really over this time?" He searched her eyes, but her face was turned downward and tears were falling on her hand as she held his. He caressed her fingers and softened his voice. "I'd like to fix this, that's what I want, Lu, but what about you? No more squabbling over dancing partners and gypsies. Let's be a solid couple. Whadya say, Lu?"

Lulu continued holding Vern's hand but she did not look up at him, even though she had ceased crying. There was something inflexible about her lips and her nostrils flared as she breathed deeply and shook her head. "I don't know, Vern," was all she said.

After a few moments of silence Vern began to speak in a slow, calm voice. He let go of her hand, but squeezed her fingers before he let go. "Well, you think about it for a few days, then, but I want you to know that I loved you the first day I met you when you lost your hat to a spring breeze, and I collected it for you. Your eyes were sparkling blue in the sunlight as you thanked me." Vern shifted his weight forward on the edge of the couch and lifted her chin with his fingers, looking into her eyes. "And the first time we made love on my sofa, with your red hair falling on my face as I kissed you, I fell into a dream of your lovely body next to me, happy and alive with passion. I was in heaven, Lu, and I think I always will be when I see you or even when I think of you."

Still, Lulu said nothing. She was looking at him, but her eyes only wandered his face before she turned her head away again. "I remember, Vern, but now I don't know."

Vern waited for her to continue, but she said nothing else. He picked up his hat and stood up. "Like I said, you let me know in a few days how you feel."

She nodded silently, and glanced up at him briefly before he started out the parlor door and down the hallway, and out onto the front porch. The screen door swung shut and he tread down the few steps and over the front path. He heard the door open again. "Vern," Lulu called. He looked back and saw her hurrying towards him, her damp eyes blinking, her lips softened and trying to smile. "I still love you, Vern, and I do want to make things right." She now stood facing him and placed her hands on his shoulders.

The sidewalk in front of the Palmer's house seemed like a sky bridge at the edge of a sunlit Heaven, where an audience of smiling cirrus clouds was calling out to him, cheering him on as he bent down and pressed his lips to Lulu's and then said, "I really love, you, Babe."

"Oh, Vern, I'm sorry I was such a drunken brat to you, but I thought if I stopped and got serious about my life, you'd be there for me, not carrying on with that woman."

He nodded as she spoke and said, "Yeah, I get it, and it won't ever happen again. She had some sort of spell over me, I guess, like the horrible dreams we had, remember that?" He closed his eyes and rubbed them with his fingers. "But it's over now. Can we move on?"

She nodded and hiccupped, "yes, we can, Vern. I love you."

"So let's kiss and make up and plan a wedding, ok?"

Lulu's eyes opened wide and brightened, her soft lips spread into a wide grin and the words, *"yes… yes… and yes!"* rolled out of her mouth.

"Let's tell your folks and then you go upstairs and get your things. We're gonna have a celebration dinner tonight in town."

# 39

A languid fog had crept in after the last set and the doors of Champlain's Bliss on East 86th St. opened as the clock struck 2 a.m. Anton's band was packing up and the patrons were still hovering around the dance floor drinking and laughing. "Say Chaz, how'd you like those shimmy moves I did during our dance?" a well- powdered babe in froth of chocolate lace called to a man who had left the floor and was heading to the bar. She put her palms down and clumsily swerved into a nearby table as she leaned forward awaiting his attention.

"Nice going, Hon," he said, looking back to smile at her. "Last call, can I buy you a drink?"

The woman hesitated, then reluctantly followed another young woman in yellow who was tugging at her arm. "Bye bye," she giggled and wove through the thinning crowd with her friend. "See ya next time."

"I'll take you home, my star, my wild bird," Anton teased as Carlotta tied the belt of her blue silk evening coat around her waist and placed an aqua hat laden with peacock feathers over her wild locks. She glanced at him in his shimmering white satin suit and fuchsia tie, nodded and grabbed her purse and violin case. He naturally took her hand and led her outside towards several waiting cabs lined in front of the club.

"Forty-seventh and Eighth," he instructed the driver as he opened the door for Carlotta. "Right?" he whispered to her as he sat down beside her.

"Close enough," she answered. "Thank you."

"Wonderful gig tonight, don't you agree, my dear?" he said. You seemed to enjoy yourself."

"I did," she answered, turning towards him with a grin. "When's the next one?"

"Oh, we have two next week. One at Jay's, Friday and another one just over here on Saturday." He tapped on the window and pointed to a bar on the same block whose neon sign beamed the name in flashing pink letters into the hazy light of dim streetlights. "La Fiesta," he added. "It's a new joint, very nice inside."

"Sure. I'm available."

"Rehearsal on Wednesday again at my house, then Friday and Saturday we work."

"Yeah, fine," she said, noting the uptick in his tone at the words, 'we work.'

"It's great playing with you, my dear. We mix well together, and you really are a star, my dear."

She felt the heat of his hip touching hers as they sat together and spoke. The sensation began to spread through her body, over her waist and torso, down her thigh, her calf and her toes. She instinctively touched the toe of his shoe with hers, and felt the compulsion to lean into him, and aided by the cab's sharp turn around a corner, she fell comfortably over his arm. He placed his arm around her shoulder and gave her a squeeze, turning to look at her. "Did I tell you how lovely you look tonight, Carlotta," he said quietly.

The cab stopped a few doors down from her building and the driver asked, "this good, Mac?"

"Sure, sure, just give us a minute."

"A minute is not enough," Carlotta found herself thinking, caught as she was in Anton's aura. Quietly, she remembered when they first met and she had been almost repulsed by the attraction she felt for him and his swarthy skin, his slick smile and long, spindly fingers. She now felt overwhelmed with intrigue.

"My dear, it has been a wonderful night having you perform in my band. I am honored to have you join our group." He took her fingers and lightly kissed them, then opened the car door and helped her out. "I can't wait to see you on Wednesday," he added, taking another second to brush her hair off her cheek and touch her lips with his.

"C'mon, Mac, meter's running," the driver reminded Anton.

"Ok, one minute, Sir." He took Carlotta's hand again and said, "Which one is your building?" She pointed to a brick building two doors down, and he escorted her there in a brisk walk, waiting until she took out her key and opened the door.

"Well, goodnight, then," she said, facing him while holding the door opened behind her. He waited for her to enter but she stayed in place on the street, leaning forward and looking into Anton's eyes, which skimmed over her face, a smile growing on his lips.

"Goodnight, my darling Carlotta, my beauty-bright." He kissed her lightly again and dashed back into the cab, waving as he drove away.

Carlotta flopped down into her bed with Boris who awaited her on her pillow, purring and blinking.

She stroked the cat and thought of Anton's expression as he bade her goodnight, and his open admiration of her musical talent. She ran a few strands of her hair over her lips and relived way he had kissed her and called her his 'beauty-bright,' while walking her to her door. His gaudy suit and brazen smile softened in her memory as she began to hover between sleep and consciousness, fading into a dream of luxury and politeness sought by the finest of ladies.

Somewhere luxurious lengths of hot pink silk enveloped her naked body and pure white moonlight kissed her hair while a chorus of black cats howled out a stark melody.

\*\*\*

Out of a heavy sleep she awoke to a dark rain tapping on her bedroom window in the early hours. The clock read 5 a.m. Boris was already up and sitting on the sill, his eyes watching something through the glass. Carlotta rose and walked to the stove and put on the kettle for tea, but noticed something out of place on the kitchen table. It was her black mirror out of its velvet bag. She picked it up placing it in the pouch and drawing the string. "I don't remember looking at this last night," she said to her cat who only wagged its tail, his eyes still fixed on the unspecified object. She stood for a moment with the article in her hand shaking her head a few times and rubbing the soft velvet with her fingertips. Pressing her lips together Carlotta placed it inside her purse, then reached down further and felt for the ankh which she briefly squeezed before answering the call of the screaming tea kettle.

Still puzzled by the sight of the unwrapped mirror, she sat down at the table with her tea and stared blankly at her purse as she sipped, her brow furrowed and her fingernails clicking against the sides of the teacup. Her thoughts wandered to the episode of riding home with Anton the night before, and his dashing back to the cab before she could invite him in. While his manner had been very gentlemanly towards her she reminisced about the way she felt when she fell over into him during the cab's turning of a sharp corner. Neither one of them had pulled away, but remained sitting close and then had put his arm around her and told her how beautiful she looked.

Leaning back and rubbing her shoulder into the back of the kitchen chair, she began wondering if there had been any deeper meaning in those events. Carlotta put down the cup and ran her hands lightly on her satin nightgown, over her hips and down her thighs. Remnants of a dream began to invite her into a reverie of walking half asleep last night to her purse and taking out the obsidian seer, trying to gaze into it from the moonlight. Yet she remembered nothing of what she had seen, only the feeling of yearning still prevailed. She again felt in her purse for the looking glass, but only clasped it for a moment in her hand allowing it to drop back down into her handbag as Boris whipped his head to one side at the sight of a large, black bird flapping its wings that was gliding past the window.

# 40

Carrying her violin, Carlotta walked out of her building and onto the curb, lifting her hand for a cab. Every car full, she walked a few steps then turned around with her hand in the air again but to no effect, repeating this measure several more times as she walked down the city blocks until a checker whizzed over and stopped abruptly next to her. She took ahold of the handle ready to open the door, but stopped and shook her head. "Nevermind," she said, pursing her lips. "I need the walk." The cab screeched away to the other side of the street and another patron swiftly took her place.

She walked on pounding in rhythm over the sidewalk with her pumps and sighing hard several times frequently looking down at her feet instead of straight ahead. Her steps seemed to beat out, "An-ton, An-ton." When she reached St. Mark's Place she stopped, looked at her wrist watch, muttering, "Just in time." She then stood for a moment, smoothing her hair with one hand, then leaned the instrument case against her leg and smoothed her palms lightly over her dress. She turned into the street arriving a few minutes later in front of Anton's door. The crow's head that was the door knocker awaited her rap, which she gave, yet turning away from the eyes of the heavy black bird as she did so. She dropped her hand to her side and clenched her fist, feeling the sweat of her palm over her fingertips.

"Hello, my beauty," Anton said when he opened the door. "Come in." he took her hand and led her into the hallway and to the stairs leading to his basement. "Lovely as always, my dear," he said raising her hand to his lips and kissing her fingers. "Now we play!" He gestured for her to take a place near where his guitar was resting on its stand.

She quickly exchanged greetings with the two other band members and prepared to tune her instrument, eyeing Anton whenever she thought he was not looking, wishing they were alone together to see if the heat from his thighs would be drawn her hers as in the cab ride home from their gig last weekend.

He met her eyes now and again, but his mind was fixed on the band tuning up. "Let's go," he said striking a chord on his guitar. Carlotta engaged her fingers and played with the expertise she had learned so many years ago as a child, never doubting her abilities, yet continuing to steal glances at Anton whenever his head was turned towards his guitar and not in the direction of his bandmates, waiting for his announcement that rehearsal was over and refreshment was at hand.

At last he placed his guitar back on its stand, and applauded his band. "Splendid, splendid, everyone," he said chuckling, his eyes bright as he nodded at each member. "We are ready for Friday night, yes? Now upstairs for food and drink," he said motioning for Carlotta to ascend the staircase before him.

Anton gently touched her arm as he offered her a glass of wine. "Red for you, my dear?" he asked as he handed her a glass.

"Yes, thank you," she said shifting her feet closer to his.

"You played exquisitely, Carlotta. You will earn a reputation for your talents very quickly."

"Thanks to playing out with you," she answered smiling directly into his eyes.

He moved closer to her saying, "No, your talent is rare." He then turned and poured wine for the others as they busily dished out portions of chicken paprikash and dumplings from a steaming casserole Anton had just taken from the oven.

The aroma of the familiar dish wafted into the room and into Carlotta's memory. "Smells delicious," she said turning her face away from the dish "I haven't had this in some time." She spooned out a small portion for herself and tried not to flinch as she took a bite.

"That's all you wish for, my dear?" Anton asked noting the meager serving on her plate.

She nodded her head at Anton with a quick, bright grin, and gagged down a first bite. She was remembering the many times as a child her mother had cooked this for one of her several gentlemen callers. She would feed Carlotta a few scraps of the traditional dish alone in her room. "Eat well, child. It cost your Mama dearly to buy this food." And with that she would shut the door on her young daughter. "Coming, yes, I'm back," Carlotta would hear her coo to the beau of the evening.

"Good stuff, Anton, maybe you shoulda been a chef," the bass player said after a few bites.

"Are you saying my chicken is better than my guitar playing?" Anton laughed.

"No, but close," he answered raising his glass for another pour.

"Yes, excellent," added Carlotta as she placed her empty plate in the sink, but I should be going." She smiled and took a last sip of her wine, fetching her violin case from the floor where she had placed it. "Oh, I must have left my purse downstairs," she added making her way towards the stairs.

"Carlotta, wait," said Anton, here it is on this chair." She smiled and went to retrieve the handbag, but Anton stopped her.

"Could you stay a bit longer and talk with me?" he said, his eyes darting over hers.

A warm tingling spread over her bosom, running upward over her throat and neck, and almost paralyzing her lips when she began to speak. "Yeah, sure," she said, her eyes beaming back to his. The bass player and drummer finished their plates, washing the last bites down with gulps of wine, then flew towards the front door after exchanging handshakes and quick good-byes.

"Thanks, doll" said the drummer tipping his hat to Carlotta. "You make the band sing like there ain't no tomorrow."

"Great to have you with us," chimed in the bass player. "Good-night."

"Sit down, my dear." Anton pulled out a chair for Carlotta then began clearing some of the dishes from the table. "Nice practice," he continued. "It is very special to have you in my band." He poured her another glass of wine and sat down in a chair facing her.

Carlotta took a sip and looked out of his kitchen window to the alley at the back of the house, which contained some small gardens. The warm spring breeze carried in the light fragrance of lilac blossoms, and the fair clouds and pale blue sky were just beginning to melt into a froth of evening lavender as a few heart-shaped leaves of a catalpa tree waved faintly over the window sill with a rhythmic tapping sound. She leaned slightly out towards the refreshing, scent breathing in its vitality and clearing her head of the chicken dish that had driven her to recall the painful memories of her childhood. "It's a wonderful band, sure."

She leaned back in her chair and surveyed his angular cheekbones and slender build, but was in a quandary about what to say. He was not like other men she had been attracted to. Anton was more gentlemanly towards her, more outwardly respectful. She sat in wait for his advances, but twenty minutes had gone by and he was just talking about music to her, how important it was to him and glad that he could share that with her. He brought up nothing about the spells she had asked him to help her with, nor did he touch her, other than tapping her fingers once in a compliment about their velocity over the string board of her violin as she played, yet his smile was warm and his conversation about music was enjoyable.

She felt a longing surging up in her throat, a hunger to be kissed and feel his desire. Her throat became dry, and as he continued his music talk she grew to believe that he had no such longing for her or he had changed his mind and she had misinterpreted his politeness as a cover for his passion. She shifted forward in her chair, one hand gripping the seat as if holding it in place on the floor, the other lying uncomfortably in her lap, fingers opening and closing.

"Well, I should be going, Anton. Such a nice evening of music with you," she said with a crack in her voice. She hid her feelings behind a placid expression, trying to keep her tone aloof as well, but she was feeling unnerved by his lack of sexual interest in her, and even though she had shifted her hips and tossed her hair several times, licked her lips while looking deeply into his eyes, it had proven fruitless. Anton, although engaging her with his smile and his eyes, merely sat in front of her and talked about the practice session and upcoming gigs.

After a time she arose, plucked up her instrument, her handbag, and walked into to the hallway towards the door. "Thank you so much, Anton. See you Friday", she said turning her head back as she hastened towards to the street.

"Yes, my dear, let me get you a cab." Anton started out of his chair to follow her, but she had eclipsed him, opening the front door and whisking it shut before he could catch up. He did open it again, only to see her bound down the street without looking back. He watched as she turned up the avenue and disappeared into the city.

Tears of humiliation seeped from her eyes, running down her cheeks and neck as she trudged up the avenue to her apartment, sometimes wiping her eyes with her fingers or tossing her head as if to say, "No, no.....but *why?*" She noticed a few people turned their heads towards her as she let out a loud sob, but she continued walking until she reached her block and felt down into her purse for her keys, holding them tightly in her fist.

Once inside she immediately took out the ankh and her black mirror. "Why?" was all she said as she looked into the glass. She searched the mirror for an image that would change her circumstances or at least give her an explanation, but all she saw was her tear streaked face. Carlotta looked up and saw amongst her collection of framed pictures of relatives, one of her mother seated on the couch holding a drink. She lunged over to it and with a swat dashed it to the floor, breaking its glass. A certain memory of her mother carrying a drink from the kitchen and sinking into that velvet sofa by the window came to mind.

It was just before they had gone to Romania after her grandfather's death to claim his valuables. "Play a tune for me, girl," she had demanded, "you are good for nothing else," laughing into her drink. She reached out and pointed her finger at Carlotta, and said, "Well, maybe men know what else you are good for, like I told you years ago. You could have been the highest paid lover in this whole city and supported us in style, but you refused your Mama, you lousy slut." The drunken mother had stood up and attempted to strike her daughter in the face, but Carlotta dodged her and flew out of the apartment and down the stairs. From the street she heard the window open and her mother's rant continuing as she disappeared down the block. "You hear me, girl? You are nothing, and no man will ever want you except for his pleasure. "You should have earned more money for us. I could have set you up with royalty... I knew the rich pockets for you to pick, you nobody, you slut."

# 41

The phone rang. Carlotta put down her cup of coffee, leaned over to the other side of the couch and lifted the phone from where it sat on the end table. "Hello," she said.

"It's Anton, Carlotta. You left very suddenly last night before I got a chance to invite you out to dinner this evening."

"Oh, hello, Anton." She moved closer to the phone and twirled the ends of her hair as steam from the coffee drifted over her face.

"It's very early," she said, clearing her throat and taking in the aroma of her morning drink as she thought of what to say.

"I knew you would be awake, my dear. I hope you don't mind. I'd like to see you this evening."

"Ok, but my spells are completed. Is it about the gig Friday?"

"No, my dear, I would just like the pleasure of your company at dinner. Could you meet me at Jay's, say 7pm?

Carlotta paused and ran her finger over the rim of her cup. "Sure," she answered, "I can meet you then."

"Excellent! I am looking forward to it, my beauty. Until this evening, then."

"Yes," she said and held the receiver to her ear until she heard the click of the call being ended. She took her cup and sank back into the couch, sipping quietly and staring into the kitchen as the last wisps of vapor from the coffee pot on the stove drifted towards the ceiling.

\*\*\*

Just before 6p.m. Carlotta put her violin and bow back into the case, undressed and walked into the bathroom. She looked at herself in the mirror above the sink as she tied her hair up before her shower, turning her head slightly from one side to the other and noting her cheekbones, her full lips, and the translucent effect of her eyes in the light of the late afternoon sun, recalling the words Geoffrey had used when describing her appearance, 'sumptuous beauty.'

But was it really true, or were those only fake words used to flatter and entice her? At one time she had believed that he had really cared for her, like the night he had given her the diamond cuff and kissed her repeatedly and gazed into her eyes. They had just returned to his house after an evening of 'sex magick' at the club he had introduced her to. "You were magnificent," he had said as she undressed and got into his bed.

She had wanted to make love again, but he stopped her. "No more, my darling Kitty, you wore me out with our show tonight. Everyone sighed with envy when you chose me for your partner." She remembered how she had drawn him away from a pink-skinned blonde lady with a flashy grin who had wanted him as her playmate for the evening. Geoffrey had smiled wistfully at the blonde, but followed Carlotta to the center of a pentagram drawn on the tile floor where she began seducing him in front of the rest of the club members as they encircled the couple and chanted, "May our wishes come true through this rapture." Bodies fell on top of one another in a delirium of lust as each one recited their spells, their wishes of magic. Carlotta said hers silently as she fell into daze helped on by the amount of hashish she had smoked upon entering the clubroom, "I want Geoffrey to love only me. Only me… only *me*."

Carlotta turned her head away from her reflection and put her hands over her face. *"How could I have done that? Anton would be disgusted if he knew,"* she thought, remembering his words to her during their first meeting at the Rabbit Hole when he cautioned her against ever using her spell knowledge for nefarious intent. It had indeed been bad intent to yearn for such a corrupt man as Geoffrey, who treated her like a plaything all along, deriving pleasure from her willingness to satisfy his carnal whims. And worse intent yet, to have involved Vern in her sex magick gimmicks in order to reconnect with Geoffrey after he had so callously dumped her after a mere three months. "Come on now, be off," her English lover had sniggered, dismissing her with a motion of his hand.

Carlotta showered quickly, remaining fixated on the odious things she had done, wasting her body and her energy on senseless desires gotten by tawdry behavior towards herself and others. She wrapped a towel around herself and went to get her purse, picking out the black mirror. She waved her hand over it three times and began to breathe into it until it fogged up. Her lips began to form words but she stopped abruptly and replaced the object back in its pouch, shaking her head. "No more. No more of this," she said slowly turning and walking towards her closet, the eyes of her cat opening as she walked by and stroked his fur in passing.

# 42

"Sure, Lu, that'll be fine. Tell your parents we'll get married this summer in their backyard under the catalpa tree, then." Vern said, "I don't want a big church wedding." He reached around her shoulder and picked up his beer bottle from the end table, kissing her cheek in the process.

"Mother wants a tent and waiters and a champagne breakfast."

"Yeah, I guess," he said swallowing a few sips of beer, but I thought we'd have a real celebration afterwards at Jay's. You know, a party with a great band and all."

Lulu frowned and snuggled closer to Vern. "Ok with me, but Mother wants a formal wedding."

"Well she's not the one getting married, is she?" chuckled Vern, holding her in a close embrace. He leaned her over the arm of the sofa pressing his lips to hers.

Lulu slid down into the cushion and laced her fingers with his. "How about formal and *small?*" she said.

"Anything you say, Baby, just tell her we want to do it soon so you can redecorate this place and move in." He loosened his fingers from hers and gently nudged her deeper down into the sofa, straddled her and pulled her top up over her breasts. She shrieked with joy as he loosened her brazier and bit each nipple. "Vern let's go eat first, I'm starving!" She wriggled away and threw both of her arms around him and kissed him several times as she adjusted her clothes.

Anton was standing at the bar and shuffling a deck of Tarot cards as Vern and Lulu entered. "Hello, kids," said Jay as he watched Anton strike the pack on the bar immediately in front of him. "Looks like I'm getting my fortune read."

Anton flipped the stack to one side and with two of his long fingers and quickly fanned out the cards into a flat row, extending it two feet to the side, and said to Jay, "Choose six cards, my friend one at a time."

Lulu veered towards the bar, but Vern led her to a nearby table.

"Let's sit here a little out of the way," he said ushering her to a table near the dance floor, again glancing at Anton and Jay as he pulled out a chair for Lulu. "I don't wanna get in the way of these card tricks." He ordered two club sodas from a waiter, but kept looking over at the bar.

"Do you know that strange looking man, Vern?" asked Lulu, also beginning to be intrigued by Jay's curious expression as he drew out the first card.

"Uh, not really. He's a musician, plays a mean jazz guitar, I'm told," recalling the night he had met Nick there when Carlotta was performing with the all-female band and noticing how she seemed to pay special attention to this man. He tapped his fingers on the table and picked up his menu. "Let's eat and run, Babe, I'm beat. We can come back tomorrow as it's Friday and do some dancing, ok?" He looked over his menu at her and briefly took her hand and smiled.

Lulu nodded and said, "sure Vern, I'm gonna get the steak, how about you?"

"Yeah, sounds good."

"I am telling the current fortune of Mr. Jay, here," Anton announced to the nearby patrons, turning back towards his colorful cards.

"*Current* fortune?" asked a man at the bar, "What does that mean?"

Anton turned towards the man tapping the deck loudly on the bar and said, "It means that things can change. Have you never noticed that about life?" His tone was polite, but his words were blunt, and his Eastern European enunciation was emphasized by certain words, such as 'have' and 'life.'

Jay chose the six cards requested, and awaited further instruction. Anton picked up the first card and turned it over.

"Wheel of Fortune," said Anton, displaying the card with a picture of a giant wheel amongst some clouds and patches of blue sky.

"What does it mean?" asked Jay.

"This is the card of Destiny. In this case, it is perhaps telling of good luck in your business," answered the fortune teller, flashing his teeth as he spoke. He turned over the next card. "The Hermit," he announced. "You wish to know what to do in some situation."

Jay, looked at Anton, then back at the cards on the bar. "Go ahead," he said, waiting for the next card to be turned over. "That's a Devil," he exclaimed as Anton turned over the card.

"No worries, Mr. Jay," it only means that you feel something is out of control, but it is not too late to change course." The gypsy gentleman flashed his smile at the on-looking bar patron, and then said, "Next one, Death." It depicted an animate skeleton with its ample grin staring right out at Jay, who rubbed at his jaw and opened his eyes wider. "A time of absolute endings and new beginnings, that is all it means," Anton explained. "Here you are, Mr. Jay." Anton held up a card showing a magician, tapped it and said, "This is what is going against you: everyone else's expectations of what you must do." He looked at Jay meaningfully as he drew out the final card. "Ah, the High Priestess. This is the likely outcome for your dilemma. Follow your intuition, Mr. Jay. Listen only to your heart in this matter, and all will be well." He spoke his words carefully while raising one eyebrow and tipping his head slightly forward as he gazed at Jay.

"What matter would that be, Jay? Something about the club or the neighborhood?" asked the intruding man as he twisted his barstool and leaned in closer to the card display. He watched as Jay wiped the palms of his hands on his apron, then again spread out the six cards, eyeballing each one and pursing his lips.

"It's about hiring my new band. Jay was on the fence about it, but we play here tomorrow night." said Anton, grinning and pointing to a set of shot glasses on the bar. "Let's toast, shall we?" The forecaster gathered the cards, shaped them into a deck and placed them back in his pocket.

Jay laughed and, then turned up several shot glasses, filling them with vodka and passing them to each of the bar customers. "On the house. To my good fortune having your band play here," he laughed, raising his glass.

At that moment Carlotta walked up to the bar. "Hello, Anton ... Jay."

Anton held out his hand and drew her next to him, kissing her lightly on the cheek. "You are lovely, my beauty bright," he said, looking her over in her sleeveless dress of coral satin, noting her shell pendant at the neckline.

Jay looked at Carlotta and pointed to a jigger. "No thanks, Jay, not just now," she answered.

Anton took her hand and led her to a table, passing Lulu and Vern on the way. He noticed Lulu putting down her glass and turning her head as Carlotta passed, her glaring eyes following as Anton seated her. Vern brushed his hair off his forehead, looking down as they walked by.

"I am very happy to see you tonight, Carlotta," Anton said as soon as they were seated. He took her hand across the table and kissed her fingers.

She stared into his eyes before speaking. "What did you want to see me about, Anton?"

He continued holding her hand and smiled. "Nothing in particular, I just enjoy your company, my dear." She slowly withdrew her hand and did not answer.

"In fact, I would like to see more of you, not just at practice evenings." He blinked his eyes and leaned a little over the table towards her.

"Oh," she said, thinking of the way Geoffrey had introduced her to the Herald of Illusion Club only a few days after having met her. Vern, too, had succumbed to her advances easily even though she had frightened him with her boldness after the nightmares, and Lulu having gone to the hospital because of them. She twisted the ends of her hair, letting it flop over her shoulder and said, "I'd like a Corpse Reviver for starters, if Jay has some of that absinthe in. What about you?" she asked Anton, who raised up two fingers to the passing waiter.

When the pale green creations were set before them, Anton raised his glass, saying, "May this witch's brew bring us a special *magic*."

Carlotta squirmed in her seat at the word, 'magic,' wondering if he had been reading her thoughts. She suspected he had those capabilities, and he was looking at her intensely, his eyes darting over her face.

"On what shell we dine?" he asked, changing his demeanor and picking up his menu. "Clams to start?" She nodded her head and took another sip. Anton looked over Carlotta's shoulder and asked, "Do you know that woman with the red hair? She keeps turning her head to look at you."

Carlotta nearly choked on her drink. "No, just seen her in here a few times. Could we order a couple more of these?" she said, holding up her glass.

"Surely, my dear, but I get the feeling she wishes you ill." He watched Lulu as she walked by their table to visit the ladies room, noting the way she gave Carlotta a side long glance, her head forward, but her eyes raging. "If she does, we will easily fix that."

An earring dropped from Lulu's ear and made a pinging sound as it hit the floor, but Lulu kept walking. Anton bent over and retrieved the piece and clasping it in his hand saying, "Allow me."

"No, Anton, please leave it alone," she said, "I don't want any trouble in this place." Her lips quivered and though her voice was low, the tone was fierce and raspy.

"You will see," he said. "It will not be difficult." He awaited Lulu's return to her table, then clutched Carlotta's shoulder as he got up to approach the couple.

Carlotta turned around in her chair and gripped its back with both hands and watched, repeatedly licking her lips, now dry and stiff. She saw Anton kneel to the side of their table and revealed the earring he was holding between his fingers.

"I believe you dropped this, my dear lady," she heard him say in a soft voice. He was smiling and holding up the earring, dangling it in front of Lulu's face. Lulu stared transfixed at it with a vacant expression in her eyes. "Is this yours, miss?" Anton asked, still dangling the item in front of her. Vern also seem mesmerized by the object, but he averted his gaze and watched as Lulu raised her palm and Anton dropped the earring into her hand. He briefly passed his hand in front of Lulu's face.

"Why, thank you, sir," Lulu said, beaming with surprise. "How very, very kind of you." She turned around and smiled at Carlotta and waved. "You're a lucky lady," she giggled. Anton gave a slight bow to the couple and returned to Carlotta, now quaffing down her second cocktail.

"Your hand is trembling, my dear. All is well, I promise." He reached out and touched her other hand which rested on the table in a tight fist. "She remembers nothing of your paths crossing some months ago, and her man will be grateful, as well."

She nearly choked when he mentioned Vern in passing with the last remark.

"Oh, God, *you know?*"

"I have no knowledge of any facts, Carlotta, but I can read the dissonance between the three of you." He paused and nodded, "But you need tell me nothing, for it does not matter."

"I have not always been cautious of my actions," was all she said while reaching down into her purse and drawing out the ankh. "Here, perhaps you can make better use of this than I will," remembering the way she had used it and her mirror to bring Vern to her bed.

"Thank you, my dear." He took the ankh and kissed it, then replaced it back in her hand. "I have no need of this."

She sat across from him trying to regain some composure, but her eyes darted over the object and then his face. She clutched it for a moment before returning it to her purse. "Thank you," she said, her eyes now cast down at the remains of her second drink. She turned around a glanced at Vern and Lulu, laughing and talking as the waiter passed by and took Vern's payment. Lulu waved goodnight when they walked towards the door, as if nothing out of the ordinary had happened; not the change in her attitude towards Carlotta, her awareness of Vern's infidelity, nor the nightmare that had sent her to the hospital several months ago.

"Our band will have a number of engagements here, Carlotta, and now you have no fear of retribution. Take comfort, my beauty." He raised his glass to her and took a swallow of the opaline cocktail, and nodded to the waiter that they were ready to order.

"But why--I mean how…"

Anton held his hand up and frowned, saying, "No more, Carlotta, no more worries. The only thing that matters is that you know my intent is to honor you."

She fidgeted with her fingernails, sat back into her chair, and sucked the last drop of the green potion, still haunted by her acts with Geoffrey at the Herald of Illusion Club. *"He will never want me if he really knew. It was a depraved thing to do, and selling the dope and behaving like a street walker,"* she thought to herself while wondering what to say to Anton.

"I hope you will allow me to show you how much I appreciate your talents and you, as a lady. The past is of no consequence." She gave Anton a blank stare. It seemed like hours were passing before her, in her silence as she looked at the man seated across from her, with his deep widow's peak and heavy eyelids. His lips turned slowly up at the corners, then opened into a full grin. "You are beautiful, inside and out." He took her hand and said, "Come sit here next to me." He got up and pulled her chair out, but she was slow to move. Leaning over her shoulder he said, "Do I have to cast a spell on you, too?"

His playful demeanor sparked a burst of laughter from her, and she stood up facing him as he moved the chair out of the way. She reached up and touched his face. "Will you kiss me first?" she asked standing on her tiptoes and raising her lips to his.

"At last!" he exclaimed, and pressed his lips to hers and held her body close.

"Hey, bank's closed," a man shouted from the bar. A few of the other male patrons were clapping and whistling as they looked on at the pair. Jay had his hands on his hips shaking his head and smiling, but the pair continued their kissing. When she finally broke away her eyes were glowing iridescent gold under the light of the chandelier. She smiled brightly at Anton and sighed, placing her hands over his shoulders and drawing him close once more.

# 43

Carlotta leaned back into her sofa holding a hot, fresh cup of espresso and breathed in its earthy notes. Boris slowly stretched himself over the sofa arm, blinked several times at his mistress, then settled into a black puff, tucking his paws beneath his chest. The apricot light of morning just beginning to peak over the window sill behind her, together with the vapor from her cup rising upward over her face might have given an onlooker the impression of a phantom, an illusory beauty hovering between dreams and reality. And she was in a dream-like state, thinking of the evening before, and the walk home from Blue Jay's with Anton. She touched her cheek where Anton had caressed it with his fingers, recalling the strange feeling not at all like a man's hand, but of sleek bird feathers brushing over it.

She slowly sipped her coffee and half-closed her eyes, gradually falling into a reverie of Anton's kisses and gentle words the evening before. His statements streamed through her mind, 'the past is of no consequence,' and 'you are beautiful inside and out,' as if spoken in a foreign language that she paused to grasp the meaning of.

Suddenly, there was a bang on the building entrance door and a voice shouted, "Carlotta!" Jolted from her day dream, she dashed to the front window and saw a blonde ponytail hanging over a man's black trench coat. It quivered every time the man's fist whacked the door. "Carlotta, let me in for God's sake." The shout dissolved into a whine but the banging continued.

She opened the window and said, "Geoffrey? What are you doing here? It's 5 o'clock in the morning."

"Yes, Kitty Cat, I've been to such a miserable party.....I need to see you," he whimpered, slurring his words.

She tossed on her robe and trudged down the stairs and opened the door, but only enough to poke her head out.

"Good God, Geoffrey, what do you want at this hour?"

"Oh, you never answer your phone and it's been weeks since I've seen you." His eyes were glazed and bloodshot. "Do, let me in, my darling, I've missed you so much." Geoffrey moved in closer to the door opening and raised his hand to her face as if to pull her towards him. "Kiss me, Kitty," he gasped with all the fervor of Hollywood's latest heart throb.

Carlotta turned her face away and tried to close the door when a loud voice came from another apartment, "Hey, what's the hubbub, we're tryin' to sleep," it said while Geoffrey continued his wailing.

"Please leave, Geoffrey," said Carlotta in a loud whisper.

She leaned her body against the door and tried to close it, but the unwanted guest continued. "Let me hold you, my dearest I need you so much."

"Okay, I'll stop by sometime, now go, please." She threw her weight on the door and tried again to close it, but Geoffrey pried it with his shoulder and elbow, until at last it burst open, knocking Carlotta against the inner wall of the foyer. She raised her arms up and crossed them over her face as he approached to draw her out of the corner. "Get out or someone will call the police," she said, jaw clenched.

He reached backward and steadied himself on the end of the bannister, nearly toppling over onto the stairs. He reeked of gin and rancid oysters as he swayed forward again trying to stagger towards Carlotta. "The party was so lonely without you, my dear," he whispered in a thin rasp, "and none of the ladies were the least attentive to your poor old Geoffrey!"

Carlotta turned to walk past him up the stairs. "I'll give you ten minutes and a cup of coffee," she sighed. "Come on." She pounded over the flight of stairs and went in, not looking back for Geoffrey.

He flopped down on her sofa and slouched over the arm. The cat hissed and darted away, causing Geoffrey to shudder. "Where did you get that odious creature?" he asked pausing for a moment as Boris hissed again with ears back and fangs showing. Geoffrey dusted off his trousers and dispersed some dark gray fuzz left behind by the departing animal. "Good, God, what a nuisance!" he added, before quickly tempering his tone. "Oh, my dear, I thought you didn't love me anymore…." His words trailed off but she ignored his extended hand and walked past him into the kitchen area and immediately began to refill her moka pot with fresh ground espresso.

"Sugar?" she asked, her back to him as she prepared the drink.

"Why, *never*," he exclaimed. "Black, black, black! Don't you remember?"

Carlotta did not answer but turned around as the brew began to bubble on her stove top. "What are you doing here at this hour, Geoffrey?"

"I told you, darling Kitty Cat, I've missed you, and I was trying to call you to invite you to the party last night with me." He lifted his head only a little and his lips formed a pout, his wasted eyes stared at her as he held out his hand towards her again. "Do come and let me kiss you."

"Here's your black coffee. You need to go home and get some sleep, and I wouldn't have gone to that party with you anyway."

"Oh, but *why not?* You used to enjoy them so much, watching me flirt, knowing I was going to take only you home with me for a divine night of passion. Remember?"

"Yes, I remember, but that's over. I'm in a jazz band now and I give my time to music, not degeneracy."

"Tisk, tisk," he giggled. "Too good for it all now, and the Herald of Illusion Club where you so reveled in casting your wanton spells?" He threw his head back on the arm of the couch again and laughed out loud. "You loved me then, I remember well, and your musky scent as you stripped naked and fell into my bed."

"You disposed of me like a piece of trash."

"Nonsense, I just get a little bored sometimes," he said, sinking lower into the couch. "Now sit beside me and hold the saucer while I have a few sips of your stimulating hang-over elixir." He sniffed into the air and awaited her offer of the morning drink, then patted the cushion and attempted a smile, but simply closed his eyes for a moment. "Of course I still love you, you must know that. After all didn't I give you that stunning diamond cuff?"

Carlotta bounded into her bedroom and opened a drawer. She reappeared with the object in her hand and held it up from where she was standing near the kitchen entrance. "You mean this?"

"Why it's more elegant than I remember," he chuckled. "I must have loved you very much."

She stepped a few feet towards Geoffrey and threw it in his lap. "Here, take it back and go." She glared at him, her eyelids taut and her nostrils splayed.

"Why, Kitty, how dare you talk to me in that manner." Geoffrey made an attempt to sit up, and puff his chest out, but he only succeeded in heaving a rattling sigh.

"I need you to go. Thanks for coming over and saving me the trouble of having to deliver your bracelet to you." She advanced towards him as she spoke, her voice escalating. She leaned forward over his extended body as it slouched on her sofa, until the last words were screamed into his face. "Take it and go!"

Geoffrey only sneered at her as he pulled himself up from his sprawl on the couch, and made no attempt to leave.

There was a knock on Carlotta's apartment door. "Hey, miss, you ok in there?" She quickly stepped over to the door and opened it wide.

"Thanks for checking on me, Mr. Green. The gentleman was just leaving, weren't you, Geoffrey?"

As if paralyzed, the rejected visitor sat quietly in his upright position on the sofa and continued to glare with his bloodshot eyes at Carlotta.

"C'mon, Pal," said the downstairs neighbor, "the lady wants you out."

"Indeed," said Geoffrey, "what *am* I doing in this filthy part of town?" He cleared his throat, rearranged his ponytail on top of his collar, swept his coat over himself and tied the belt, and drawing a pair of white gloves from his pocket, he sprang through the open door and down the stairs. The windows rattled with the slam he gave the build-ing door as he exited.

A thin, shrill rant flew into Carlotta's open window. "You'll be sorry for this," it echoed, "*indeed,* you will be sorry!"

# 44

At precisely 6:30 that evening Carlotta's bell rang. She ran to the window and saw Anton waiting outside holding a mixed bouquet of scarlet and orange flowers. Her heart beat faster as she reached to buzz him in, and instantly opened the door as he ascended the flight of stairs to her apartment. He was wearing black evening attire, a white shirt and bowtie, and a satin top hat. She beamed when he stood in front of her. "Oh, you are so handsome, Anton," she said her lips parted wide.

"And you, so exquisite in your turquoise dress, my dear peacock." She smoothed the beaded skirt over her hips and chuckled, touching the silken white dahlia that was clipped in her hair just over one ear. He leaned forward placing one finger beneath her chin, and kissed her lightly.

"Are you ready for a little dinner before our gig?" he asked, offering her the bouquet.

"Yeah, sure, but come in for a minute and let me get a vase." She fingered the long stem of a bird of paradise and looked up at Anton, her eyes sparkling. "My favorite flower, thank you."

She hurried into the kitchen and filled a tall crystal vase with water and began to arrange the flowers as Anton walked a few steps in towards the couch. "And who is this little creature?" he asked as Boris stood up from his spot on a cushion, purred and advanced towards the new guest. Anton reached out and stroked the cat.

"That's Boris," she said, "seems as if he likes you." She glanced up from her task to see Boris rubbing up against Anton's leg. "He doesn't do that with everyone," she added, thinking of the encounter with Geoffrey earlier that morning. "Maybe you can visit him again after the gig tonight," she said, placing the vase on her kitchen table.

He chuckled and gently pulled the cat's ear as Carlotta walked towards the door, grabbing her violin and bow case. "I would like that," he smiled, offering her his arm as she opened the door.

Anton stopped in the doorway and kissed her again before they bounded down the steps and into the warmth of spring air, fragrant from the abundance of blossoms that hung heavily on the trees and skimmed their shoulders and arms as they walked down the avenue sidewalks together towards Blue Jay's.

"Extra! Extra! Paper, Madame, Sir?" A newsboy with a tattered brown cap falling over an abundance of tawny hair said in a raspy voice as the couple passed. He nearly stepped in front of them showing the headline, ***Wealthy Socialite Dies While Flagging Cab on 6th Ave.*** Anton casually stepped to the side and tipped his hat to the boy, but Carlotta snapped her head to look at the photo of the reported victim, nearly tripping over an uneven piece of pavement as she recognized the smug smile and blonde ponytail of her former lover beneath the caption.

Anton steadied her and asked, "You ok, my dear?" She only shook her head and coughed, as a sudden flash of heat attacked her throat and cheeks. She smiled weakly at Anton, but quickened her pace.

"Sure, just need a drink of water," she whispered, still coughing, anxious to divert his attention from her reaction to the headline. She did what she knew how to do, so well; she reverted to a placid expression with her eyes looking forward as they continued their walk towards Blue Jay's, refusing to let on to Anton of her shock of this news. She stopped coughing and said, "Just fine now, maybe some spring pollen caught in my throat." But she felt Anton's eyes darting over her as he opened the club door for her, believing he could read her disquiet over the extra that had been presented to them.

Once inside Carlotta immediately went over to the tiny stage and began setting up the area with a couple of chairs and some stands with sheet music. Anton went directly to the barkeep and brought back a glass of water, handing it to Carlotta with a slight smile. "Ok, let's get a bite, shall we?" he said, pointing to a table nearby.

As Anton was seating Carlotta, Nick and Lulu walked in. Carlotta shot Anton a sidelong glance and stiffened her neck.

"Oh, hiya!" called Lulu, waving as she pranced over to the bar, arm in arm with Nick. "Youz playing tonight?" She smiled openly at the pair as they passed, then looked out over the club. "It's already filling up," she said to Nick. "Do we want to eat at the bar?"

Nick gave a hasty nod to Carlotta and Anton. "Sure, Babe, we can do that." He cleared his throat and tapped his hat over his thigh several times and pulled out a barstool for Lulu.

Carlotta's cheeks reddened at his brusqueness, and she looked down and said to Anton in a low voice. "You didn't make him forget?"

"No, just the lady," he grinned. Let him remember his actions so he does not cause himself such troubles ever again." He laughed and took Carlotta's hand across the table, kissing her fingers adding, "You are all that matters to me." He winked at her, taking two menus from the passing waiter. He handed one to Carlotta, who received it mechanically. She opened it but barely glanced at its contents, still stung by the headline of Geoffrey's accidental death knowing she had thrown him out onto the street in his drunken state.

Anton stared at his menu and quietly said, "It's not your fault, my dear."

Carlotta simply nodded without looking up and thought to herself how distasteful his appearance had been, banging on her door at the early morning hour, in his wrinkled evening attire which reeked of gin and hashish. She quivered in disgust remembering the things she had done with him, and openly. Feeling Anton's eyes upon her, she looked up and forced a smile. "I think I'll have the trout special."

"Two trout specials, and club sodas, " he said as the waiter walked up to their table. "Now, let's relax a little before we play," he added to Carlotta, taking her hand across the table.

By the end of the first set Carlotta had put the matter of her former lovers behind her, enjoying the attention she got when playing her solos and watching the Friday crowd dance to her wild melodies. She knew that Anton had barely taken his eyes off her when her fingers ran up and down the neck of her marvelous violin, playing with all the passion of a modern-day Paganini, the jazz tunes of today with a Bohemian flare.

As she placed her instrument back in its place for a short break, she heard a pair of ladies' pumps spring down next to her. It was Lulu, beaming straight at her as she turned around and faced her. "Wowza, my dear, you sure can stir up fire with that fiddle! Would your band play at our wedding party in a few months?" Lulu continued to smile and fluttered her eyelids at Carlotta, the tall feather accenting her Rhinestone headband waving as she tilted her head from one side and then the other, awaiting an answer.

Carlotta stared blankly at Lulu, her mouth beginning to open but unsure of what words she could muster. "Uh….. let's ask Anton. It's his band." She drew back and tensed her body, her lips rigid as she glanced at Anton.

Lightly touching Carlotta's her arm, he said to Lulu, "Why, we would be very honored, dear lady. Where is it to be held?"

"Here! At this club," she answered, her rouged lips turned up and glimmered like cool cherry ice under the light of the large chandelier.

"How gracious of you to ask us," he said with a slight bow. "You will let us know when."

"Yeah, we will, and thanks," she added with a lively dip and jazz hand wave.

The dismayed Carlotta balked at his answer and simply shook her head. "I guess you know what you're doing."

"Nevermind my pretty," he said pulling her to him and kissing her. "After the next set we'll go back and tell Boris, ok?" His gentle laughter was contagious, as he locked her in his embrace and playfully swayed her to and fro. Her body relaxed and she reached her face upward to kiss him.

"Hello, Carlotta," a man's voice called just as she and Anton picked up their instruments once more. She turned around to see Nick waving at her as he and an elegant blond lady passed by on their way to the bar. "I thought we'd catch a few tunes this evening.

"Why, hello, Nick," she answered holding her violin in one hand and the bow in the other. He looked happier than she had ever noticed him looking. "Is this your wife?" Carlotta asked.

Nick took Robbie's hand and led her closer to the band area. "Yes, this is Robbie," he said placing his arm around his wife and smiling.

"So nice to meet you, Robbie," Carlotta said. "I was glad to hear that you were able to find your way back to Nick." Carlotta's usual cool stare broke into a lustrous smile, her eyes bright with wonder as she beheld the formerly lost woman in front of her.

Robbie smiled back and simply said. "Thank you for encouraging Nick not to give up."

Carlotta watched the couple as they walked to the bar. A peaceful warmth swept over her through her limbs and torso, extending to her neck and head. She breathed deeply several times. In her sighs, the resentment of her life seemed to seep out of her heart through her breath, dissipating into the fanciful haze of the club's chandelier as its glow fell over the patrons of Blue Jay's, lulling all with the ethereal light of fancy.

Anton's eyes were fixed on her as she played her introductory solo and standing next to him she was aware that he noticed the heat of her body, her wild locks sometimes flying over his shoulder and arm as he awaited his cue to take over with his guitar, all the while feeling his unmistakable admiration as she played. Acutely aware of a change in herself, as a sleeping bird awakens after sheltering in a thicket from a night of cold, endless rain, now spreading its wings and flying to the uppermost branches of a flowering tree under the brightening dawn with confidence that all was well in her life.

# 45

"Why, hello again, Boris," Anton said as he removed his hat and placed it on an end table near the cat. Boris rose up from his place on the arm of the sofa to rub his furry back beneath Anton's outstretched hand and purred.

Carlotta went into the kitchen and poured out two snifters of brandy. "A nightcap?" she said as she offered one to Anton. His fingers grazed hers as he took the glass, dispersing a charge of electricity over her hand. She smiled, and noted the grace of his long, well-manicured hand, and polished nails, wishing to enjoy them brushing over her naked body. She sat down on the couch and kicked off her shoes. "It was a great gig, tonight, don't you think so?"

Anton nodded and sat down beside her, his hand finding its way over the back of the couch and onto her shoulders. "Yes, I could not be happier with our band," he said, "and you?"

Carlotta giggled and wrinkled her nose. "Sure, me too," she said leaning into his embrace.

"You are a rare talent, Carlotta," he said holding her tighter and kissing her cheek. "And we have another gig tomorrow night. Did you wish to get some sleep before it gets any later?"

She shook her head and looked up at him. "I'd rather sit here with you."

"Close your eyes, then," he said before he kissed each eyelid and then her lips. He placed his drink on the end table, took her glass from her hand and said, "Would you allow me to see your looking glass?"

Carlotta blinked and moved her head back a little and pursing her lips as if questioning his request, then arose and withdrew the seeing-eye from her purse on the kitchen table. "I thought spells were over for now," she said, standing in front of him as she handed him the velvet covered object, waiting to see what he would do with it.

"No spell, just a time in the future," he said.

Just at that moment a sizzling sound came from the open wid-

220

ow followed by an abrupt clap of thunder. She glanced out to see the night sky, now brilliant with violet streaks of flashing light through the unexpected heavy rain that pounded the roofs and streets, and was beginning to drench the window sill. Anton got up and closed the widow, shaking some errant rain drops from his cuffs as he stepped back to Carlotta. "Well, you are 'stuck' with me now, as they say."

Opening the pouch and taking out the black mirror, Anton handled it carefully at the rim and sat down again. "Sit next to me, my dear, and let us gaze into this together," he said drawing her onto the sofa beside him. He held the item up until they could both see their reflections within, Carlotta looking deeply into the glass and Anton glancing into it, as well, and then back at Carlotta. He kissed her cheek and then placed the obsidian seer face down on the end table and took her hands, brushing her lips with his. Another violaceous fire bolt blazed again followed by more thunder, crackling like heavy crystal chunks breaking out of an immense sack from above and echoing into the rain driven streets. Carlotta turned her head towards the window again, just as Zeus pierced the sky with another blazing javelin and more bursts of thunder, extinguishing the glow of every lightbulb in the area.

In the darkened room, Anton picked up the mirror and held it up again just as a succession of flashes lit the sky. "Look," he said, "and tell me what you see."

Carlotta viewed the image before her and gasped. "I see *this!*" she answered and kissed him full on the lips. Anton smiled beneath the warmth of her lips, held up the reflector to view the image and saw the two of them lying naked on the couch engaging in passionate kissing. Within a few minutes Carlotta peeled off her dress, her panties and bra, and Anton kicked off his shoes, tore off his suit, and everything beneath, awaiting Carlotta's touch. She quickly enticed him with more kisses, and drew his body to her with both her hands.

"Hello, my beauty bright, my elegant peacock," he whispered, taking a minute to gaze into her face before reclining on the sofa with her beneath him.

An hour or so later when the storm outside had ended, Carlotta took his hand and led him to her bed, curling up beside him with her head over his heart, listening to the velvety sounds of his heartbeat, like fluttering wings beating through the air. As their bodies melded deeply into her mattress, she allowed rest to present itself and a reverie overtook Carlotta's thoughts as drowsiness entered her limbs and eyes. She fancied a pair of large, peacock-like birds with shimmering white and electric blue feathers sitting on the roof edge of the brownstone across the back alley and looking in the direction of her apartment. The plumed creatures nudged each other briefly, and as if of one mind, suddenly took flight, soaring very close together en route through her open bedroom window, alighting on her bed.

# 46

"That's right, we were married three weeks ago," said Vern holding up Lulu's left hand and displaying her wide diamond wedding band to several people standing nearby, "on the hottest day in August in her parent's back yard."

"So you waited 'til a freezing night in November to celebrate?" said Vinnie from the other end of the bar. "But I'm sure Jay has lots of cool champagne to go around, too." Seated beside him, his wife tittered and waved at Vern with both hands.

"Thank you for inviting us, *Mr. and Mrs. Garvey!*" she said, her China red nails flashing as she moved her fingers.

"So glad you could be here, Mrs. Dawes, to keep your fella there in line." laughed Vern. "Have at it Vinnie, party goes on all night long."

"Whatda ya know! A lot of regulars won't like being left out on a Friday night."

"You and the missus drink up, Vinnie. Open to the public at 10 p.m. Jay'll be outta the bubbly by then!"

Jay motioned to a waiter saying, "This bus is ready to roll, Sam," pointing to a tray of glasses bubbling with pink champagne. "Serve this fine officer and his wife first," he said as Vinnie held up an empty glass and grinned. "He'll keep us outta trouble."

"Sure, sure, like I always do for yuz, Jay!" Vinnie took two glasses from the waiter's tray and handed one to his wife. "Let's have a toast for the happy couple," he shouted turning towards Vern and Lulu, who had gone to stand beside a table graced with a large, white, three-tiered cake, a perfect replica of the club's chandelier, complete with an etched lotus design on the sides. A small Lalique sculpture of embracing lovers was at the very top. "You kids gonna cut the cake?"

"Thanks, folks, we'll cut up that beautiful confection later. Let's have some dancing first," Vern said while holding Lulu with one arm and raising his other arm in a broad gesture with open palm and a quick waggle.

"You are stunning in that sparkling dress, *Mrs. Garvey*," a light voice said from behind. "Steel gray and silver sequins, my favorite winter combination." Lulu turned around to see Robbie just gliding in on Nick's arm. Several long strands of pearls swayed over her aubergine velvet dress as she walked up and gave Lulu a light kiss on the cheek, a marcasite hair ornament glittering over her Greek-inspired chignon.

"Robbie, *you're* the fashion plate," Lulu giggled with raised eyebrows, her lips forming a perfect 'O.' "And that dress looks familiar."

A lovely pink blush pervaded Robbie's cheeks as she leaned closer on Nick's arm. "I saw it in one of your elegant window's at Bonwitt's last month and had to have it," she answered.

"Congratulations, Vern," said Nick as the two men shook hands.

"Happy days, glad to see you both here tonight," Vern answered with a wide smile, "now let's dance!" Vern led Lulu to the dance floor as the music began.

The band started off with *When My Baby Smiles at Me* and Vern fox trotted his bride around the floor once, then signaled to Anton to step it up. With a nod to Carlotta, Anton tapped his foot, changed tempo and people abandoned their tables and gathered on the floor to join the newlyweds. Waiters paraded trays of champagne around the perimeter of the dance floor as passing hands reached out for more glasses of the festive libation amongst an abundance of fringe, beads, feathers, and sequins which caught the dim light of the chandelier, turning the room into a colorful jewel box during the spirited dancing.

With careful presentation of the tunes, Anton seemed to command the guests' movements, sweeping them further and further into the depths of his melodies, their expressions and steps became unbridled madness as their zealous feet stomped out the infectious rhythm of each tune. Anton kept nodding to Carlotta to ratchet up the fury, as more and more partyers spilled out of their seats and onto the floor, immediately catching the Charleston fever and joining in with absolute spontaneity spurred on by the band and the wild, gypsy jazz numbers.

Just after 9 p.m. Anton announced that the band was taking a break and would be back shortly, but that did not stop the activity on the deck. Folks picked up more drinks from the waiters who continued making the rounds with trays of champagne and steamy hors d'oeuvres, drifting savory aromas over the floor as the crowd stood talking and drinking, awaiting the restart of the band. Nick and Robbie had gone to the bar and were chatting with Jay as Carlotta motioned to Anton to follow her there.

"I love your band," said Nick, reaching out to shake Anton's hand. "She's the greatest fiddler in town," he added, giving a slight bow of his head to Carlotta. "I've had the pleasure of playing with her myself at a few jams."

Anton smiled broadly, showing his long, yellowed teeth which looked like mellowed ivory under the bar light, and put his arm around Carlotta. "I was so fortunate to find this lovely lady," he said leaning over and touching his lips to the flower in her hair. "Not only for my band, but as my fiancé." Carlotta beamed as she held out her left hand and displayed an unusual ring, a substantial star ruby encircled with small diamonds.

"Oh, how beautiful," exclaimed Robbie, taking Carlotta's hand to get a closer look at the exceptional ring. "When's the happy day?"

"This January," she answered. "Anton's taking us down south where his cousin has a cottage on the gulf shore, for a small wedding and a honeymoon." Her golden eyes glimmered as she smiled up at Anton.

"Congratulations, that'll be a nice getaway from this New York winter," He said to Carlotta, noting her changed demeanor. Although clad in a slinky black dress and a red headband that was dripping with swags of jet beads over her long locks, her stance was solid and calm, quite unlike the way he remembered her always smoothing her skirt over her hips with her hands, as her breasts rose and fell under her sighs, tossing her hair and staring pointedly with her cat-like eyes during his earlier conversations with her.

"Nick," she said, reaching down into her purse. "I have something for you." For a moment he started, recalling the odd black mirror she had thrust into his face the time in the park when he had run into her while walking his dog. She withdrew her hand in a fist, holding it out just over Robbie's lap. "This belongs to you," she said, opening her fingers and displaying the ankh in the palm of her hand.

"But I thought we agreed—" said Nick, looking at the object and then at Carlotta.

"I have no need of this, Nick, the charm has done its work and now needs to be returned." With eyes half closed she smiled, her full, upper lip parting slowly above her overbite. "It belongs to you and Robbie."

Nick, gawked, his soft, brown eyes growing wide in awe of her gesture. "Why, thank you, Carlotta," he said taking the object and placing it in Robbie's hand with his own clasped over hers. "I don't know what to say," he added, looking at his wife, "except that I am thankful to have her back home." Robbie pressed her cheek into Nick's shoulder and stifled a sob that had been welling up in her throat.

"Keep it in your pocket, Nick, where it belongs," Robbie said as she handed it back to her husband.

"Hey, folks, when's the music gonna start again?" shouted a flushed Lulu as she and Vern strutted up to the bar. "I'm ready for another dance!" She added and took Vern's hand. "Could ya get me another club soda with lime, Sweetie?" she asked him, wrapping her arms around him and kissing him full on the lips. Vern shuffled his feet and laughed as Lulu accosted him again, Then raising one arm he twirled her, then dipped her backward, her leg flying into the air. "How's that for a fast move, Baby?" he asked, gazing into her eyes.

"Oh, I got lipstick on you!" she laughed, wiping his cheek with her finger.

"Great band," Vern said to Anton, glancing briefly at Carlotta, as well. "So nice you were able to play this party for us." He quickly lifted his finger to Jay and stepped over to an empty space at the bar, awaiting his drink order.

Out of the corner of his eye he saw Lulu sway closer to Carlotta. A flash of heat fluttered over his face and throat as he dared to watch the scene play out.

"Lemme see your ring, Hon!" said Lulu with a sing-song lilt in her voice as she grinned and took Carlotta's fingers, examining the ring.

When Vern looked away and directed his attention back to the bar, Jay was vigorously wiping it down, his head bowed slightly over the area he was cleaning, but his eyes were on Vern, and his lips pulled into a tight grimace.

"What's up with Cat?" he said pointedly, bending his head towards Carlotta and Lulu.

226

Vern gulped and wiped his forehead with his handkerchief. "Well, guess she's finally got herself a real beau, huh?" He felt Jay's eyes on him as if challenging him to give a further explanation, but Vern just tapped on the bar and looked over at the two women again as Jay placed a beer and a club soda in front of him.

"Yeah, she caught a live one this time," Jay said, still staring straight-faced at Vern, who looked away and said nothing. "You sorry about that man?" he guffawed after a few moments of Vern's silence, throwing his bar towel over his shoulder.

"Hell, no!" Vern answered in a loud whisper, looking again at Lulu and Carlotta admiring each other's rings and exchanging a few words.

Jay straightened his posture and folded his arms. "You remember I told ya to stay clear of her—"

"Sure ya did, Jay, and *voila,* I took your advice and all's well, see?" With his palm open and fingers taut, Vern pushed his hand up closer to Jay's face. "Stop before you ruin my party," he chuckled taking another gulp of his beer.

Jay threw his head back and laughed, then turned towards the band which had started to play again.

Vern slapped his hand on the bar, picked up his drinks and said, "Ya really know how to throw a shindig, thanks Jay." He smiled, nodding back at Jay as he whistled along to *Sweet Georgia Brown* and strutted back to Lulu who was bopping to the music at the other end of the bar.

***

The soiree was still in full swing at 10p.m. when the club opened to the public. The Friday night crowd poured in, barely giving the door a chance to close between arrivals as the throng gathered at the cloak-room, ready to hand over their outerwear to the attendants who busily received the winter garments, dusting of pellets of snow from their hats and lapels before placing them on hangers and shelves.

The dancers, still hot with jazz fever barely noticed the gust of cold air that chilled the room, until a newcomer, still brushing the hoary precipitation from his trouser legs and shoes gave a loud order to the folks still caught up in the bottleneck at the coat check, "Hey, close the door, will ya? It's cold as hell in here now!" The few dancers who heard his roar over the music, turned to look out the open door of Blue Jay's and into a sheet of frozen vapor blanketing the street and sky in a glaze of white sparkle.

*"Snow already?"* a dancing lady called, her head turned towards the door and stumbling over her partner's feet as he attempted to give her a twirl under his arm. "It's barely November!" The door closed briefly on the sugary sky, quickly opening again as more partyers gathered within, brushing off their coats and awaiting their turn at the cloakroom door.

Anton's band played on feverishly, one tune after the other, Carlotta bending deeply into her prized instrument, her hair swaying wildly over her shoulders as she fiddled, fusing the descant of her homeland music with the modern jazz strains. Anton stood close by, their hips touching from time to time, each energized by the heat of the other's body and performance as they cast their musical spell over the hoofers, absorbed in frenzied dancing under the gossamer light of the tiered chandelier. Ladies' teeth glistened in smile, red lacquered nails rose into the air with jazz hand movements through the undulating shadows of their gentlemen partners, creating a modern bacchanal spree captivating everyone in the club.

# 47

No one noticed the slim, grayish figure of a man gliding in through the front door and over to the bar. He held up one finger and a barkeep mechanically placed a greenish drink in front of him. "Your absinthe, Sir," he said and stepped aside. The customer paid him no notice but had already turned his attention to the band, focusing on Carlotta. He stared blatantly at her, reaching his hand around to touch the stem of his cocktail glass, but never lifting it for a sip.

His lips formed words but he made no sound. "Kitty Cat, Kitty Cat," he repeated several times. He bowed his head slightly and tipped the dusky rim of his top hat, which he had not bothered removing upon entering the club. His fingers absently brushed over the white bowtie—or was it white?

No, it was ashen, like the rest of his attire, his frail-looking complexion, and the lifeless ponytail that trailed down his back.

The colorless man continued to gaze at Carlotta and mouth the words, 'Kitty Cat,' but she had not noticed him. At last a wail flew from his lips, "*Caaaarloooottaaaa,*" it called, echoing over the bar and into her ears alone. The sound arrested her and she ended her solo abruptly with a grating note, instantly feeling Anton's eyes upon her as she fixed hers upon the shadowy man at the bar, who was now breaking into a hysterical laugh. He reached into his pocket and drew out a dazzling diamond cuff and held it out to Carlotta. "You've *killed me,* Kitty Cat," he howled to the violinist.

Anton nudged Carlotta with the edge of his guitar, but she remained motionless, her eyes wide as she beheld the smoky phantom cackling out her name for none but herself to hear. Another man strode up and bent over the bar and seemed to displace the feeble specter as he ordered some drinks, unknowingly leaning into and occupying the first customer's place. But the gray stranger reappeared, this time standing directly in front of Carlotta, waving the bracelet immediately in front of her nose, the acrid smell of the antique bed filling her nostrils until she wheezed. "Remember me, remember me, as I am now so you must be," he recited in a sing-song voice, "Prepare for death and follow me!"

Anton and his band continued to play with Carlotta still trans-fixed on the man, her instrument dangling in one hand and her bow in the other. The floor beneath her felt as if it were crumbling as was her new-found life, and she had the sensation of sinking into a foggy pit where there was no sound save the voice of the dead man, who pointed to the floor and said, "Behold *this,* and remember our nights at Herald of Illusion." Looking down at the floor, which appeared like a sheet of glass lit from below, she saw beneath her a world of naked bodies writhing on satin sheets, and reaching upward and moaning in agony. It was the anguish of eternal loss; not only loss of love, and negation of redemption, but a state of final spiritual ruin and she felt it infecting her limbs as she watched the figures under the transparent floor. The beat of the music softened to a dull thud until she heard it no more, now feeling something drawing her to the scene below. Geof-frey's voice spun through her ears, "You will not escape me

One heavy tear fell from her eye and onto the floor with the crash of a crystal ball. "This is your fortune, my child," she heard the shrill voice of her mother call. She staggered forward and listened to the jingle of silver bells and felt the weight of her old ankle bracelets dragging her down. "Dance now, girl! *Dance in Hell!*" She lifted her hand into the air and felt the vibration of a tambourine against her fingers. "Come to me and dance for the dead."

A guest on his way back from the bar glanced at the stunned Carlotta beginning to move her feet and shake her lifted hand. He called out to Anton, "Hey, man, get that doll to fiddle again, will ya?" He seemed to walk straight through the still looming tormenter in front of Carlotta. Anton nodded to the drummer to take a rhythm solo and Carlotta heard his shoes hurriedly tapping over the floor to her and felt his fingers on her arm. Anton guided her to a seat at the end of the bar, yet only momentarily did she break the gray man's locking gaze.

"Stay here," Anton told her. She stood next to the seat, still paralyzed with foreboding of what this appearance of this ghost had brought: the disintegration of her new life with Anton, and the happiness she had found through her talent. Grimly, she recalled the nights she had he spent with Geoffrey at the Herald of Illusion, where she studied the dark art of casting spells through her unscrupulous seduction of men.

The floor was spinning under her feet and a surge of nausea swept over her while many clammy hands reached up and tried to grab at her ankles. "Oh, God, how could I have done those things?" she muttered into space. Carlotta bowed her head and looked again at the writhing figures below. She locked her arms over her waist, her red nails gripping sharply into her flesh, as if to hold her person in place, unwilling to succumb to the death call of her former lover.

Anton again motioned to the drummer, and now the bassist to keep the feverish momentum of the jazz beat alive as the floor was still crowded with dancers moving frantically to the diluted, but lively music. Nick had left his table, and walked towards the stage area and through the unseen man now hovering again in front of Carlotta. He surveyed the sparse band and the debilitated violinist. "Anton," called Nick, what's up? Carlotta, are you alright?"

The apparition beckoned Carlotta with his hand murmuring, "I joy in recalling our nights at the *Herald of Illusion Club,* for I too, learned the magic power of fornication between those sheets with you, my dear!" He pressed his mouth against hers and inhaled the breath from her parted lips, appearing to expand in stature as he did so. Carlotta clasped her throat with both hands and fell onto the barstool, gasping as if she were suffocating. *"Yes, I did it willingly!"* she shrieked, now looking directly into the eyes of her tormenter.

With a swipe of his finger, Anton outlined an invisible pentagram over the top of the assailant's head and whispered a few words into his ear, at which he slowly turned his grinning face, and glided a few steps away in front of the table containing the untouched wedding cake. Carlotta watched as Anton gripped the back of the phantom's neck, seeing his indistinct figure growing more solid as it stared at her and suction more of her breath from the short distance between them. "Geoffrey, please, *stop,*" she whispered, but he persisted.

With a quick snap, Anton twisted Geoffrey's neck, let go, and watched him crash into the table, almost knocking over a passing waitress, whose lingering screech rang through the club, even rattling the chandelier as the white cake exploded all over her and nearby dancers. The minimal band had stopped playing, the house lights went up and the party-goers awoke abruptly from their frenetic hoofing, screaming and trying to push away from the scene of a decrepit man with a broken neck lying in the middle of the destroyed cake. The dazzling cuff bracelet had fallen from his hand onto the floor, glistening softly under the brightened lights of the club.

The once lulled patrons became a horrified mob, some moving closer towards the fallen corpse, his neck bent unnaturally to one side, his lifeless eyes still gawking at Carlotta. Jay and Vern rushed over from the bar and stood with Nick, all looking on helplessly as the pandemonium swelled. Some folks began moving in to get a closer look at the dead man in the smashed cake and others pushed towards the front door, shoving and trying to elbow their way out of the club.

With alacrity Anton swept his hand over the corpse which dissolved like snowflakes on a sunlit street, the wedding cake appearing again on its table, perfect and unharmed. There was an immediate hush in the crowd, people stopped and looked at each other in bewilder-ment as their arms relaxed and feet stood in place, heads turning from the exit door they had so fiercely clamored toward, now looking per-plexedly back into the club. A lady in pink stepped forward and said, "Was there a fire alarm, Mister Band Master?" She placed one hand on her hip and waved a finger in the air as she pirouetted in place. "C'mon, now, Hon, party's not over yet, give some more tunes!"

"Sure thing, Pal, how 'bout another Charleston?" another flapper called, grabbing her fellow and leading him back to the floor, swaying in exaggerated rhythm as she moved. Others followed suit, laughing, their dazed eyes glittering under the house chandelier.

"Say, what just happened?" another lady asked as she ambled back from the front door. "Were we leaving for some reason?"

A man shook his head and took her in a Charleston hold. "Dun-no, Babe, I was just waiting for you to come back," he said whirling her onto the dance floor.

Carlotta stood in place staring into nothingness as the partyers came to life again. She felt something warm reach around her waist and a distant voice seemed to say, "Remember what is important in your life…." She started and turned to see Anton holding her firmly with one arm. He held out his other arm towards the crowd and with a wide grin, said, "And now, ladies and gentlemen, my lovely lady and I will play a special duet for you. It's called *The Wild Cat.*" His words passed over her as if in a dream. She allowed the tense breath in her lungs to escape and accepted Anton's hand as they walked back to the stage area. She felt him place her beautiful violin in her hands while kissing her cheek and whispering, "You are beautiful, my star, inside and out. Now let's play." The gloom on Carlotta's face melted away, her golden eyes darting over Anton's face. She reached up and touched his cheek with her ruby lips and stepped onto the stage area and took up her fiddle.

"Just one number for now, everybody," Lulu called out holding up a silver knife, "We have to cut this wedding cake." She walked up to where Vern was still standing with Jay and Nick near the stage. "Say, what happened, fellas? Did yuz just all come up here to watch the band on their break, or what?"

Vern brushed his hair over his brow and shook his head. "Beats me, I just followed Nick and Jay." Jay just shrugged, but Nick turned his eyes to Anton, who beamed at him as he strummed his guitar.

"Nick?" Lulu asked, but Nick just smiled back at Anton.

"Oh, I was going to request a particular number after their break, that's all, Lu." He put his hand in his trouser pocked and jingled the ankh that Carlotta had returned to him earlier. "Uh, I hadn't heard them play *Sunshine,* tonight, I guess," he answered, his eyes still on Anton.

He looked back at Robbie who was still seated at their table, and waved her over. She nodded and walked towards Nick, kissing him on the lips when she arrived. "What's going on here?"

He felt the heat of her body as she took his hand and leaned against him, and drew a long breath of the jasmine perfume that lingered in her hair. Robbie looked up at him with half closed eyes and suppressed a yawn, then chuckled, "It was a grand evening, but I'm about ready to go home with my husband."

"Just one dance first," Nick said, turning towards her and moving her slowly to the waltz melody in his head, completely out of step with the band's brisk tune. As Nick turned he briefly caught Carlotta's sparkling eyes. She blinked and gave a nod towards Nick, then turned her attention back to Anton. He watched them as they played the duet, feeling the dynamism between the two of them as they performed. "Good for you," murmured Nick, smiling briefly at the pair as he turned Robbie outward and ended their waltz with a bow.

"Ok, let's slip outta her, it's nearly 3a.m." Nick said taking Robbie's hand.

Nick turned to Vern to say goodnight, but Lulu had pulled the bridegroom towards their cake and cut a slice before the duet was finished. She laughed and shoved a bite in his mouth and he did the same to her. A collection of couples, including Nick and Robbie, stood by and clapped, but some folks were still dancing as the ritual was performed. "Thanks everybody," called Lulu as the guests passed by her and thanked the couple for the evening. "See yuz soon, Nick, Robbie," she called out as the two waved goodbye and headed for the door.

The whispering breeze greeted them outside, and the building tops were crowned with the glitter of frosty snowflakes. The two walked out on to the street, their shoes softly crunching in the thin layer of snow that had fallen on the sidewalk. Robbie placed her gloved hand inside of Nick's coat pocket as he took her arm and asked, "Say, what was going on with the band and Carlotta getting up and standing near the bar looking so dismal? Is that why you rushed up there?"

"Uh, yeah, I think so…I don't really remember, except that she seemed to be suddenly ill," answered Nick. He listened to the distant blare of music as the door of Blue Jay's opened and closed again, and then the sound of his footsteps in the snow. "Seems she recovered ok, though," he said recalling the smile he exchanged with her just before he led Robbie out of the club. "Yeah she's fine, I'm sure."

Robbie smiled up at him and said, "So grand to be going home with you, my love, on such a winter's night. Shall we walk or get a cab?"

"Let's walk, then," said Nick, drawing her closer as they approached  Fifth Avenue. "Just look at the buildings against the sky, Robbie."

To the east the endless row of buildings were lit at the tops by a ribbon of radiant magenta that had crept up beneath the fading moon and cast a soft glow over the very tops of a snow-frosted collection of buildings, some tall, others only a few stories high. A murky fog hung at street level melding the lower portions of the structures into the lingering darkness of night with the sidewalks, giving the impression that they were suspended in mid-air, their many windows peering like sleepy eyes into a universe called New York.

# About the Author

Celeste Plowden holds a BFA in Art History with a minor in English literature and further studies at Parsons School of Design, New York, for Textile Design. During her lifetime she has been a fabric designer, real estate title examiner, fine artist, showroom model, singer, dog lover, and perpetual student of early modern history. She writes stories of romance with dark connections to supernatural beings and uses her knowledge of history to paint rich settings for her characters which dwell in places she has lived, New York and London.